BRYHER: TWO NOVELS

LIVING OUT
Gay and Lesbian Autobiographies

Joan Larkin and David Bergman
GENERAL EDITORS

The Other Mother: A Lesbian's Fight for Her Daughter
Nancy Abrams

An Underground Life: Memoirs of a Gay Jew in Nazi Berlin
Gad Beck

Bryher: Two Novels: Development *and* Two Selves
Bryher

The Hurry-Up Song: A Memoir of Losing My Brother
Clifford Chase

In My Father's Arms: A True Story of Incest
Walter A. de Milly III

Midlife Queer: Autobiography of a Decade, 1971 – 1981
Martin Duberman

Widescreen Dreams: Growing Up Gay at the Movies
Patrick E. Horrigan

Eminent Maricones: Arenas, Lorca, Puig, and Me
Jaime Manrique

Taboo
Boyer Rickel

Secret Places: My Life in New York and New Guinea
Tobias Schneebaum

Bryher: Two Novels

Development and *Two Selves*

Bryher

Introduction by Joanne Winning

The University of Wisconsin Press

The University of Wisconsin Press
2537 Daniels Street
Madison, Wisconsin 53718

3 Henrietta Street
London WC2E 8LU, England

1   3   5   4   2

Printed in the United States of America

Library of Congress Cataloging-in-Publication Data
Bryher, 1894–1983
[Novels. Selections]
Bryher: two novels / Bryher
000 pp.   cm.
Includes bibliographical references.
ISBN 0-299-16770-4 (cloth: alk. paper)
ISBN 0-299-16774-7 (paper: alk. paper)
1. Autobiographical fiction, English. 2. Lesbians—Fiction. I. Title
II. Series.

PR6003.R98 .A6 2000
823'.91421—dc21   99-052229

The editor and the University of Wisconsin Press gratefully
acknowledge the permission of Perdita Schaffner to reprint these
novels.

INTRODUCTION

Write a book. And find she had a friend.
                                    —Bryher, *Two Selves*

BOTH *Development* and *Two Selves* have been absent
from the literary landscape since the period of their
first publication during the early 1920s. This is a result
partly of the larger marginalization of the texts written
by the women of the modernist period, but also partly
because their author, as critics have only recently begun to note, remains one of the least recognized figures in the modernist landscape.[1] In accounts of the
modernist period Bryher has been acknowledged primarily only in relation to her partnership with the key
female modernist H.D. and her assistance of other
female modernist writers, including Dorothy Richardson and Marianne Moore. Yet the range of her interest
and her energetic intellectual engagements with the art,
literature, and discourses of her time are quite simply
phenomenal and deserve more rigorous critical discussion in their own right. As Nancy, Bryher's central protagonist in these novels, realizes above there is a profound correlation between writing and a keen sense of
friendship between women.

TWO NOVELS

Nancy, as a young woman in these novels, has yet to fulfill either her literary or her emotional potential, but Bryher herself was undoubtedly a figure central to the community of female modernists in Europe in the early twentieth century and their writing, promoting friendship and enabling literature and its creation in a number of different ways. She also, along with so many of her peers, engaged in the process of locating definitive literary language and form with which to represent female and lesbian subjectivity—as both *Development* and *Two Selves* prove. The reprinting of these two autobiographical novels in this volume represents an important step in the recentralization of Bryher in discussions about and readings of the burgeoning body of female modernist texts. *Development* and *Two Selves* were written in 1920 and 1923 respectively. Together with the later novel *West* (1925), they form the trilogy of autobiographical fiction that maps Bryher's coming to consciousness as a woman and artist, culminating in her meeting and subsequent partnership with H.D.

BRYHER IN CONTEXT

Bryher was born Annie Winifred Ellerman in 1894, daughter of the British shipping magnate John Ellerman and his common-law wife Hannah Glover.[2] She was brought up in wealthy but rigidly constrained circumstances in the family homes in Mayfair in Lon-

INTRODUCTION

don and in Eastbourne. After a trip to the Scilly Isles
with her school friend Doris Banfield, she adopted the
name of the most remote of the five inhabited islands,
symbolically associating the landscape of this small
outcrop of islands in the Atlantic Ocean with her own
freedom from familial ties. She finally changed her
name simply to Bryher by deed poll in 1951, at last
throwing off all vestiges of paternal control and identity at a time when her own career as a historical novelist was becoming established. Nancy's story, which
is traced through *Development* and *Two Selves* (and on
into *West*), is a fictionalized account of Bryher's own
childhood, adolescence, and early adulthood. When
not living in either of the family homes, Bryher was
taken traveling with her father across Europe, Africa,
and the Middle East. Her childhood was unconven-
tional; she did not attend school until the age of fifteen. Queenwood, the boarding school to which she
was sent, prompted a traumatic shift in her sense of
self and autonomy. The experience, which she later described as "a violation of the spirit," left her with fervent feelings about the nature of education and intellectual and emotional development.[3]

In 1913 at the age of nineteen Bryher bought a
copy of the first Imagist collection, *Des Imagistes.*
Reading this new poetry made her "drunk with joy,"
since this work heralded, in her words, "the approach
of a new age."[4] She had been writing poetry herself
since her adolescence and, inspired by Imagism's re-

invigoration of poetic form, persuaded her father to fund the publication of her first collection, *The Region of Lutany,* in 1914.[5] Three years later in 1917 Bryher obtained copies of the two Imagist anthologies edited by Amy Lowell after Pound's departure for Vorticism, as well as a copy of Lowell's own critical work *Six French Poets.* Lowell's work impressed Bryher greatly and prompted her to produce her first piece of extended literary analysis, *Amy Lowell: A Critical Appreciation* (1918). Lowell proved to be an all-around inspiration to Bryher, who with typical forwardness, wrote her an enthusiastic letter and followed it up with samples of her own poetry. Lowell responded encouragingly, providing Bryher with suggested readings from amongst the very best innovative modernist works, including the first three novels of Dorothy Richardson's *Pilgrimage* series and *Sea Garden* (1916), the first collection of poems from the American Imagist poet H.D.[6]

H.D.'s poetry was to profoundly captivate Bryher. In *The Heart to Artemis,* she records the significance with which this work soon became imbued for her:

> There will always be one book among all others that makes us aware of ourselves; for me, it is *Sea Garden* by H.D. I learned it by heart from cover to cover. . . . I began the morning and ended the day repeating the poems. It was not until some months later that I discovered from Amy Lowell's *Tendencies in Modern American Poetry* that H.D. was a woman and American.[7]

INTRODUCTION

Bryher also learned that H.D. lived in Cornwall. Obtaining H.D.'s address from Clement Shorter, the publishing husband of her childhood friend Doris Banfield, Bryher took the audacious step of writing to H.D. and requesting a meeting. Both H.D. and Bryher, along with biographers and critics, have documented and fictionalized this meeting and the resultant life-long partnership that arose from it. It is clear in these writings that both women felt to some degree "saved" by the other. Bryher's clear desperation at the degree of parental control she was still experiencing at the age of twenty-four and her overwhelming feelings of wasted desire and talent are articulated in *Development* and *Two Selves.* Only the very slimmest of hopes of "finding a friend" remain for Nancy. Yet, in a prevision of the importance this meeting will hold, Nancy recognizes that this "adventure" is worth one last risk. In the subsequent novel *West,* Nancy acknowledges that Helga Brandt, the fictional H.D. "saves" her life: "only an American had bade her live."[8] H.D. herself, pregnant as a result of her affair with Cecil Gray and estranged from her husband Richard Aldington at the time of the meeting, explores the extraordinary advent of Bryher's arrival in her life in the two posthumously published novels, *Paint It Today* and *Asphodel.*[9] In these texts Bryher appears respectively as Althea and Beryl de Rothfeldt. In *Asphodel* Beryl's arrival signals to Hermione Gart (H.D.'s fictional self) that "a light is shining at the far end of a long, long tunnel."[10] Yet also in this fictional account Bryher's promise to take care of both H.D. and her daughter Perdita Schaffner is balanced by the promise H.D. extracts from Bryher to move beyond her suicidal feelings and take up the reins of her life.

Bryher's ensuing life with H.D. was one characterized by wide-ranging intellectual and literary endeavor. In addition to offering, at the least, emotional and physical companionship, and perhaps as important, H.D. also provided Bryher with a literary context. Through H.D.'s contacts Bryher was asked to translate Antipater of Sidon's "Six Sea Poems" for the Poets Translation Series of the Egoist Press. Perhaps more important, her ensuing friendship with Harriet Shaw Weaver, editor of the *Egoist,* proved to be the start of her prodigious career as literary patron. In 1921 she edited and funded Marianne Moore's first collection, *Poems,* and also provided subsidy for the publication of H.D.'s *Hymen.* Bryher's patronage was to extend across publications, publishing ventures, bookshops, and personal subsidy for friends and acquaintances experiencing financial hardship while writing.[11] Not least, she was committed to utilizing her inherited wealth to sustain many different female modernist projects; perhaps one of her most notable beneficiaries through the 1920s and 1930s was Dorothy Richardson. Bryher's regular "loans" undoubtedly secured the ongoing production of Richardson's lifework, *Pilgrimage.*

INTRODUCTION

During 1921 Bryher and H.D. met Robert McAlmon, with whom Bryher entered into a marriage of
convenience to sustain her freedom from parental control.[12] While McAlmon proved to be a complicated
choice of marriage partner in emotional terms, his interest in literature and avant-garde writing provided
Bryher with the most fascinating contacts and literary
projects. Together with McAlmon, Bryher founded
and funded the Contact Publishing Co., which ran in
Paris until 1928. Throughout its history the Contact
series published many of the most important modernist writers: H.D., Mina Loy, Mary Butts, Djuna
Barnes, Gertrude Stein, Ernest Hemingway, and
James Joyce. McAlmon's *Contact Collection of Contemporary Writers,* published in 1925, included work
by Bryher, H.D., Mina Loy, Dorothy Richardson,
May Sinclair, Djuna Barnes, Mary Butts, and Gertrude Stein.[13] McAlmon stayed in Paris, eventually becoming estranged and later divorced from Bryher.

Her interests, however, extended beyond book
publishing to the dissemination of avant-garde writing
through books and magazines. To this end she provided financial support for Sylvia Beach's Shakespeare
and Company bookshop in Paris, a nexus for modernist writers and a point of contact for the reading public
interested in new, experimental material. As Andrea
Weiss has shown, throughout the 1920s Paris became
an identifiable center for the overlapping communities
of lesbians and female modernists.[14] Bryher, more so

than H.D., took the opportunity to immerse herself in this subculture, although her reception into the expatriate literary community in Paris became increasingly compromised as relations with McAlmon became acrimonious.[15]

In 1927 Bryher and H.D. met the young Scot, Kenneth Macpherson. H.D. and Macpherson began an affair, and Bryher, desperate for a divorce from McAlmon, suggested another marriage of convenience with Macpherson. This partnership, perhaps more suitable from the start, was to work a good deal better than that with McAlmon. The meeting with Macpherson coincided with Bryher's interest in the emerging art of cinema and the growing field of psychoanalysis in the late 1920s. As Laura Marcus has argued, the new art of cinema and the discourses of psychoanalysis map one another as "twin sciences and technologies of fantasy, dream, virtual reality and screen memory."[16] For Bryher, both provided innovative ways of thinking about human subjectivity and progress. Macpherson, who had already been analyzed briefly by the German psychoanalyst Hanns Sachs, introduced Bryher to him in 1928. She subsequently underwent four years of analysis with him in Berlin.[17] In addition to what proved a productive and enervating analysis, the connection with Sachs also provided Bryher with access into the European psychoanalytic community and its ideas. Bryher argues in *The Heart to Artemis* that her experience of the repression at

INTRODUCTION

school in Queenwood (documented so articulately in *Development*) was to make her an "adherent" to Freud even before she had encountered psychoanalytic thinking. Ten years later, she notes, she became one of the first subscribers to the *British Journal of Psychoanalysis* and read Freud in translation as soon as new works became available. Bryher finally obtained an introduction to Freud through the sexologist Havelock Ellis, whom she had known since the early 1920s. She was to remain an enthusiastic advocate of psychoanalysis, seeing it as a transformative discipline with great potential for social good, and believing it should be widely accessible to all: "I don't want to preach communism, I only want it to be possible for workers, and this includes badly paid intellectuals, to come in contact with p.a."[18] Committed to questions of access, Bryher donated money to various psychoanalytic schemes, including setting up the Hanns Sachs Training Fund for trainee analysts. She was also keen to fund the analyses of friends. Through the late 1920s it is also clear that she considered undergoing analytic training herself; a process she called getting "a dog-collar."[19] In 1933 she approached Freud about the possibility of H.D. undergoing analysis with him. Freud's subsequent acceptance and the ensuing analysis are movingly documented in H.D.'s *Tribute to Freud* (1956).

Bryher's interest in film centered on its social, educational, and political potential. Together Bryher,

TWO NOVELS

Macpherson, and H.D. started the film journal *Close Up* (1927–1933), which as Jayne Marek has argued was to become "the chief contemporary forum for debate about the social implications as well as the theory and practice of cinema."[20] Edited by Macpherson and Bryher, and funded by Bryher, the journal published reviews and articles by an international list of contributors, including writers such as Dorothy Richardson and filmmakers such as Sergei Eisenstein and G. W. Pabst.[21] Important for Bryher, it offered an outlet for her political articles about war and its effects. During the early 1930s she wrote several articles that called attention to the worsening political situation in Europe and argued for constructive debate about the nature of war. In her pamphlets *Film Problems in Soviet Russia,* published in 1929, and *Film in Education,* published in 1937, she expressed her view of film as a unique cultural form through which political and social ideals could be mobilized. Another of the key interests of the *Close Up* group was the production of film. To this end the POOL film group was also set up in 1927, producing three short films and one full-length film *Borderline* (1930) in which Paul Robeson and H.D. play central roles and Bryher appears as "a cigar-smoking proprietress."[22]

Until 1939 and the outbreak of World War II, Bryher spent most of her time in Territet, Switzerland, in the Bauhaus-influenced home, "Kenwin," which she designed with Kenneth Macpherson. Her interest in

INTRODUCTION

patronage and editing remained strong. In 1935 she bought the review *Life and Letters,* merging it with the left-wing magazine the *London Mercury.* Under her control its title changed to *Life and Letters Today* and published many distinguished European writers: André Gide, Jules Romain, Jean-Paul Sartre, Paul Valéry, and Franz Kafka. Its British contributors included Dorothy Richardson, Mary Butts, Siegfried Sassoon, and the Sitwells; and its American contributors included Marianne Moore, Elizabeth Bishop, May Sarton, Muriel Rukeyser, and T. S. Eliot. One of Bryher's most notable discoveries for *Life and Letters Today* was the Australian writer Patrick White. Despite the disruptions and deprivations of war Bryher managed to keep the magazine afloat and functioning as an organ of innovative literature. Throughout the 1930s her political life also remained central. Her base in Switzerland provided an ideal conduit for the escape of Jewish refugees from Germany. In all, Bryher helped over one hundred people flee the Nazi regime in Germany, amongst them notably Walter Benjamin. She left Switzerland for her own safety just as war was declared in August 1939, returning to London and H.D. to survive the war years there.

At this time, while H.D. was working on her own poetic response to the war, *Trilogy,* Bryher began the body of work which was to dominate the remainder of her career—the writing of historical novels. The intense experience of war witnessed firsthand through the Blitz in London prompted Bryher's literary explorations of nationality and Englishness. Questions of history and identity seemed to crystallize for her in the time of war. In all, Bryher went on to produce nine historical novels, which explore real historical events through fictional "minor" characters.[23] No doubt in the writing of historical fiction Bryher was to some degree revisiting a passion from childhood, in which the boys' adventure stories and particularly the work of the nineteenth-century writer G. A. Henty fired both her imagination and her sense of injustice at being born a girl. As an adult Bryher created an archive of manuscripts and materials on nineteenth-century "boys' books" and adventure stories titled "Dusty Diamonds," which was exhibited at the Grolier Club in New York in 1965. Her keen interest in boys' fiction and her eventual creation of historical persona through male characters can be read suggestively alongside her own thinking on gender identity and sexuality, which I shall come to discuss.

After a breakdown at the war's end, H.D. retired to Kusnacht in Switzerland, supported as ever by Bryher both financially and emotionally. Bryher herself returned to Kenwin to continue to produce her novels. In 1961 after a period of worsening health, H.D. suffered a stroke and died. Bryher, traveling from Vaud, arrived shortly before her death. For whatever reasons, H.D.'s death seems to have freed Bryher to turn finally to the recording of memory through

INTRODUCTION

autobiography. One year after H.D.'s death, she published *The Heart to Artemis: A Writer's Memoirs,* which chronicles her life up until the Second World War, following this with *The Days of Mars: A Memoir, 1940–1946,* published in 1972. Bryher lived alone at Kenwin until the time of her own death in 1983.

READING *DEVELOPMENT* AND *TWO SELVES*

Amongst contemporary audiences, *Development* and *Two Selves* attracted very different critical receptions. *Development* was published in July 1920 in Britain and in December 1920 in America. It was reviewed very widely for a first novel, prompting responses in both newspapers and literary periodicals.[24] *Two Selves* was published through the Contact Press in Paris in 1923 and received only one review in the *Manchester Guardian.* Other than this it seemed to escape the notice of literary reviewers, though Marianne Moore, who had previously reviewed *Development* in the *Dial* in 1921, wrote to Bryher at the time of its publication regretting that she had nowhere to place a review of what she regarded as a good novel.

Amy Lowell's preface to *Development* ensured that the novel was read (by readers familiar with such terms) in the context of the literary movement of Imagism. The reviewer for the *New York Times Book Review* comments: "since it would appear that the especial form of authorship which Nancy, the heroine of the book, is to adopt will be that of free verse, who more fit than Miss Lowell to tell us what we ought to think about W. Bryher's book."[25] Indeed Bryher's devotion to Imagism and its techniques clearly inflects her prose style throughout the novel. Constance Mayfield Rourke, writing for the *New Republic,* regards this as the strength of an otherwise "difficult, inverted book" and argues that Bryher's construction of Nancy displays "the typical imagistic power to startle, the typical cerebral intensiveness without intensity, the same fatal abundance." Though she has "the poet's sensuous equipment" it is used indiscriminately and thus becomes "tortuous."[26] Writing in her preface, Lowell regards the novel as "a singular book," rightly identifying it as a *Bildungsroman* and placing it within the same tradition that produced *Jane Eyre* and *Obermann.* Lowell reads Nancy as an Imagist born. She has, from the first, "all sorts of intuitions and understandings" that lead her to view color and words in Imagist terms. Words, indeed, become "pigment" and "tone" to Nancy who then struggles to realize this artistic calling as a girl in the midst of late-Victorian society. Recognizing the novel as thinly disguised autobiography, Lowell regards both author and protagonist as "a baffling and intriguing personality." Lowell suggests this partly because of Nancy's dogged attempts to "free her spirit" in both artistic and social terms;

INTRODUCTION

this eccentricity arises, in part, out of her sense of herself as a boy and her grief at the lost opportunities in her childhood as a girl.

While no contemporary reviews fully take up this latter point (though I shall do so in subsequent analysis), all Bryher's contemporary reviewers acknowledge her attempt to record the struggle of both the artistic temperament and femininity—with varying degrees of praise and criticism of the picture of "personality" that results. In "The Making of a Vers-Libriste," the reviewer for the *Nation* regards the novel as providing "access to a literary psychology which, in this special form, is both new and important." By contrast, the reviewer for the *Saturday Review* regards its focus on Nancy's stifled and frustrated psyche as "a warning against the danger of too close a preoccupation with the analysis of one's emotions." Such self-absorption results, for the *Times Literary Supplement* reviewer, in a central character who has "an inhuman priggishness."[27] Similarly, the *Athenaeum*'s reviewer regards Nancy at fourteen as "an awful example of what . . . indulgence may end in."[28] Certain reviewers of the novel felt uncomfortable with Bryher's use of autobiographical fiction. The reviewer for the *Times Literary Supplement* argues that "Miss W. Bryher is not really entitled to call *Development* a novel," while the *Saturday Review* notes that "genuine autobiography is not easy to disguise."[29] Such discomfort with the uneasy boundaries between "life" and "text" are reminiscent of the mixed responses to Dorothy Richardson's *Pilgrimage* series. The resonance between *Development* and Richardson's work is instructive since Bryher was a fervent advocate of Richardson's modernist project.[30] The reviewer for the *New Republic* identifies a clear link between Bryher's Nancy and Richardson's Miriam Henderson: "*Development* is not a novel, as it is called. It is a personal record. It belongs more particularly with Miss Richardson's *Pilgrimage*." Yet unlike Miriam Henderson, who is simply "not worth writing about," Bryher's Nancy is of more interest: "Inarticulate as she is, here is a personality of complicated power. Thwarted and divided, she makes war."[31] Nancy's "war" is primarily waged against society and the strictures it places upon her as a young woman. As the reviewer for the *Bookman* notes, Nancy is not "an ordinary girl" but rather "a very modern girl."[32]

Responding to the novel's inherent feminism, Marianne Moore's review in the *Dial* questions Bryher's construction of discourses of femininity and women's role:

> One's dress is more a matter of one's choice than appears; if there be any advantage, it is on the side of woman; woman is more nearly at liberty to assume man's dress than man is able to avail himself of the opportunities for self expression afforded by the variations in colour and fabric which a woman may use. Moreover, women are no longer debarred

from professions that are open to men, and if one cares to
be femininely lazy, traditions of the past still afford shelter.[33]

Moore's rejection of Bryher's feminist commentary
on girls' upbringing was echoed to some degree in
the twelve-day-long furore about education in girls'
schools that took place in the *Daily Mail* after publication of *Development.* Picking up on Bryher's account
of Nancy's time at Downwood girls' school, the *Daily
Mail* ran two articles on the novel entitled "Cramped
School Girls."[34] Both identified Bryher as an ardent
critic of the system of girls' education in England, who
in her "remarkable little book" makes "a vigorous on-
slaught" on the establishment. Over and above the cal-
iber of Bryher's writing, which the paper regards as
marking her out as an artist, it regards "the school
chapters" as the most important, conveying as they do
the "dull cramping formalism" of girls' education. The
reasons for the *Daily Mail*'s interest in sparking debate
about *Development* undoubtedly arose out of general
debates about the education of girls in Britain during 1920. Both articles on *Development* followed on a
contentious debate about the caning of girls by male
teachers that had raged in the paper, both in articles
and readers' letters, throughout May 1920. Readers of
this commentary on *Development* duly took the bait
and letters proceeded to appear in the paper over the
following week.

For the most part Bryher received vehement criticism from headmistresses, schoolteachers, and parents for her ignorance about the current realities of girls' education, arguing that she evidently had knowledge of nothing other than a dated nineteenth-century system. After several days of outraged and indignant attacks, Bryher herself responded in defense of her account of Queenwood insisting on the veracity of her portrayal: "I went to 'Downwood' in May 1910 and left in 1912. Every incident in the school portion of my book 'Development' is founded on actual fact."[35]

Despite the consternation which *Development* caused both to contemporary readers, and indeed the Ellerman family themselves, the book sold well (perhaps *because* of this consternation), and Bryher was pleased with its reception. Writing in *The Heart to Artemis* she states:

> My instinct about writing had been correct. I knew that *Development* was not a book of which Mallarmé would have approved but I really objected to the human wastage of school. My family bowed to the inevitable. I had committed the unpardonable Victorian sin and made myself 'conspicuous'. (I enjoyed this very much). I was allowed to join H.D. in a small apartment that she had rented in Kensington, not far from where the Pounds and Mrs Shakespeare were living and where I tried, without success, to write my second book.[36]

This second book, billed at the end of *Development* as a sequel entitled *Adventure,* was to become *Two Selves.*

INTRODUCTION

Unlike *Development* it caused no ripples in the world of education. Its review in the *Manchester Guardian* notes the autobiographical link with Bryher herself and, like certain reviewers of *Development,* finds Nancy an egoist whose struggle towards artistic identity becomes "tiresome." Her emotions are "too storm-wracked" to be legible either to herself or the reader.[37] This reviewer fails to take up the major and undoubtedly engaging themes of the novel: Nancy's continuing "war" with society as a woman, her engagement with the new modernist movements of Imagism and Futurism, her readings of H.D.'s poetry, and her exploration of confused gender identity. It has thus fallen to late twentieth-century critics to explore these questions to some small degree in their scholarship.

Being a Boy

Towards the end of *Development* Nancy undergoes a transformative and epiphanic experience that takes place on a midnight shrimping trip off one of the Scilly Isles. While preparing to go out to fish, Nancy achieves a previously impossible sense of selfhood: "The lance hooks jangled in the darkness. Nancy followed the others up the road, knowing she was a boy." It is clear that from the outset of *Development,* which opens with Nancy at the age of four years, that her subjectivity has been characterized by an internal split between male and female identities. Yet it is during this trip to the Scillies that Nancy seems to come to a point of understanding about herself, a kind of self-knowledge symbolized by the night: "It was her first adventure with night; a strange, a wonderful experience, full of the mingled dream and reality she desired." Nancy's encounter with "the night" might perhaps be suggestively read alongside a later modernist text, Djuna Barnes's *Nightwood* (1936), in which lesbian sexuality is complexly overwritten by the signifier of "the night." Robin Vote, one of the novel's key characters and the object of the frustrated desires of Nora Flood (Barnes's fictional self), has special connections to the night, which symbolize both her enigmatic sexuality and her dangerousness. Throughout her affair with Robin, Nora characterizes the night as a place of sexual excess and desire.[38]

Such a conflation of darkness, nighttime, and lesbian desire may well also be at work in Bryher's *Development.* What is clear is that this epiphany does little, subsequently, to help Nancy's sense of gender dysphoria. By the beginning of *Two Selves,* the split between surface femininity (however compromised) and internal masculinity has become entrenched:

Two selves. Jammed against each other, disjointed and ill-fitting. An obedient Nancy with heavy plaits tied over two ears that answered 'yes, no, yes, no,' according as the wind blew. A boy, a brain, that planned adventures and sought wisdom.

Nancy's desire for "adventure," articulated throughout both texts, will of course culminate in the event that seems to form the teleological purpose of Nancy's desire—the meeting with the enigmatic woman poet, who has eyes "with the sea in them" and who has awaited Nancy's arrival. Such an ending suggests that both texts represent a pilgrimage to identity.

Yet the question remains what kind of identity? Nancy's "split" subjectivity is based both upon a profound gender dysphoria and the desperate and overwhelming need for "a friend" who will ultimately prove to be a woman. These novels seem to articulate narratives of identity that can be read either in terms of lesbian sexuality or transsexuality. Susan Stanford Friedman has read the duality of this image of two selves as a motif through which to articulate the "Victorian trap of feminine obligation"; a trap which prohibits women from any kind of creativity.[39] As such, Friedman regards Bryher's "splitting" of subjectivity as an attempt to register the tension between exterior capitulation and interior rebellion. Undoubtedly Friedman is right to identify questions of social and cultural constraint as being imbricated in Bryher's configuration of Nancy's subjectivity here. Throughout both novels Nancy is acutely aware of the delimitations that patriarchal society places upon her cultural and social landscapes.

It seems to me, however, that it is necessary to consider this configuration of subjectivity in the light of Bryher's avowed lesbian identity. In her important article on *Two Selves,* Diana Collecott reads the text as a lesbian "quest narrative" and contextualizes it amongst other material Bryher was producing in the early 1920s, notably her essay "The Girl-Page in Elizabethan Literature" and her draft prose-poem "Eros of the Sea."[40] Collecott argues that it is clear from the material that Bryher produces during this period that she is exploring the boundaries of gender and sexual desire through her writing. In this regard it is extremely useful to read Bryher's construction of lesbian sexuality through the contextual frames of sexological and psychoanalytic discourses of inversion and female homosexuality.

Within the discourses of sexology, lesbianism and male homosexuality are rendered through the term "inversion." Two of the notable theorists of inversion, Richard von Krafft-Ebing and Havelock Ellis, both locate a powerful correlation between lesbian desire and gender identity. For Krafft-Ebing inversion is a pathological condition. However, Ellis through his theorizations of both male and female homosexuality seeks to find a way of interpreting inversion which will prove, incontrovertibly, that such a condition is innate and to

INTRODUCTION

some degree "natural." Despite their differing agendas both Krafft-Ebing's and Ellis's notions of the female invert inevitably map masculinity onto the lesbian body and personality, using case histories to work up their theories of "confused" gender identity. Throughout the case histories recorded in his chapter on female inversion in his *Sexual Inversion* (1897), Ellis records childhood "masculinity" as an early indicator of innate inversion. In the case history of "Miss M," he notes the following:

> As a child she did not care for dolls or for pretty clothes, and often wondered why other children found so much pleasure in them. "As far back as my memory goes," she writes, "I cannot recall a time when I was not different from other children. I felt bored when other girls came to play with me, though I was never rough or boisterous in my sports." Sewing was distasteful to her. Still she cared little more for the pastimes of boys, and found her favourite amusement in reading, especially adventures and fairy-tales.[41]

Here Miss M's adult sexuality is interpreted through the masculine identifications and behaviors of her childhood, implying that her "condition" is one that has been with her since birth. The influence such theories might have had upon Bryher is perhaps made clear, even in this short extract, by its interesting resonance with the account of Nancy's childhood recorded in *Development*. The degree to which Ellis's theories were important to her is made even clearer by the details of her friendship with him.

Bryher met Havelock Ellis in 1919 through H.D.'s friend Daphne Bax, maintaining a correspondence with him that was to last until 1939. As Bryher was later to conclude in *The Heart to Artemis,* "Ellis opened new ways and relieved the anxieties of hundreds of uneasy minds."[42] Ellis's sexological investigations into human sexuality were to be amongst the first sympathetic theorizations of male and female inversion. Bryher and H.D. were to form a close friendship with Ellis, renaming him "Chiron" (healer of Achilles) and inviting him on a trip to Greece with them in 1920.[43] During her first meeting with Ellis in London, Bryher raised the question of her gender identity and her lesbian desire. Recording this conversation in a letter to H.D., she writes:

> Then we got on to the question of whether I was a boy sort of escaped into the wrong body and he says it is a disputed subject but quite possible and showed me a book about it. . . . We agreed it was most unfair for it to happen but apparently I am quite justified in pleading I ought to be a boy—I am just a girl by accident.[44]

There is a curious mirroring between Ellis's act of introducing Bryher to sexological narratives, which provide a kind of revelation about her sexual identity, and the revelation experienced by Stephen Gordon in Radclyffe Hall's *The Well of Loneliness* (1928) as she unwittingly stumbles across a copy of Krafft-Ebing's *Psychopathia Sexualis* in her father's study:

> Then she noticed that on a shelf near the bottom was a row of books standing behind the others; the next moment she had one of these in her hand, and was looking at the name of the author: Krafft-Ebing—she had never heard of that author before. All the same she opened the battered old book, then she looked more closely, for there on its margins were notes in her father's small, scholarly hand and she saw that her own name appeared in those notes—She began to read, sitting down rather abruptly. For a long time she read; then went back to the book-case and got out another of these volumes, and another. . . .[45]

Hall's text, certainly the most famous and infamous lesbian novel of the 1920s, provides a useful parallel to Bryher's novels. Hall was similarly influenced by Ellis's sexological pronouncements on inversion, and her protagonist shares with Nancy a profoundly unsettled gender identity, regarding both her body and her emotional constitution as masculine. Making a new and innovative reading of *The Well of Loneliness,* Jay Prosser has argued that Hall's text is read most legibly as an early narrative of transsexual identity.[46] Like *Two Selves* it collapses lesbian desire and gender dysphoria in a way that may well seem problematic in terms of late twentieth-century formulations of lesbian identity. The difficulty encountered in trying to prise the two narratives of lesbianism and transsexuality apart in these texts is explained by the entanglement of these identities during the first part of the twentieth century. As Judith Halberstam notes in her recent formulation of the term "female masculinity," the discourses of both lesbianism and transsexuality were conflated, both in the minds of theorists and of lesbians themselves, until the 1940s when medical and surgical advances made gender reassignment surgery and effective hormonal treatment possible.[47]

It is certainly clear from Bryher's papers that both transsexuality and homosexuality were areas that continued to trouble and intrigue her. From 1929 until the 1970s, she collected newspaper articles and reports on "sex-change" operations and stories of individuals who crossed gender identities. Indeed these stories seem to arrest her attention in a way that homosexuality did not since she was not to supplement this collection with articles on homosexuality until 1949.[48]

In utilizing sexological theories of inversion that construct the lesbian as a figure defined primarily through her masculinity, Bryher places both *Development* and *Two Selves* in what I would argue is a legible tradition amongst lesbian modernists. In a range of ways Virginia Woolf, Dorothy Richardson, and Djuna Barnes (amongst others) all use codified masculinity and gender dysphoria to delineate lesbian identity within certain of their texts. Woolf's *Orlando* (1928), for instance, "dodges" the imposition of masculinity upon the lesbian body (glorified through the charac-

INTRODUCTION

terization of her sometime lover Vita Sackville-West)
by staging a fantastical and explicit sex change in its
main character. Within the early novels of Dorothy
Richardson's *Pilgrimage* series (1915–1967), Miriam
Henderson's body becomes a screen on which masculinity is projected in her large hands "like umbrellas"
and her "lack" of femininity. In Barnes's *Nightwood*
the inversions of masculinity and femininity in the
characters of the cross-dressing Dr. Matthew Mighty-
Grain-O-Salt O'Connor and Robin Vote, who is at
times described as a boy, evoke sexological construc-
tions of inversion and homosexuality.

In addition, versions of lesbian masculinity can
also be located in lesbian artists of the modernist
period. In Romaine Brooks's portrait of the lesbian
painter Gluck, entitled *Peter (A Young English Girl)*
(1923), Gluck is represented as a cross-dressing figure
marked by a certain aristocratic masculinity. At this
time Brooks also painted a portrait of Radclyffe Hall's
partner, Una Troubridge, that is similarly codified
through masculinity. Gluck's own work itself utilizes
the signifier of masculinity as a marker of lesbian identity. Her *Medallion,* painted in 1937 to celebrate her
relationship with Nesta Obermer, represents the heads
of both herself and Nesta on a stylized background,
both with short, slicked hair and strong masculine fa-
cial features.[49]

The uses that Bryher makes of the discourses

of sexology in order to reach some kind of self-understanding are supplemented by her readings of the discourses of psychoanalysis, which were to provide her with other useful narratives of gender identity and sexuality through which to read both herself and her friends. Freud's most sustained analysis of lesbian sexuality and his last case history was "The Psychogenesis of a Case of Homosexuality in a Woman." This case history was published in the *International Journal of Psycho-Analysis* in 1920 and was translated by one of Bryher's acquaintances, Barbara Low. While we cannot be sure that Bryher read this case history when it came out, we certainly do find reference to it in the correspondence between Bryher and H.D. at the time of H.D.'s analysis with Freud. As Susan Stanford Friedman has argued, Freud seemed to use his theoretical apparatus from this case history in his work with H.D., regarding her symptoms as arising out of the same psychic configuration as the "beautiful girl" of the case history, who has repudiated her desire for the father in favor of a resurgence of pre-Oedipal desire for the mother.[50] Writing of her "mother-fix," H.D. writes to Bryher: "F. says mine is absolutely FIRST layer, I got stuck at the earliest pre-OE stage, and 'back to the womb' seems to be my only solution."[51]

Reading this case history alongside Bryher's sense of her own gender identity is instructive. In his analysis Freud attempts to move away from what he regarded as the crude biological narratives of sexological "inversion" and to develop a more sophisticated understanding of the identifications and desires of the female homosexual. Yet despite this intention, he still utilizes the signifying index of masculinity to construct lesbian identity. In psychic terms the young homosexual girl seems to have performed a transsexual leap in the re-routing of her desire from father to mother:

> This girl had entirely repudiated her wish for a child, her love of men, and the feminine role in general. It is evident that at this point a number of very different things might have happened. What actually happened was the most extreme case. *She changed into a man and took her mother in place of her father as the object of her love.* [emphasis mine][52]

While undergoing analysis with Hanns Sachs, Bryher reached a "block" in the analysis because of a similar transformative "switch" in her early psychic history. Writing to H.D. about her analysis with "Turtle" (her nickname for Sachs), Bryher explained, "my analysis sticks because almost as far back as memory I am 'male' but there must have been a point Turtle says, where I decided to be 'male.'"[53] Working with Sachs, Bryher finally recognized that this switch takes place at about three years of age, though she was ultimately unsuccessful in locating the event that caused it. This sense of psychic and physical masculinity continued to be the most profound factor in Bryher's understanding of her identity. During H.D.'s analysis with Freud, H.D. was to discover that within her unconscious, Bryher was figured as a man. Bryher's reply to this revelation was that it made her "glad."[54] Freud himself was to pass judgement on Bryher's gender identity during this analysis. In *Tribute to Freud,* H.D. records that Freud himself characterized Bryher as a masculine figure, exclaiming upon being shown her photograph: "She is *only* a boy."[55] The importance which Bryher attached to this crossing of the gender divide and the terms of lesbian desire is made clear in a letter to Walter Schmideberg in which she indicated the pressing areas of investigation into which psychoanalysis should move in order to grow as a discipline. She noted with disappointment that:

> No research has been made in p.a. with regard to the girl who is really a boy. Freud made one study, and there are a few occasional references, that is all. . . . Turtle knows much but never writes about it.[56]

Within her reference to Freud's "Psychogenesis of a Case of Homosexuality in a Woman," it is clear then that Bryher conflates some kind of transsexuality with lesbian sexuality, seeing the two perhaps as a seamless continuum. What is also clear is that in her own fictional accounts of her coming to identity, the dominant discourses of inversion and female homosexuality provide important points of reference through

INTRODUCTION

which to construct this record of the journey to lesbian identity.

The "Ends" of Writing

As a coda to this reading of *Development* and *Two Selves,* it is important to note, as Susan Stanford Friedman does in her reading of *Two Selves,* that masculinity must also be read for women in the early twentieth century as something evoked through the act of writing. Friedman suggestively links Amy Lowell's "The Sisters" with Bryher's *Two Selves,* noting that for both to write was to act "manwise."[57] Here again, Bryher's complex correlation between lesbian sexuality, masculinity, and writing can be seen to work within a tradition of lesbian modernism. We can trace the complex signification of lesbian sexuality and writing through the works of Virginia Woolf, Dorothy Richardson, Djuna Barnes, H.D., and Gertrude Stein, amongst others. Writing, indeed, becomes the "end" of Nancy's quest, imaged both in the body and the poetry of the fictional H.D. There is, indeed, a kind of textual causality at work in Nancy's final journey in *Two Selves,* up the "Phoenician path" to the "grey cottage that faced the south-blue sea." H.D. has already "entered" the text, embodied through her poetic voice, three chapters before the chapter "Meeting." She is, indeed, woven into Nancy's consciousness prior to the

point of their meeting when she finds "strong, satisfying music" in a poem that is given no title:

> I saw the first pear
> As it fell—
> The honey-seeking, golden-banded,
> The yellow swarm
> Was not more fleet than I
> (Spare us from loveliness).[58]

These lines, from H.D.'s poem "Priapus," appear in the
first Imagist collection *Des Imagistes*—the collection
that provided Bryher's first introduction to H.D. at the
age of nineteen. There is, in this unacknowledged
quoting of H.D.'s lines, a kind of circularity at play
within the text, a sense of a previsioning of final union
that foregrounds the importance of writing and poetry.
Nancy, we understand, must "write a book. And find
she had a friend." Yet the hope of either endeavor is
waning dreadfully by the end of *Two Selves:* "Cycles
and cycles of days. Nothing happening. Words beat in
her head. She could not say them." In this despairing
"wordless" state Nancy takes a chance on "adventure"
and decides to keep the appointment with the poet
who might become a "friend." Then, chastening her
desire outside the door to the cottage, she reminds herself that "poets, of course, were not what they wrote
about." Yet the figure beyond the door—who is young,
beautiful, entrancing—will ultimately allow her to
find a way to vocalize the words she cannot say. We

INTRODUCTION

know this because Bryher herself finds this language
in the texts of *Development, Two Selves,* and *West,* in
the self-reflexive recording of the real-life meeting that
shaped her life to come. Her "development," which is
brought to fruition by her union with H.D., is memori-
alized in fictional form and brought to a point of ending by writing:

> *If she found a friend, an answer, the past years would vanish ut-
> terly from her mind.*

Words, friendship, desire: all infinite possibilities
which open out the future, and make sense of the past.

NOTES

1.   Evidence of Bryher's key position in the networks of modernism is provided by the sheer breadth of her correspondence,
spanning many of the major literary and intellectual figures of the
first half of the twentieth century. This correspondence is held in
the Beinecke Rare Book and Manuscript Library, Yale University.

2.   For fuller biographical accounts of Bryher's life, see Bar-
bara Guest, *Herself Defined: The Poet H.D. and Her World* (New
York: Doubleday and Co., 1984); Rachel Blau DuPlessis, *H.D.:
The Career of That Struggle* (Bloomington: Indiana University
Press, 1986); Gillian Hanscombe and Virginia L. Smyers, *Writing
for Their Lives: The Modernist Women, 1910–1940* (London: The
Women's Press, 1987). For Bryher's own account, see *The Heart
to Artemis: A Writer's Memoirs* (London: Collins, 1963) and *The
Days of Mars: A Memoir 1940–1946* (London: Calder and Bo-
yars, 1972).

3.   Bryher, *Heart to Artemis,* 122.

4.   Ibid., 157.

5.   This was followed by a second collection, *Arrow Music,* published by J. and E. Bumpus in 1922.

6.   Both introductions turned out, in their own ways, to be important. Bryher was to go on to become a longstanding friend and patron to Dorothy Richardson, providing sufficient financial assistance to allow parts of *Pilgrimage* to be produced in times of hardship.

7.   Bryher, *Heart to Artemis,* 187.

8.   Bryher, *West* (London: Jonathan Cape, 1925), 1.

9.   H.D., *Paint It Today* (New York: New York University Press, 1992); *Asphodel* (Durham, N.C.: Duke University Press, 1992).

10.   H.D., *Asphodel,* 206.

11.   For a fuller account of Bryher's editorial and financial support of "little" magazines, see Jayne Marek, *Women Editing Modernism: "Little" Magazines and Literary History* (Lexington: University of Kentucky Press, 1995). The terms of Bryher's patronage and questions of cultural production remain to be theorized.

12.   For McAlmon's account of this marriage and his life with Bryher, H.D., and Perdita, see Robert McAlmon, *Being Geniuses Together, 1920–1930* (Baltimore, Md.: Johns Hopkins University Press, 1997).

13.   For McAlmon's somewhat mixed career as a publisher, see Robert E. Knoll, *Robert McAlmon: Expatriate Writer and Publisher,* (Lincoln: University of Nebraska Press, 1957); Sanford J. Smoller, *Adrift among Geniuses: Robert McAlmon, Writer and Publisher of the Twenties* (University Park: Pennsylvania State University Press, 1975).

14.   Andrea Weiss, *Paris Was a Woman: Portraits from the Left Bank* (London: Pandora Press, 1996).

15.   Bryher recorded her reminiscences of early twentieth-century Paris in *Paris 1900,* trans. Adrienne Monnier and Sylvia Beach (Paris: La Maison des Amis des Livres, 1938).

16.   Laura Marcus, "Cinema and Psychoanalysis," in *Close*

INTRODUCTION

Up, 1927–1933: Cinema and Modernism, ed. James Donald, Anne Friedberg, and Laura Marcus (London: Cassell, 1998), 240.

17.   For an excellent account of Bryher's involvement with the psychoanalytic community and her own plans to become an analyst, see Maggie Magee and Diane C. Miller, "Superior Guinea-Pig: Bryher and Psychoanalysis," in *Lesbian Lives: Psychoanalytic Narratives Old and New* (New York: Analytic Press, 1996), 1–33.

18.   Letter to Walter Schmideberg, 1937. Quoted in Magee and Miller, *Lesbian Lives,* 26.

19.   For an account of Bryher's attempts to begin training, see Magee and Miller, *Lesbian Lives,* 1–33.

20.   Marek, *Women Editing Modernism,* 118.

21.   The most important articles from *Close Up* can be found in the excellent annotated collection *Close Up, 1927–1933: Cinema and Modernism,* ed. Donald, Friedberg, and Marcus.

22.   Anne Friedberg, "*Borderline* and POOL films," in *Close Up, 1927–1933,* 218. Donald, Friedberg, and Marcus include stills from *Borderline* in their discussion of the film, including one of Bryher.

23.   For a discussion of Bryher's use of antiquity in her historical fiction, see Ruth Hoberman, *Gendering Classicism: The Ancient World in Twentieth-Century Women's Fiction* (Albany: State University of New York Press, 1997).

24.   *Development* was reviewed in the following papers and journals in Britain and America: *The Times Literary Supplement; The Saturday Review; The Athenaeum; The Bookman; The Spectator; The New York Times Book Review; New York Evening Post; Boston Evening Transcript; The New Republic; The Nation; The Dial.*

25.   *New York Times Book Review,* 23 January 1921, 25.

26.   *New Republic,* 26 January 1921, 270.

27.   *Times Literary Supplement,* 24 June 1920, 401.

28.   *Athenaeum,* 30 July 1920, 144.

29.   *Times Literary Supplement,* 401; *Saturday Review,* 24 July 1920, 79.

30.   Indeed Bryher provides some of the most insightful and

TWO NOVELS

nuanced contemporary commentary on *Pilgrimage* in *Heart to Artemis,* regarding the book as "a searchlight" amidst the gloom of the Great War.

31. *New Republic,* 270.

32. *Bookman,* August 1920, 172.

33. Marianne Moore, *Dial,* 21 May 1921, 589.

34. See *Daily Mail,* 26 and 28 June 1920, 3 and 5 respectively.

35. Bryher, letter to the *Daily Mail,* 2 July 1920, 6. For the full correspondence regarding Bryher's portrayal of "Downwood," see *Daily Mail,* 29 June–7 July 1920.

36. *Heart to Artemis,* 194.

37. *Manchester Guardian,* 18 January 1924, 7.

38. Another characterization of sexual excess and deviance through "night" can, of course, be found in James Joyce's "Circe" section of *Ulysses* (1922).

39. Susan Stanford Friedman, *Psyche Reborn: The Emergence of H.D.* (Bloomington: Indiana University Press, 1987), 35–36.

40. See Diana Collecott, "Bryher's *Two Selves* as Lesbian Romance," in *Romance Revisited,* ed. Lynne Pearce and Jackie Stacey (London: Lawrence and Wishart, 1995), 128–42.

41. Havelock Ellis and John Addington Symonds, *Sexual Inversion* (London: Wilson and Macmillan, 1897; North Stratford, N.H.: Ayer Company Publishers, 1994), 88.

42. Bryher, *Heart to Artemis,* 287.

43. This trip was to end in disaster after H.D. experienced her famous "visions" in Corfu. Ellis was to travel back to Britain alone, while Bryher brought H.D. home overland. H.D. later recorded this experience in *Tribute to Freud* (1956).

44. Letter to H.D., dated 20 March 1919. Quoted in Magee and Miller, *Lesbian Lives,* 5.

45. Radclyffe Hall, *The Well of Loneliness* (London: Virago, 1990), 207.

46. See Jay Prosser, *Second Skins: The Body Narratives of Transsexuality* (Cambridge: Cambridge University Press, 1998).

47. See Judith Halberstam, *Female Masculinity* (Durham,

INTRODUCTION

N.C.: Duke University Press, 1998). Though, as Prosser notes in his detailed historical account, certain transsexual subjects called upon medical help (and received it) as early as the 1860s; see Prosser, *Second Skins,* 140–55.

48. These clippings are taken from a range of papers including *The Times, The New York Times, The Evening Standard,* and *The Illustrated London Times;* the sources of some are not attributed.

49. See Diana Souhami, *Gluck: Her Biography* (London: Pandora Press, 1988).

50. See Friedman, *Psyche Reborn,* 121ff. See also Lisa Appignanesi and John Forrester, *Freud's Women* (London: Virago, 1993), 389–90.

51. Quoted in Appignanesi and Forrester, *Freud's Women,* 390.

52. Sigmund Freud, "The Psychogenesis of a Case of Homosexuality in a Woman," in *Case Histories II: "Rat Man," Schreber, "Wolf Man," Female Homosexuality,* Pelican Freud Library, vol. 9 (Harmondsworth, Eng.: Penguin, 1979), 384.

53. Letter to H.D., dated 27 April 1931?. Quoted in Magee and Miller, *Lesbian Lives,* 12.

54. Letter to H.D., dated 16 March 1933. Quoted in Magee and Miller, *Lesbian Lives,* 21.

55. H.D., *Tribute to Freud,* 170.

56. Letter to Walter Schmideberg, dated 1937. Quoted in Magee and Miller, *Lesbian Lives,* 26.

57. Friedman, *Psyche Reborn,* 43.

58. For full poem, see Peter Jones, ed., *Imagist Poetry* (Harmondsworth, Eng.: Penguin, 1972), 612.

BRYHER: TWO NOVELS

DEVELOPMENT

DEVELOPMENT

A NOVEL BY W. BRYHER

LONDON
CONSTABLE AND COMPANY LTD.
1920

PREFACE

AMY LOWELL

THIS is a singular book; in many ways, a remarkable book. To any one interested in the reasons why of personality (as I confess myself to be), it cannot fail to provoke attention. The autobiographic novel has an illustrious ancestry, the autobiography masquerading as novel is almost as numerous a clan. Is *Development* the granddaughter of *Jane Eyre* or of *Obermann*? If the former, Nancy is a finely conceived character-study; if the latter, we are face to face with a young lady the least to be said of whom is that she is unlike anybody else.

This is the record of the growth—not yet of a soul, that may come—but of a mind. Through a series of deft touches, we see a small, lonely, imaginative child gradually evolving into an artist. From the first page in which the little girl of four is sitting in a box which "was really a boat," to the last chapter of aphorisms— chippings of the artistic egg—slowly, very slowly, the character is built up for us. A strange, contradictory character, supersensitive to a certain set of impressions, quite cold to others; a character overweighted on one side, leaning heavily to a bias, and yet always with the desire to stand upright, to fill the empty

DEVELOPMENT

places, to tread clearly and evenly, to see the world as a whole. Little by little the girl realizes her limitations, strains against them—pitifully inadequate struggle for so gifted a being in an environment where her subtle psychological needs are evidently but vaguely understood. And yet, is that true, after all? For the result has certainly been the creation in Nancy of all sorts of intuitions and understandings, of a delicate colour sense, of a rare perception of the possibilities in words. I think I have never met or read of any one with a keener or more conscious realization of the various beauty of words. They are to her what pigment is to the painter; what tone is to the musician. To most people, even to most authors, words are chiefly symbols; to Nancy, they have an essence of their own, a vibration in themselves quite apart from their connotations.

Nancy is evidently a writer born. "When I am older I will write a book" is the burden of her childhood's years. At nine years old she starts her first literary venture. Her mind is filled with the clash and clamour of Pope's *Iliad,* augmented by a boy's story-book of the second Punic War. She falls in love with Carthage, and so she begins her story: "Hanno was a Carthaginian boy. He was nine years old. He was very glad because he was going on his first campaign." Nothing precocious happily, for precociousness in nine cases out of ten ends in abortion. Her hopes are beyond her power of expression. The later Nancy records this epi-

PREFACE

sode with charming humour, particularly the end where the little girl, lying awake, suddenly remembers that she has forgotten to mention Carthage itself, and creeps out of bed to add to her one accomplished paragraph: "Carthage was a great city."

Nancy speaks of her childhood as "epic," and so indeed her imaginings undoubtedly made it. The family were in the habit of spending their winters abroad, and Nancy is taken to Italy, Sicily, Egypt, Spain. She develops a thirst for history, undoubtedly fostered by the long hours spent in museums. At first she rebels at these, and her mind wanders away to a puppy she has seen on the steps or to the donkey she has ridden the day before. But at last her curiosity betrays her, history books make armour and pottery comprehensible; she learns of the past not only through books, but through a series of object lessons. "Fairy Tales delighted her but little," she records; fact is the thing which charms. It is always the actual which stirs her, even if the actual be written in the past tense. Always, from beginning to end, her creative power moves about the real. Here are a few examples of her gift for words playing upon a thing actually seen:

> "A clock had long ago struck ten in the clear Scillonian air. The black stems of scattered masts were lit by gold buds."
>
> "The air was filled with a sudden richness, the scent of slumbering grass."
>
> "Sunset carved the eastern islands out of grape-blue darkness with a gold knife."

9

DEVELOPMENT

She speaks of waves as "dented blue or curved racing green"; says of the Scillies that "untouched by any spirit of historical antiquity they breathed freshness; as though, a bubble on the lips of the sea, each had been blown to reality that morning." The two poems in the book are fine, imaginative studies in the creation of atmosphere, in that power of understanding the essence of places which is the author's especial excellence.

But the epic childhood is suddenly broken. Nancy is sent to school. She resented this bitterly; in fact, the author is at no pains to hide the fact that she still resents it. And yet it is evident that this brooding child needed human contact if ever mortal did. One can imagine the bewildered family cudgelling their brains as to what to do with this hypersensitive, bookish, lonely little person. School was not a success. She set herself to hate it, and did so most successfully. And yet it did something for her. For the first time in the volume, persons, not mere shadows, walk through her pages. The head mistress, Miss Sampson, is excellently drawn. Her speech to the Sixth Form on the occasion of the "row" is one of the best things in the book; and later, when lecturing the school on the necessity of keeping things in their places, she breaks off to ask, "Has any one seen my fountain-pen? I have mislaid it for two days," Nancy for the first time makes use of irony, just the touch needed to balance her emphasis of beauty, the touch which marks the novelist.

PREFACE

Irony once discovered, Nancy does not spare herself. With relentless analysis, she says, "The indifference of others assured Nancy in her belief she was a poet; expression broke to lines of echoed verse and worse thought." She calls herself "a child of eighteen," and such she appears really to have been. For all her critical faculty, evidenced in the chapter "The Colour of Words," she seems incapable of growing up. The book is indeed development, but the end is not on the last page, that is to come, perhaps in the next volume promised, perhaps in others not yet written.

The "echoed verse and worse thought" are published, which proves the family to have been more sympathetic than wise, and Nancy's irony plays cheerfully about the ineptitudes of reviewers. But most delightful of all is the portrait of Mrs. North, who, after turning over the leaves of the precious volume, but reading nothing, lays it aside with the confident dictum: "Child, you will be a great poet." Mrs. North is a real joy as she flutters through a scene or two. Admirable the picture of her at a schoolgirl tea, where "she rushed up" to a group of her guests, "a plate in each hand, knelt on one knee before them, and chattered."

If Nancy's childhood was epic, the chapter "Salt Water" is lyric. Here the artist has full play, and we feel that Nancy is at last coming into her own.

The chapter on "Vers Libre" is only partly concerned with that all-absorbing topic. It is really the reaction of Nancy's first contact with the moderns, in

DEVELOPMENT

this case the masters of modern French poetry. The criticism is often most trenchant; it is no immature child who says of Régnier: "His prose had all the quality of poetry, was often more emotional than his verse." This is art; this she understands. But it is a child again writing of Fielding who can speak of its being "amusing" to read of Amelia. Amusement is scarcely an intelligent emotion to experience before the stark and terrible tragedy of which that sad lady is the heroine.

Indeed our author, or her puppet, is a baffling and intriguing personality. As a little girl, "she was sure that if she hoped enough she would turn into a boy," and the fact that the transformation has not taken place seems to be a strange and ever-present grief to her. Much of her energy is taken up in warring against the pricks of place, sex, and opportunity. In a sort of vague insight, she realizes that expression will free her spirit, but the wide ranges of creative imagination are denied her. She cannot make through the power of vision. "It was intolerable to write of any mood she had not personally experienced" is the keynote and the barrier of her artistic impulse, but to it we owe this illuminating bit of autobiography. How will she plan her literary future? Poet, novelist, critic—she has the potentialities of all three. Which will she be at pains to develop? An unusual young person, whether she be heroine or merely author, and one whose farther steps every reader of this book will wish to follow. No better

PREFACE

study of the growth of an artist's mind has been written, I think; it is all here, all the helps and all the hin-
drances. Whether as novel or fact, the book is a true
record of a talent gradually breaking into flower, of a
life slowly growing into cognizance of itself and of that
which it was created absolutely to do.

CONTENTS

BOOK I
EPIC CHILDHOOD

15

DEVELOPMENT

BOOK II
BONDAGE

BOOK III
TRANSITION

CONTENTS

17

BOOK I

EPIC CHILDHOOD

"The world is yet unspoiled for you."
H.D.

CHAPTER I

THE AGE OF DISCOVERY

I

ADVENTURE and the salt edges of the sea beat against the window clamorous through the rain.

Nancy was sitting in a box at the edge of the nursery table, listening to the *Swiss Family Robinson* being read to her aloud. The box was really a boat, and by the exercise of some imagination, the uncompromising squareness of its edges rounded into a tub, and helped by the noisy swirl of raindrops against the glass, there was no difficulty in believing that the distant chair (which was land) could scarcely be attained. The wind caught words and drowned them in its vehemence. Outside was hurricane.

It was fun to play; it was fun to hear of strange islands, buffaloes, boys slashing a path through sugarcanes; but the morning was wistful with the half-expressed desire, "If only I could have lived in an age when something happened."

Her rightful inheritance, the world of venturing

story-books, was dead. Her days passed unpleasantly free from danger. True, when she was fourteen she would run away and be a sailor, but that was ten years distant; it was so long to wait that sailing ships might be then, as she had heard them say, "extinct."

She could never remember a time she had not wanted to go to sea. Waves, dented blue or curved racing green, the fishing ships that moved bird-like across the water, seemed all that was left of a time when stowaways went to sea, climbed masts, rode through forests and tramped over the mountains in far places, or hunted for seals and whales. She grew tired of play, tired of listening to mere words. Would nothing ever happen any more?

The door flung open. Amid quick sentences and ensuing tumult Nancy was thrust into her outdoor clothes, into an old cap worn only on wet days, and taken, bewildered, breathless, to the actual edge of the sea.

"Wreck." Lip to lip against the masterful wind scattered the alarm. Already the lifeboat waited to be launched; crowds filled the desolation of the beach. The blue asphalt of the front was flooded with puddles, but for once all were too excited to blame Nancy if she splashed in them. The sea was a wide mass of luminous metal, faint silver here and there where a flickering light caught it, or a grey hollow revealing the tumult underneath; and beyond the clamorous horizon, sailors, actual sailors, even now prepared to launch their boats, and were in real danger of never reaching shore.

It seemed a page from a story-book that Nancy watched instead of read. That with her own eyes she could see peril and preparations for rescue had all the texture of an imaginary dream. Hail and spray rapidly beat a sense of salt reality into her thought till, exultant with discovery that wildness was yet alive and might be hers, she hurried joyously along the beach to be lifted up to see the men in cork belts and sou'-westers ready to begin their voyage. A parting of the waves, a vivid shout, and the lifeboat slid into the water, vanishing in the hollows, or flung, a struggling fish, upright against a roll of wave. Gusts of wind caught Nancy as they turned towards home, lifting her till she wondered if she would blow away, like the toy vessels children sailed and lost in summer-time. The savage rain stung her eyelids and blent with wind and sea and sky in an immense and thundering force, but she did not care, roughness was beauty to her, adventure had returned.

Next morning oranges heaped gold among the rank sea-grass or rolled from broken barrels on the wreckage in the sand.

II

Storm ever remained a profound association of infancy, storm and a longing to run away. There were

DEVELOPMENT

days when she desired utter uncontrollable freedom so much that she had to escape from sight, were it but to hide at the bottom of the garden till the fit had passed, days she longed to be a boy and go to sea. This was not to be traced to any strictness, she had more liberty than most children; it was simply a touch of natural wildness the restraint of later years was never to eradicate.

Her one regret was that she was a girl. Never having played with any boys, she imagined them wonderful creatures, welded of her favourite heroes and her own fancy, ever seeking adventures, making them, if they were not ready to their hand, and, of course, wiser than any grown-up people. She tried to forget, to escape any reference to being a girl, her knowledge of them being confined to one book read by accident, an impression they liked clothes and were afraid of getting dirty. She was sure if she hoped enough she would turn into a boy.

Her days were spent in the garden, on the beach, or in the lanes, picking wild flowers or blackberries, or playing at "exploration," her favourite game. Before she was five she taught herself to read, picking it up as she turned the pages; weaving her own romances round each picture, till the reins of the real stuffed donkey mounted on rockers threatened to hang in idleness, forgotten.

Fairy tales delighted her but little. Unconsciously she cared for nothing but what had actually happened, or what was possible to happen. The long walks, when, to make up for play, her father told her of foreign places with magical names, outrivalled in enchantment any legendary fables. Best of all she loved the hours when, ranging the contents of her Noah's ark carefully, two by two, upon the floor, her mother spoke of gondolas and palaces and streets where girls let down a basket from the upper windows to draw up lettuces or carrots, of a city ruined by molten lava ages and ages ago, and of a museum there where lay the bread baked, the lamp used, the day of its destruction, now crusted to hard metal with the volcanic liquid, which Nancy herself would see some day, when she was just a little bigger. Spring evenings when she came in with spoil of early primroses, she would hear of sharp snowy peaks above the resinous pine forests, gentian, and wild Alpine roses. Thus, to Nancy travel grew wonderful as a book, an inevitable thing, her proper heritage.

Infancy is the real period of exploration, but discoveries crowded so thickly upon Nancy that she ceased to think of them as such; in fact, when in years to come she remembered childhood, unconsciousness was the only word that was any adequate picture of the first fourteen years of her life. Yet the white and tenuous roots, desire of expression, love of freedom, a wish to go to sea, forming the base of her individuality, were already very deep. The days, the little days before they changed to the larger radiance of childhood,

DEVELOPMENT

passed in happiness, complete with a peace that held no restlessness, while month by month flung to her, basketwise, impressions and fresh beauties, sea flowers, the roseal flush clouding the August peaches, a lane heavy with nut or blackberry, March, when the spirit of childhood seemed itself enshrined in the primroses—colour of moonlight—and the soft warm feel of sand, the transparency of seaweed under her bare feet. Her one unrealised desire was possession—like a boy—of a pocket-knife, her one disappointment was the refusal of a live pet monkey; yet there was ever a poignant sadness about these little days, when years later she remembered them, of something for ever lost, of a promise never to be fulfilled.

But always truant among her dreams even of ships and sailors was the thought, "When I am older I will write a book." With years curious things seemed to happen, but there was the ring of a boast about this desire, something of the impossibility of a fairy tale, remote in its chance of ever coming true.

III

"Please may she come and play with me?" The speaker pointed a jam-stained finger at Nancy, peeping in half-frightened amazement between the bars of the gate. Nancy had played but seldom with other children, she was not sure that she wanted to go with the stranger.

THE AGE OF DISCOVERY

She heard a whispered consultation, while the child from next door regarded them with impudent eyes.

"Nancy, run along and play with the little girl, she wants to show you her garden."

A little unwillingly she trotted off.

"What's your name?" asked her companion, licking the jam from her fingers.

"Nancy."

"Mine's Sylvia."

She was a strong assertive child, half a head taller than Nancy and bigger in proportion.

"I've been wanting to play with you for a week. Didn't you hear me call through the hedge yesterday?"

Nancy shook her head. Unafraid of any one grown up, she was a bit shy of this infant with her queer rough speech.

The friendship lasted a few brief weeks. At first the novelty of a playmate who, unlike a toy elephant, could argue, quarrel, and on occasion fight, prevented much resentment at the way Nancy's carefully cherished animals were scratched and broken. The end came on a summer evening after tea. Nancy possessed a tricycle which she was wont to ride about the garden, but since Sylvia had come, fear the garden beds might be destroyed had forbidden its use. That evening, on promise of behaving quietly, they were allowed to take it up and down the quiet road outside.

Sylvia snatched the handle at once.

DEVELOPMENT

"You ride it up and I'll ride it down," suggested Nancy.

"Right," nodded Sylvia, racing off. Nancy ran behind her to the top of the road, watched her sweep round a little clumsily, up and back a second time.

"It's my turn now," Nancy interrupted, as Sylvia moved to ride down the road again. Sylvia laughed defiantly.

"I've got it and I'm going to keep it."

It was the injustice that stung Nancy. It was her turn and her tricycle. Furiously she snatched at the handle, at the seat. The tricycle fell over, Sylvia caught at Nancy's hair, blow followed blow, there were yells of anger, both were lost in a whirlwind of waving arms. Soon a crowd collected; the grocer's boy, leaving his parcels, urged them on. Small, but quick and reckless, Nancy danced round her opponent in circles, uttering shouts of triumph, about to knock Sylvia to the ground when some one gripped her collar, gripped Sylvia likewise, and led them both, howling and incoherent, up the road. Nancy's mother, hearing a noise, had feared an accident, had arrived in time to see the ending of the fight. Twenty minutes later Nancy lay dejectedly in a dull and darkened room, a full hour before her proper bedtime, meditating on the injustice of the world. It was not that she minded being led up the road in disgrace so much, she knew she was never punished at home unless she deserved it, but that Sylvia, to whom she had surrendered toys and leadership for

28

all these weeks, should dare to ride away with her tricycle, in defiance of all justice, and that their fight should be stopped just as she would have knocked her down, perplexed her unshaped ideas of morality. She hoped, kicking the bed savagely, that Sylvia also was in a darkened room; there was a savage joy in desiring that Sylvia got no supper. Henceforth, her games should be shared with her toy elephant, a safer and a quieter companion.

IV

With seven the age of discovery deepened into childhood. Rumour hinted at a possible journey that winter to Milan and Venice, perhaps the Italian Lakes. Toys grew more and more neglected; even her stuffed animals were laid aside for books. On her birthday she was given a volume of tales from Shakespeare, not Lamb's, but a more elementary picture-book that disputed the right even of the *Swiss Family Robinson* for chief place in her affections. The elemental tales of the plays, growing even as she grew, passed so utterly within her nature that it was hard to realise, after a few months, there was a time when Viola and Imogen had been unknown. The mere fact of the frequent assuming by the Elizabethan maiden of "the lovely garnish of a boy" captured an imagination eager enough to copy; she was ever impatient of the end where they changed to a girl's attire. Odd bits of the stories would attract her—Pericles finding his armour, smelling of brine and sand; the journey of Imogen to Milford Haven; Caliban snaring sea-mells among the wilder parts of the island. Perhaps a sense of the eternal beauty of the mere names moved her even in infancy; disdaining the other literature of childhood she lived in Illyria, fanciful, yet so vivid, an unimagined reality. Near Christmas-time they went away.

V

From a train brilliant with light they huddled into a gondola, into the violet denseness of a stormy night. A peculiar state of wind and tide had combined that year to flood the great square; St. Mark's shivered with the touch of water, and the wind had a northern keenness about it as they left the station. Nancy's first impression of Venice was that gondolas were uncomfortable things; she could see nothing in the blackness, only the unrestful water stirred in miniature splashes against the bow. Up a canal, through a door, right into the flooded hall of the hotel, and amid a chatter of vivid Italian Nancy was lifted on to dry land, halfway up a staircase piled, as far as the steps were dry, with rescued furniture.

Much of this first Italian visit passed into vague remembrance obscured by later and more vivid hours at Naples or at Rome, but the outlines of Venice, boldly carven, never quite passed from thought. St.

THE AGE OF DISCOVERY

Mark's was perhaps her first conscious impression of richness. St. Mark's contrasted with Milan, that colder city, seen on the way home. Child-like, it was neither the pictures nor the quaint drawings, the moulded lions nor the gondolas with their long clumsy oars, that attracted Nancy's eyes, but the fluttering mass of pigeons in the centre of the square. Every afternoon she would climb the Campanile, making it a game to see how fast she could run up; then, her hands brimming with grain, she lured a flight of metallic wings across to the far edge of the square, watching the soft and eager heads as three or four birds perched on her arms or sought the spilt gold on the pavement. It was a sad day when she turned from this, from the sunshine and the water to the coldness of the North.

It was not until the following year she became really intimate with Italy, coming to Rome, to the Forum, where she gathered an antique bit of marble, to Naples crowded with the open life she loved, the aquarium where whole hours were spent watching the sleepy sea-anemones, sea horses, crested as a wave, the feeding of the octopus, and the strange southern iridescent fish darting and shifting in the bubbling water. From this, from days at Capri or at Baia, some weeks at Florence, with enforced confinement to the museum, came near to being an irksome end to her second winter spent abroad.

CHAPTER II

HISTORY

"I HATE Michel Angelo." The custodian looked shocked, a passing visitor smiled. Nancy stared at the head of the faun with more than a little fear she would surrender to some compelling power in the rough marble, gazing up at her with such inscrutable eyes, but she was tired of Michel Angelo, the name followed them everywhere, besides nobody could explain to her what a faun was. Outside in the sunshine there was a puppy playing, a brown puppy chasing its tail, and though she was aware it must long ago have strayed into one of the dark Florentine streets, an unconquerable hope that it lingered on the steps prompted her to be impatient of each delay. A live puppy held a vastly greater interest for her than a cold statue. "I hate him," she repeated, looking for sympathy to her mother who had delivered her from the tyranny of museums on more than one memorable occasion.

"We shall only be another half-hour now, and if you are good you shall have a new book this afternoon."

HISTORY

Contented with the promise, Nancy was silent. A book was far more exciting than a puppy she could not touch.

Museums were cold places, there could be no playing in them. There were statues, many of them broken, all with long uncomprehended names. The shelves were lined with pottery, red or black, and curiously fashioned green bronze lustred with age. Always in answer to her persistent inquiries she was told they were "vases" or "lamps." Even to herself she lacked power to put into words her desire, impetuous to escape into speech, to know who had used these vessels, when and where the shields, the breastplates hanging on the wall, had been worn. What did they eat, what did they wear, how did they live? Childhood is not articulate, so she thought instead of the brown puppy playing in the sunshine, the soft flickering movement of a donkey's ears. To her eyes these carvings were relics of a dead, uninteresting world, yet there existed an imperious sensation of a domain passed, as one might pass a garden, ignorant that behind the stone hedges bees swarmed in velvet murmur amid hives, whence the blood of the sun trickled in stalactites of honey and stung the delicate powder silvering the bloom of the violet grapes. Chance put into her hands a key.

Among the two or three English books a child might care to have, Nancy chose that afternoon one, by no noted name, that retold to infancy such portion of the Iliad as could be understood by it, with the addition of many earlier and later stories, the fall of Troy, the Amazons, myths of the Greek Gods. She was attracted by the picture on the cover, struggling men in armour resembling that abounding in Italian museums, and carried the book triumphantly away.

Ever a quick reader, picture after picture shaped in her mind, never to fade; interest quickened till it flamed, ardent, invincible. Lovelier than the opening petals of the almond, richer than a southern morning, impressions poured into the white and rounded vase of her imagination, clamorous and hot with sweetness. It was her first revelation of the power of literature, of her own power and desire of a richness that could never be satisfied, a new world, or an older one understood at last. She read of Greek children, of their games, their days passed in enviable wildness; of the strengthening of young Achilles on the hearts of lions, the marrow of bears; of fauns and satyrs, music and the Nereids of the sea. Troy pictured itself to her, the ships, the tents on the shore, full of the little details children love, the woollen cloths, the carven bowls, the unyoked horses. She delighted in the combats, the funeral games, especially the wrestling and the chariot race, the burning of the ships, and, supreme moment, the fight over the body of Patroklos. She could see it, feel it, till her days passed in a crashing of bronze, a clatter of sandals, till to have seen the sun-browned body of a warrior catch the light at the corner beneath the heavy perfection of his harness would have surprised her less than the group of guide-equipped tourists plaintively wondering what they ought to admire.

Parts there were that appealed to her less strongly than others, the loveliness of Helen, for instance, boys and warriors alone reigning in her fancy, and Paris, whom she heartily despised, but it was the foundation of a knowledge of antiquity never again to be ignored. Marred but by a need of constant reassurance, it was more or less a truthful picture of a distant age, it awoke a dormant interest in history, which became the engrossing passion of her days; history, only another fashion of desiring a complete knowledge of life. Actual existence is too complicated to do more than puzzle a child of eight. Nancy, in fact, was not consciously aware it existed. It is too full of shades and tones; a child desires the crude outline, the hard curve there can be no mistaking, and this history, with store of vivid narrative, epic of flight and battle, offers in abundance to a childhood unconcerned as to why an event happened, which cause was right, content to look merely on a broad whole, or take a side perhaps and follow the conflict with an eager interest.

Perfectly willing now to spend the entire day in a museum, provided she could pillage its contents to fit and fill her own imagination, with this book and a companion volume in which she learnt of Odysseus and his travellings, the whole of antiquity seemed to draw aside its veil of years with slow and unreserving movement, and taking its place, with sun and wind and grasses, among the natural emotions of child-hood, she herself played in a primitive world.

Two books, however rich in impressions, could not content her long. There were gaps in the story, the perpetual and dreaded threat, "Wait till you are older and you will read things for yourself," etc., combined with the incompleteness of her knowledge to keep her in a state of literal hunger for information, until, just following her ninth birthday, she saw in a window Pope's translation of the Iliad. After some stormy minutes, with the derision of several grown-up people ringing in her ears, Nancy having found an unspent shilling in her pocket, bought and carried the book away.

Children are ever the best judges of what in literature is most suitable for them, what they can understand. The appeal of much written for infancy is really to adult sensation, while most of Shakespeare, an epic such as the Iliad, will fill the imagination of a child in a radiant and pristine sense no scholar can recapture. Vividness, both in narrative and detail, that is what a child desires. It must be able to see pictures.

The heroic couplet does not jar the insensitive ears of a child of nine. Nancy read Pope's translation all day, dreamt of it at night. Troy, represented by a large mud pie, occasionally was taken in the garden, usually on an autumn morning when the gardener made a bonfire, because the smoke was the burning city, and the sparks looked like falling towers from the two steps at the end of the lawn which were the Greek ships putting out to sea. On wet afternoons the chariot of an arm-chair whirled madly to battle, Nancy crouching beneath a picture-book held for buckler that sheltered her from a rain of imaginary arrows. Compelled at last to acknowledge that she had read and re-read the book till she could absorb it no more, another chance discovery taught her Greece and Troy were not the only nations of the ancient world.

It was really a boy's book of adventure that drew her enthusiasm to a fresh direction, a tale of the second Punic war and Hannibal's advance on Rome. The fascination of this modern-hearted figure, set, strange contrast to his nobleness, amid the most savage race of a savage antiquity, early eclipsed her delight in even Achilles himself. Achilles was a visionary figure, but Hannibal, he was known to have existed, at nine he had marched on his first campaign. (A hastily procured history-book assured her this was correct.) That at her own actual age had begun a career which, but for the cupidity of an effeminate Carthage, might have changed the story of the world, the audacity of that march through an undiscovered country, across the Alps—the stumbling, dying elephants, a memorial of their passage—almost to the gates of Rome, quickened and ripened a love of history, ever to be of her elemental roots of life.

The stories of the Punic wars, of Carthage, were in themselves picturesque. There was a richness in the word mercenaries which appealed to her imagination as she watched in thought Numidian cavalry, wrapt in lion skins and quick as a southern lizard; that primitive artillery, the Iberian slingers; the carved shields of the Carthaginian horse waiting their turn to embark on that voyage whence four years later the remnant returning, exhausted with victories, were to lose their greatest battle beneath the walls that had betrayed them to hunger.

Beside Hannibal, fiction or fairy tale was dull as an etching to an eye avid of colour; still, books that treat of Carthaginian life being inaccessible to childhood, to assuage a hunger for literature that should bear at least the name of Hamilkar or of Hanno in its pages the inspiration came to Nancy to write a story for herself.

She was balanced on the edge of a sofa that was an elephant advancing with a swaying dignity toward the Alps when the thought took form, but the whole campaign was forgotten while she pondered over the hero's name. A boy must occupy the centre of the story. To her, Carthaginian girls existed merely in a fabulous way. She would have liked the boy to belong to the Numidian horse, her woolly shawl would have made a magnificent lion-skin, but she did not know a Numidian name. Finally she decided on the Carthaginian cavalry. This took the whole afternoon.

Tea was devoted to a meditation as to the accessibility of paper; finally, a new exercise book, intended for her French dictation, appropriated, she began:

HISTORY

"Hanno was a Carthaginian boy. He was nine years old. He was very glad because he was going on his first campaign. He had a breastplate and a helmet with plumes and a buckler covered with silver plates. He rolled up a lion-skin and put it behind him on his saddle. He belonged to the Carthaginian horse." This, in Nancy's scrawled handwriting, covered two pages, and was finished just as bedtime came. She felt very proud of herself, though it was slow work and she wanted to get to the Alps. When the light was turned out she began wondering how many days it would take her to get to the battle of Cannae. It had not occurred to her then that a book could be written otherwise than straight through from beginning to end. She remembered suddenly she had forgotten to mention the city in her story. Every one was downstairs, so, with great precaution not to be heard, she crept out of bed and added to her tale in pencil, "Carthage was a great city." Then she jumped quickly into her bed again, into the warm softness of the sheets, and closed her eyes, dreaming.

CHAPTER III

HIEROGLYPHICS

HURRIED days in Naples, a sudden decision, watching for the ship in the rifts of sea between the crimson roses, going on board, coming up the first morning to see Stromboli volcanic blue within the distance; storm, leaning on the rail to watch an Arab in scarlet fez spring on deck, first hint of Egypt, these and a confused impression of hieroglyphics, Bedouins, Thotmes, and the desert merged in a vague expectancy as the train left Alexandria. Nancy was bitterly ashamed of herself. She had disgraced her first voyage by seasickness; part of the journey, in fact, she had not enjoyed at all. Her most tolerable hours had been those spent lying on deck, wrapt in a rug, dreaming, with shut eyes, of the adventure and the mystery enshrined for a child in the story of the early Egyptian vessels that rowed tropic seas to Punt.

They had wandered out to Italy in early December with the possibility of further voyage before them, Egypt or Sicily. Nancy had hoped for Egypt; Italy was wonderful, but Naples was still Europe, and Egypt

40

meant Africa, crowded, if rumours could be trusted, with camels, vultures, scorpions, and even jackals, up the Nile. To a child the mere word desert was full of fascination. To-day she had landed in this new continent for the first time.

Annoyingly oblivious of the importance of the moment, every one brought out papers, went to sleep. The train, reeking of Europe, rattled on. Nancy was thinking of the Zoo, the solemn keeper leading a dromedary with a look of infinite dreariness in its eyes. The guide-book spoke of pelicans—it was hardly to be believed these birds existed wild and uncaged where she, Nancy, might see them. Was it possible the whole country was a myth?

Tired of waiting for something to happen, Nancy stared at the plain wishing she had a book to read. The carriage was full of glaring stillness, papers rustled. Another two hours to Cairo. Probably Luxor would turn out to be just the same as Europe she thought impatiently, till out of the midst of the plain of green corn and cotton plant a mud village, full of an unmistakable Eastern silence, sprawled by a clump of date palms. A figure or two in fez or turban moved among the doorways. Along the wide road a man, vestured in indigo, preceded a shaggy camel, marching no longer drearily, but with the insolent pride of his position as chief of the desert beasts stamped in the uneven pace. Nancy stared, pressed to the dusty windows, excited, happy, till they passed from sight. Africa, she was in

DEVELOPMENT

Africa. How difficult to realise she had left Europe at last.

As they drove to the hotel a water-carrier, bent beneath the weight of his goatskin, shouted in guttural Arabic among the crowd; veiled women passed, and men with lemon slippers dangling from a pole. Too late to go out that night, she longed impatiently for morning, for the first day of a wonderful three months to which she was to owe the broad foundations of an education few children have the opportunity to obtain.

Cairo was stranger than she dared imagine. At first the usual winter rains made the roads impassable with mud; later they dried to a dust of ground ivory. Nancy poured over hieroglyphics and Egyptian history, explored an ostrich farm, went to Heliopolis; most of all she loved it when they walked or drove through the bazaars.

Poem of a city, the East is silence, there is no youth, only age and antiquity.

The dreams of the city are the stuffs of the merchants, indigo, almond and cinnamon. There is gold for remembrance of Antar, Antar, fingering his weapons, brushing aside the rough camel-skin to gaze at the dust of the desert. Ivory and tulip red, as songs murmured to a lute of ebony when Mamum ruled in Damascus.

The speech of the city is colour. In the dusk of the palace of the vendors of carpets, over a screen of ebony, mother o' pearl and ebony, trail of turquoise, trail of silver, a scimitar snaps

HIEROGLYPHICS

the darkness. Cordoba to Damascus bent once to the might
of the moon-curved steel.

The East is silence.

Silence of eyes that are impalpable black almonds, silence of silk
of cream and of cinnamon, silence of turbans folded, lustrous
and heavy as the bloom on white roses. Garrulous and guttural, the water-carriers with their goatskins, rough with hair,
bloated with water, the grunt of a camel, shrillness of a seller
of scarlet slippers, these are only the ripple and promise of a
wind that is asleep for ever. The East is silence.

Spoils of Ethiopia, Numidia, Assyria, were heaped, were wasted
in the Memphis markets. Now nothing is left of Antar, of Mamum, the marches by night, the defiance, the victories, but
crumbling moonlight over the sheath of the scimitar.

Rumple the stuffs, there is emptiness, colour, but no singing, only
terror crouching by the silence, the inscrutable silence. Thebes
and Memphis and Carthage crumbled to a colour, a savour
of mightiness, essence of parchment, of amber and cinnamon.

The opaque pearl of stillness is shattered by clumsy-vowelled Arabic. A sais passes, bronze figure escaped into life, racing in
white and impetuous scarlet. Heavily the air re-gathers to a
stillness.

The East is silence, fear and antiquity.

.   .   .   .   .   .

They had been in Egypt a week. To-day was their
first morning in the desert, their first day of real adventure. It was cold driving out to the pyramids, where the
donkeys awaited them, but once free from the crowd of
begging Egyptians they would ride across the wastes
of golden dust to Sakhara, the Step Pyramid, to the
ruins of fallen Memphis, and back by train from the

43

neighbouring station. Twenty miles in the saddle—the poetry of the thought of it. Nancy shook the reins of her donkey, quite as big an animal as the pony she was accustomed to ride, with a string of blue and vivid beads round the shaggy white neck. Behind her trotted a young Arab, in an indigo shirt, barefooted. Now and again the donkey twitched its muscular ears softly, when a fly worried it. A boy's story-book and a couple of histories had filled Nancy with pictures of a world that had been a centre of wisdom and civilisation four thousand years before. Antiquity held no terror for her, only interest; in imagination she lived within it oftener than in this modernity of railway trains and formalities. To her it was a period of unrestrained freedom, a life of riding forth, a lion-skin on the saddle, the picturesqueness of single combat. Half the morning Nancy alternated between a tale of ancient Egypt, in which she was a warrior marching into Asia, under Thotmes, and a struggle to ride her donkey as she would her English pony. She wearied out the young Arab assigned as her attendant by a series of mad gallops. She led the entire party.

The desert was so unlike the plain her imagination had pictured. It was not flat, but a sequence of delicate and sloping ridges, and the sand soft and pliable as gold dust slipped from sharp and scattered flints. Four hours after they had passed the Sphinx, the excavations of Sakhara came in sight.

Nancy was sorry to dismount. She wanted to ride

on and farther till sunset-time, then to sleep in a
tent, roughly, to set out again with morning on their
journey till, as their dragoman told them, after four
months they would come to Tunis or Tripoli. Once in
the tomb of Ti, her momentary disappointment vanished. With the ardour of a child for animals, it was
the hunt of a herd of gazelles, the return of the quaint
Egyptian craft from fowling, the sheep, the geese, and
the oxen that attracted her. She explored the tombs,
would hardly be prevented from plunging, if only for a
few steps, into the subterranean passage, now blocked
with shifted sand.

They came back by Memphis as the sky flushed
red behind the date palms. She would have retarded
every minute which drew their ride nearer to a close.
Perhaps it was this, or was it simply the desolation of
that immense and lonely figure, prone in the deserted
grass, with vegetation springing in tropical neglect between the scattered stones? For the first time something of the desolation of antiquity, the actual coldness
of ruins, something that was not quite sadness, a feeling alien, fingered her heart. Here had been a centre
of wisdom, the regal end of royal Egypt; the spoils,
the wealth from Numidia to Circassia had spilt, had
wasted on those pavements, and now, she was sitting
on a white donkey staring at a wilderness of stones.
Donkey-boys and dragoman jabbered in unison. There
was no vivid freshness of paint, homeliness of Ti
among his oxen, nor the impenetrable dignity of the

pyramids: it was desolate, an aspect of antiquity, a deadness she could not understand. In the sharp flame of the short dying of the sunlight a train brought them back to the modern city.

A fortnight later they left for Luxor by train. Nancy was disappointed at first she was not to go all the way by boat, but the prospect of reaching Thebes in a night's journey consoled her. Thebes—of all Egyptian history nothing had impressed her sailor mind so much as the expedition to Punt, and was not the tomb of Hatasu herself on the other side of the river? Then there was Rameses, the epic of Pentaur, on the great Karnak wall.

Her first impression of Luxor was a long line of donkeys ranged at the corner of the ruins, dust and flies. From her point of view the afternoon was wasted seeing the Luxor temple, when she desired to cross the Nile, and reaching the hollows of that ridge of hills, full of strangeness and the dignity of the pyramids, to come at last to Thebes. Luxor temple was dull; she could not love all ruins indiscriminately; and she spent much of the time watching an Arab boy suck length after length of sugar cane—it reminded her of the *Swiss Family Robinson,* a book now relegated to the forgotten days of babyhood.

It might have been an Egyptian boat, relaunched from the museum that morning, in which they crossed the Nile. Half-way, they disembarked, to hurry across an islet of sand. Another row, a scrambling into rough saddles and ahead as usual, Nancy turned for Thebes. Along a path too narrow for galloping, trenches for irrigation on either hand, she came at last to one of the few survivals of the Seven Wonders, the Colossi of Memnon. Emblems in their mystery and in their sadness of the whole realm of Upper and Lower Egypt, life seemed almost to breathe from the stone as it caught hues and diverse lights. What had made the sound, Nancy wondered, the sound at sunrise and at nightfall? Watching them, she had a sense of intrusion, almost of fear.

"The Tombs of the Kings." It needed no dragoman to point to the temple of Hatasu to assure Nancy they were in ancient Egypt at last; with a turn of the valley they stepped straight into a living antiquity. They ventured into passages heavy with the smell of bats. They explored temples, multitudinous tombs. They passed a curved basin where in summer the natives sleep to avoid scorpions, and an Egyptian brought a scorpion for them to see, heavy-looking but venomous, on a bit of broken pottery. Little naked children, balls of chocolate brown, with white and dirty skull-caps, played about a fallen statue. Nancy deciphered one or two of the commonest hieroglyphics, picked up a few words of Arabic. She rebelled when they turned to go back.

Days passed quickly in Egypt. As a final pleasure before they left Luxor, Nancy was permitted to ride to Karnak one evening at full moon. The others followed in a carriage a pace or two behind, giving her a sensation of delightful loneliness, almost of danger, as she trotted off through a blackness powdered with moonlight. The moulded figures loomed strangely out of the dark. Karnak had never seemed so immense; never before had she known so much of the age, the peace, the mystery of this land that had lived on the memory of a former greatness when Carthage was a young city and Rome a waste of marshes. They passed the great wall, Rameses in his chariot, on till they could look across the isles of shadowy ruins up to the moon, full and lovely in an inscrutable sky. There was a howling of wild dogs in the distance as they turned away.

It was not until the following year Nancy had more than a hurried glimpse of Nubia. They came at once to Cairo, from there direct to Assuan, spending a month on this border of a harder, more barbaric land. Here was none of the soft richness that linked Cairo to the days when the scimitar of a Saracen held dominion from Bagdad to Cordoba, nor the sense of age which placed even modern Luxor back in the beginning of history; but adventure, rides into a desert where the tossed sand was stamped by the footprints of hyaenas, sails along the golden water of the Nile. Perched high above them were great white pelicans, with bills a brighter orange than the rocks, and amid the incessant murmur of the Arab rowers, children, grave as an old temple, gazed at Nancy without a movement in the myriad tiny plaits of their black hair, shining, Nubian-wise, with castor oil. Even the stillness had a new air about it; the mute uneasiness of the bazaars had gone; nor was there a trace of the sleepful heaviness of Thebes. This was the silence of the wilder spaces, Bedouin in its pride.

"Fire!" They turned hastily half-way to the native town. Had the whole world blown into flame? The opaque river was a hot goldness, the sky blazed with flame, the land was land no longer, but burnt, visibly. Shrill and husky, Arabic and English voices mixed. Children ran, policemen ran, the crowd ran; and over the Roman ruins, the hotel, a mile away, was cut into towers and pinnacles of an ominous red.

Nancy had never seen a building burn before. Assuan had assembled in the square in front of the hotel. People whispered and rumoured of the accident. The electric light dynamo had blown up. It was a corner building, and as yet the hotel was untouched. Should a puff of wind arise as sunset came—men shrugged their shoulders, spoke of sleeping in boats upon the Nile, of hiring an Arab house. Nancy watched the violent flames leap from the holes where windows had been. There was no beauty in them, only terror. She was not afraid, but they sullied the spirit of the land—an intrusion, undesired, too cruel to own adventure. The natives chattered helplessly; precious water kindled the burning, rather than assuaged it; in a swift silence flickers crept nearer and nearer the roof of the hotel.

"Sand!" A rush of white-robed Arabs to the desert;

DEVELOPMENT

expectancy. With the first bucketful the red sparks were not so vehement; trembling invalids pressed back to the shelter of their rooms, as the immediate danger passed. An even tramp, and a company of soldiers formed a barrier round the enclosure. "Why," Nancy questioned, "are they stationed here?" "To prevent the Nubians from looting the hotel." By the light of a candle in a bottle, with the challenge of the sentries breaking the air beneath her window, Nancy was put to bed.

They turned away from the Nile, into the Libyan waste, in the cold air of the early morning. Nancy ever felt speech to be an intrusion when she rode. The even motion, the wide spaces, made her desirous of dream. Refusing to remember this was their last day, she galloped on, always a little in front, the blue beads round her donkey's neck glittering with movement. Three hours passed, and four. They had ridden up a valley, dismounted to see some caves, ovals of dark amid the gold, and were come now to the regular track, marked, half-buried with sand, with camels dead on the march, rigid in a sullen exhaustion that had wrestled with death and expired in victory.

Under a high mound of rock and sand they halted to rest the animals. They could ride no farther and return that day. Nancy pleaded to ride just a few feet farther alone, to a clump of camel's food, with rough and tenuous branches. A wild sense of liberty, unfelt before in so intensified a form, filled her heart. Thus had the youth of the world ridden forth. She wished she could gallop away into the waste of gold, away into the strangeness of that mud-built town, a week's journey distant, beyond it till she came at last to an Abyssinian sea. As if in answer to some part of her desire, a dozen Bedouins, tangled black hair streaming to the date-brown fingers pressed firmly on their sword hilts, heavy matchlocks slung upon their camels, moved from without a whirlwind of dust. They surrounded them, yelling in hoarse Arabic; thrusting their hands out for money, the fierceness of the desert in their eyes. A moment or two, and they had turned the corner, bearing their produce up to Assuan, one, lagging a pace behind, matchlock in hand.

Adventure is the poetry of life, the richest treasure of childhood. Stirred with the invincible spirit that made Cortez and made Roger, that sent the low Egyptian boats to dare the voyage to Punt, the spirit that has made the sailor and the artist, Nancy moved regretfully away, filled with dream.

Beyond the low cave on the horizon a jackal waited, immobile, for the sun to set as they returned. Nancy turned her head to watch it, wistfully conscious of a sense of farewell, in a measure right, for only as an unconscious child was peace for her in the East.

In the dust-storm, whirl of flying grit, they turned next day to Cairo, towards home.

CHAPTER IV

TRUANT WITH ADVENTURE

I

THE brown ears of Nancy's mule twitched in a slow rhythm. She was jolted upwards at an aggravatingly even pace, ahead, as usual, by some hundred yards. Light was regal about the fretted ridges, the luminous air lived; morning, jocund and defiant, leapt on the snowy points of Monte Rosa. The mountains sloped in vivid line against a gentian sky. It was no hour to waste upon a saddle; sun caught her to a hot rebellion: it was a day of movement—wild, imperious.

Zermatt was hidden by the pines. The slowness grew unbearable; the minutes should not waste in un-protesting acquiescence to a dull command "sit still." Not wilfully, but impelled by a touch of immortal madness, desire of liberty too large for childish pas-sion, Nancy slipped from off her mule and raced, un-heeding, up the hills.

Pursuit was impossible. It was hard enough to move even slowly over the stones. Only the agility of ten, seeing no danger, careless of the way, clambered in natural recklessness up the short grass slope, vanished beyond a corner, running, scrambling, climbing towards the far horizon. People called her, spoke to her. She was unafraid, but held her way in silence, up and on towards the orient ridge.

A calmer day she would have stayed to pluck the mountain pansies or gather the rich bell gentian, blue as an Arab tile; this hour even the rarer Alpine roses, colour of sunrise breathed on the snows of the Dent Blanche, tempted her in vain. Freedom: she wanted freedom. Alone, truant with adventure she ran on, seeking an immortality for which she would never know a name.

Terror a time might ever come when liberty would cease forbade her to return. Before a savage wildness the mountains had unloosed, unconscious childhood bowed assenting head. Exultant-hearted, a full hour before the rest could come, the Schwartz See with its purple blackness, its daisies and its gentian, spread before her eager feet.

Nancy burst on, past the lake, past the hotel, past the staring people, beyond the mountain pinks, till lion-wise, in crevice of sharp blue and splintered violet, the "Glacier of the Lion" sprang upon her startled sight.

Nancy stopped, ashamed, bewildered, by the inscrutable ice. Two men had climbed it once—climbed it, losing an ice axe on the way. Dazed by the impene-

DEVELOPMENT

trable pinnacles, dumbly she told herself the story, twice and then again. Courage, of which a child has daily need, is ever the virtue dearest to its heart. Her own impetuous morning became but mockery beside the huge boulders, the smooth ledges; her path to an immortal freedom was barred by the crystal snow.

Never had the edges of the Matterhorn curved so sharply in a noon all blue and gold. The hour of her recapture was at hand. Not yet had come the time when she might put forth strength in conflict with the mountain. Not yet, but it would come. One day should hold adventure captive within her hands.

II

Worn steel—dull indeed beside the damascened gold and silver mail of the Spanish kings, but conqueror was written on the blade, and Cortez himself had swung it, the very night, perchance, when, Aztec grappling Spaniard on the dark and turbulent causeway, a trembling civilisation slipped from victory through the endurance of his will. Truly by that sword had Mexico been won.

All the enthusiasm of her eleven years Nancy lavished on the weapon. The treasuries of Spain were as dust beside its glory; old and unread books beside that conquest, perilous, impossible, the seizing of a land, if ever one were seized, by one sword, one brain: the treachery, the sieges, the defiance. Hernando Cortez,

TRUANT WITH ADVENTURE

"El Conquistador," and the sea breathed through his spirit.

The wildness of his youth answered her impatience of authority. With Agathokles he linked himself in the burning of the ships, with Hannibal in the audacity of his marches, with Roger in his daring. That his expedition meant the ruin of an empire, the destruction of a wealth of learning, was not for a child's vision. For Nancy Cortez spelt Spain; he was another in the long line of leaders who, raising their land to history, were rewarded with dishonour.

Nancy looked round the armoury, perhaps the richest in the world, wishing she could have borne mail. Her ears were alert for the rustle of steel; she longed to feel the weight of a sword, to wield the curious battle-axe hanging so near her head, to fasten a hauberk about her of linked and twisting metal. Spanish sunlight smote the dark aside and flickered, rapier-pointed, the blazoned breast-plates to a golden iridescence. In that one room was shut the Middle Age.

Egypt had served as preparation for the study of the Saracens; it seemed a natural sequence the following winter should be spent in Spain. But Madrid was dark with a repression that was one side of the mediaeval centuries, and cold with biting wind. The insistent note of tragedy in the story of the land even a child found it difficult to escape. Could anything be gloomier than the Escurial, repellent lines set in a savage plain? Interest apart, the day there had been one tren-

DEVELOPMENT

chant dreariness, an explanation of the destruction of wealth and knowledge, the ruin of Mexico, Peru and Granada, by the rigid might of this Iberian power. Toledo, bright as were its streets, held much of the temper of its own weapons, thrust in a sheath and uneasy in captivity. Even the sword of Cortez, as she looked at it, seemed to point away from the North, harsh with gold and sand, to the clearer cities of an Andalusian South.

III

A single lamp swung windily amid a desolate platform. The train which had left them at Cordoba at half-past four on a December morning, jolted on. Into a blackness broken but by rain, Nancy gazed sleepily through the window of the cab. It seemed hours before they arrived at the hotel.

Their footsteps sounded harshly in the silence, as they followed the one attendant along the stone corridors into a large room, cold and lit by just a charcoal pan, three-legged and mediaeval. Nancy sat in the biggest chair in a state of delightful sleepiness that rejected sleep for dream. They might have been sitting in some old Spanish palace with a slit for window and the steel cap of a man-at-arms glittering in the shadows of the door. The hours were passing when to pretend to be of the bodyguard of Hannibal contented her; she wished she could have followed Cortez, but she needed to be herself a leader; she wanted to know and feel the actual deeds. Somehow it seemed impossible that she could ever grow up like the ordinary people she saw in England, afraid of storm, with repressed voices, such restricted lives. No; when she was older, according to her childish phrase, something would happen, something must happen, that would make these present days but a promise of adventure beside its wonder and its wildness.

Names—Toledo, Seville, Cordoba, each a mediaeval parchment—trailed dreams across her mind. In her imagination she donned mail; she could almost feel the weight of her sword; the dead embers in the charcoal pan became a beacon; she was tramping towards it through unexplored regions as she dropped asleep.

A space of elfin arches, leaf-bent, curving flowerwise, or moulded in crescent upon crescent of Arabian richness, pure in colour as the bloom of coral or a drifted shell, the Mosque at Cordoba, born of six centuries of Moorish rule beneath a softer sky, held an indefinite trace of the desert, of the date palms, foreign to Cordoban eyes. Not beggars, but some Arab scribe, royal in vesture of amber or of indigo, should have kept the outer steps. The absent lances, palm leaves in a golden air, of the Saracenic warriors, made poor the stone-paved streets.

The day was history. The fascination of all foreign places, elusive and impalpable, that drove a thousand

Spaniards to dare a western sea, was heavy in the orange trees, splintered with crystal rain. The drifting tangerines mocked with a light derision trailing lemons carved of an early moon.

Unwillingly they took the southern train. For all its fretted glory the Alhambra was so desolate, beside Seville, flaming with orange and with scarlet. There was a sensation, almost of terror, of a pitiful appeal in the Court of the Lions, in the thin columns straight as tulip stems, its sculptured fountain, with no peace, only a hard expectancy of tragic event to be, even the gipsies dwelling Neolithicwise in caves could not eradicate. Algeciras brought a welcome wildness with its fields of palmetto, of narcissus, and the dark cork forests that sloped towards the sea. Unshaken from her Italian allegiance, Nancy left, one January morning, for Algiers.

IV

Water swirled beneath the train, ominous cracks threatened the embankment. On either hand were no longer the desert spaces, but a pressure of floods, here smooth, here twisted to a whirlpool of no definite colour, and crashing like a battle-axe towards the perilous rails. "C'est dangereux, mais c'est dangereux." Up and down the crowded corridor rushed an anxious French attendant. "We're likely to be stranded here all night," a man was heard to mutter, and the two old ladies in the next compartment dropped their knitting and sat rigid with a terror they were half ashamed to show. Every one collected at the windows. Nancy turned with contemptuous voice and excited eyes: "It's the funniest desert I've ever seen; it's flooded."

Algeria had been one long disappointment. Algiers had greeted them with snow. Nancy hated cold. It was appalling in its newness, its air of French formality. Nothing had happened; there had been nothing to see; only the amusement of watching the anchored ships lined along an entirely modern harbour; the glimpse of savage monkeys along a Barbary gorge.

El Kantara had been passed, and in place of Libyan mystery they had steamed into this avalanche of water, exciting, yes, but never the Sahara. From an earthen bank a waterfall beat the window with a shower of crystal spikes. "We shall be the last lot through for a week," echoed down the corridor. The floods died in a rushing turbulence three feet deep as they jolted into the station.

Biskra looked annoyingly European. Out of the night and raging wind a crowd of negroes burst upon the luggage. The carriages swayed in the uneven mud as they drove to the hotel. "The wall has been blown in; the wall has been blown in," every one was shouting, and residents and newcomers filled the passage and gazed at the heaped débris of what had been a bedroom, the unstable eastern architecture cracked and shattered by the storm.

DEVELOPMENT

Biskra was just a parody of Egypt. Nothing could change the palms, but the streets held an air of French intrusion, the East had lost its dignity, camels stepped sullenly and not with a Libyan pride. Nancy was glad when, by way of Constantine and Bône, they came to Orient Tunis.

V

Slanting trails of rain blurred the windows, but Nancy's eyes, eager for Carthage, would not be reconciled to the limits of the carriage. For three years—a whole age in childhood—she had hungered for sight of the city, she had sworn allegiance to Hannibal in her thought. Iberian slingers had kept her from her play, Numidian cavalry, rough with gold-dust and a doubled lion-skin, had galloped across her dreams. Period after period from Phoenician settlement to Roman burning passed through her mind, too young to read aught but the strength and splendour of the story. The mercenaries, Hanno the voyager, the last siege, were too epic not to impress their wonder on any childhood happy with knowledge not only of history but of the actual South. She stared out of the window, hopeful that the impossible might happen, that antiquity would return. She wanted the war elephants to sway over the rough stones, to see the spears of heavily-armed Gauls, steel leaves erect in a thicket of branches, to watch and watch till the mist broke and out of it moved the dark horses, the purple and the silver of the Carthaginian horse.

The carriage stopped.

They scrambled out, not into a noon of amber warmth with the sea, the Carthaginian sea, a space of hyacinth at the horizon, but into a darkness of mud, a greyishness that held no violet about it, set with a few bleak stones. Nancy looked about her for the city. Not even the name of Hannibal met her eyes.

Rain fell, a quiverful of silver arrows shot by a damp wind. Guides spoke, proffering their services. "Carthage, the ruins of Carthage!" And the sea crashed and the storm with the clanging of heavy bronze.

This was the end of the conquest of the Alps, Trebia, Lake Trasimene. Clay lamps in a cold museum, and the voyage of Hanno forgotten. Coins, fragments of stone, scattered as the mercenaries, and no Hamilcar to rally them. A hunched Tunisian in alien clothing, and Punic cruelty, Punic greatness, hidden with earth, colder than the sea.

The wind, insolent conqueror, whirled over desolate Carthage. Remembering the glory of Hannibal, the beauty of the city he spent himself to save, Nancy was caught by a strange desire to cry.

VI

Nancy opened joyously the pages of the Shakespeare she had just been given and wondered where to begin.

DEVELOPMENT

Troilus and Cressida sounded exciting; Achilles, Ajax, Hector, these were familiar names. But who was Pandarus? and why did Troilus come so eagerly from war? Cressida was a girl, no fighter, and therefore unimportant, but the strange guise of her favourite Greeks was too hard for infancy, and she missed the swirl and vigour of the Iliad battle-scenes. After a hasty glance she turned to another play. Perhaps because of Egypt, perhaps because of the chance music of a single line, she began the final acts of *Antony and Cleopatra*.

Here was real fighting. Cleopatra's spirit was worthy of a boy; Antony, who threatened disappointment, died in armour. She read on eagerly; this was an adventure.

Even thus early her ears were alive to the keen beauty of word and thought. The pages seemed to burn with colour before her eyes. Lifted above all that, by her very immaturity she could but crudely understand, she was conscious of an exultation felt but once or twice before only, the knowledge these pages guarded an immortality as strong as the rich antiquity she knew; an explanation of greatness that effaced the desolate memory of the few stones left of the city that had nurtured Hannibal and betrayed him.

> Give me my robe, put on my crown! I have
> Immortal longings in me: Now no more
> The juice of Egypt's grape shall moist this lip:—

TRUANT WITH ADVENTURE

Yare, yare, good Iras; quick.—Methinks I hear
Antony call: I see him rouse himself
To praise my noble act: I hear him mock
The luck of Caesar, which the gods give men
To excuse their after wrath: Husband, I come;
Now to that name my courage prove my title!
I am fire and air; my other elements
I give to baser life.

These thoughts were powerful as a sea-wind; here was
the flame, here was the wildness of the desert, keen as
ever she had known it on those venturing Egyptian
mornings, alive, calling her in words. This was the
spirit that had taught Hannibal to conquer; in this
spirit he had accepted death. But more than the
fierceness of it, it held loveliness.

O eastern star!

All of Egypt, sombre, beautiful Egypt, was in that line.
Here was adventure safe from scorn and from
desolation.

She need not sorrow for Carthage any more.

CHAPTER V

ALMOND-BLOSSOM

A DELICATE foam of almond-blossom shimmered the naked earth, fell lightly on Nancy's hair, was blown, with what wind there was, to make of ruined Naxos a newer city of living petals. A herd of brown and shaggy goats passed under a geranium hedge, a spear's length high. A sea of lazuli beat in from Greece below the arching boughs.

Nancy watched the water, watched the almond trees, wishing she might wait, here in Sicily, for Spring. The influence of the past Italy and Egypt had embedded so deeply in her nature, had grown with these months spent in Palermo, Akragas, Syracuse. Here was antiquity; here was also the Middle Age. It was not only the fantastic carts, gaudy with saint or armoured knight, that held an air about the rude drawing as of a land emerging from the ages of barbarism, nor the peasant, brigand-eyed, his rough sheepskin trousers shaggier than the Sardinian donkey he crouched on; but the whole atmosphere, under the outer skin of railway and tramcar, was vivid with the days of both

ALMOND-BLOSSOM

Dionysius and Roger, the cultivation of olive tree or almond that had proceeded undisturbed amid the clashing of aliens, Greek and Carthaginian, Saracen and Norman, fighting for the dominion of a land yielding alone to the Greek islands in richness or in beauty. The place slept. At Solunto, at Syracuse, antiquity could claim pre-eminence, but at Monreale the spirit of the Middle Age was enshrined in blurred line and magnificence of mosaic. Here, in this land of wild geranium and growth of fennel, of temples fashioned of the spirit that led Agathokles to Carthage, palace of moulded pillar, lazuli and marble, she could swing at will from a confused mediaevalism to the clearer beauty of an earlier but not so primitive age.

Her companion had been Freeman's own abridged version of his larger history, and much of the magical enthusiasm poetry was afterwards to kindle lived for her now in mere words, with association of loveliness of heroic deed, the Carthaginian war, Agathokles and the burning of the ships, the quarries of Syracuse; or the name alone of a place, Concha del Oro, shell of gold, that brought the sea to mingle with almond and with lemon blossom, Palermo or Euryalus, now vivid with anemones.

From earliest remembrance certain phrases, names especially of places or of persons, were never free from an association of colour, fashioned of a tone, written in it; and as she grew, this feeling developed, unconsciously expanding until her whole vocabulary became a palette of colours, luminous gold, a flushed rose, tones neither sapphire nor violet, but the shade of southern water; Ionian-blue she called it, coming later to Greece, and white, with all the delicacy and fragileness of thin foam, or a heavier shimmer merging to the cream bloom of a rose petal. This, to her, was perfectly natural. She marvelled no one ever exclaimed, "I love the gold of magical!" or "What a wonderful white Sicily is!" just as so many murmured "What a magnificent crimson the painter has caught in that fold of drapery!" but with the capacity of a child for silence, spoke of it but once or twice, and the incredulous glances taking it for play, passed unnoticed. She assumed it was common to every one, if she wondered at all that it was never mentioned; supposed it was too ordinary, too usual, though to her it was an added interest, an added beauty in her life.

Travelling has much in common with adventure, and all these days of surely an epic childhood seemed immortal to Nancy, even the hours spent moving from place to place. Her imagination, sensitive to all impressions of the loveliness and the legends ready to her hand, found time to ponder as the train jerked on, to assimilate what crowded street and ruined building had heaped there in profusion, effacing all that held no importance from her memory, in preparation for the new atmosphere of another city. Besides, in Sicily, as in Spain, trains are not obsessed by any desire of speed, and in the long hours as they passed through brigand-rumoured mountains or above a sea of dark green foliage lit with sun-round oranges or the paler moon-lemons, or as they moved along a coast of waves blue as dark hyacinths, something of the spirit of the land unconsciously became absorbed within her thought.

All this tranquil winter spent so near the olive trees she had turned more and more from tales to accredited history, and her first conscious inspiration had taken shape. With the impetuousness, the ignorance, perhaps, of twelve, accepting no impossibilities, she fashioned, vaguely, it was true, but decisively the vision of an immense history of Sicily, which would become almost the history of the Mediterranean, from the beginnings of Egypt, through Phoenicia, Greece and Carthage, to the end of Saracen and Norman, the gradual dying of the Middle Age. It was not alone to be a history. All the life of the time, the customs, the armour, especially the trade, would be depicted, the tiny details she missed in the longest histories, all that she wanted to know and was told she was "too young to understand." She would labour to make it perfect, to make it beautiful, till it became the very epic of the South, till all could read in one volume the knowledge she was seeking in books, in fragments, in pictures, in stones, in the whole of the land itself. At this time a historian usurped, to her, the place that excavators and Egyptologists formerly had held. It seemed a way to keep, to touch the immortality of a greatness impos-

sible to escape, in the ruins of Akragas or at Naxos,
that heap of fallen stones, beautiful yet in its loveliness
as the light caught the snows of Etna, burning behind
it. In sleep she could have traced the map of Sicily.
All imaginary things, memory of the Iliad, even, faded
before the audacity of Agathokles, leading his defeated troops across the stretch of water, perilous with
storm, up to the very walls of almost victorious Carthage, setting the sand aflame with firing of the ships,
missing by how little the conquest of Northern Africa itself.

As for Duke Roger, better than any romance were
the fragments she could collect of his story: the castle,
perched among the roughness of the hills, the almost
careless seizing of an island, where all the Southern
nations in turn disputed for mastery. Undisturbed by
the complexities of history, her imagination was free
to absorb the entire force of the direct narrative, un-
fettered by moralities, by any weighing of issues. The
subtler shades of the hesitation of the Athenians had
as yet no meaning for her. With a natural intolerance
of indecision Nikias was pitilessly condemned.

Besides this growing consciousness of the power
of history, the actual poetry of the island; the tenderness of the colours, so unlike Egypt or the hard glare
of light and shadow in Spain, exerted its influence in a
way unfelt before. A conscious perception of loveliness
possessed her imagination for the first time. Natural
surroundings are the greater part of the moulding

of childhood, and when the sun is the sun of Naples or Girgenti, when the seas are hot with thought of Greece, with echo of Africa, when instead of bleak wind and barren marsh there is lemon flower and almond-blossom, something of the clamorous richness of the South must pass into one's very being never to be eradicated.

The ruins on the opposite hill, grey and arrogant as rain, held Nancy's eyes. The sky, transparent as an almond petal, flushed with night. Wind stirred; the spirit of antiquity, strong with loveliness, lived, touched her in its breath. The immortality of the land spoke. Naxos was immortal, so were the almond petals, and it was these she wanted, these—Greek Sicily, an old beautiful freedom, not the Sicily of the Normans, not the Middle Age.

The sharp colours softened; she grew afraid for them, angered the wild darkness should rob from her the day. It was unbearable the passion and the triumph of this moment should perish with the sun, dreams might tremble in their transience but not reality, not life. And desperately, as she fought for it, as the hills turned ominous with greyness, remembrance of the book she was to fashion drove fear back. To be wise was to possess Sicily for ever.

Childhood had spoken farewell to the South.

CHAPTER VI

APRIL

"WHAT is a pterodactyl?" The family sighed. Unexpected questions in an imperious voice were ever an ominous sign. Nancy's habit of reading anything from a time-table to a dictionary was responsible for a great deal of miscellaneous knowledge, but nobody knew where her interest would lead her next. A visitor, unwitting of the consequences, had left on the table a magazine containing some account of a recent discovery of prehistoric animals. This Nancy had found and read.

A mere explanation that a pterodactyl was a kind of flying reptile belonging to the Jurassic and Cretaceous periods was insufficient. Nancy wanted to know what it ate, what it looked like, when the Jurassic period was. The article presupposed a certain knowledge, could only be a hint to her of an unexpected world, made more delightful by its very difficulties, possible of reach but through some volume of research. Admitting no impossibilities, the undaunted enthusiasm of thirteen spoke firmly: "There must be something written on the subject, and I am going to read it."

A couple of elementary text-books appeared within a few days and were rapidly learnt by heart; the real authorities followed. For almost a year and a half she pored over skeletons, ranging from dinosaur to man, from the gigantic tree ferns to the chipped and polished flints of the Neolithic Age. That the volumes she desired were so expensive it took months of waiting and persistent appeal before they were given her, merely quickened her enthusiasm. Hitherto, the beginnings of history had been dulled by obscurity; Carthage, Phoenicia, had risen from a myth. Palaeontology offered her a firm foundation; it completed history. Besides, were not the stories of many of the discoveries a romance in themselves? She wrote a tale, nine pages long, of a boy of the Palaeolithic period; she copied drawings of mastodon and dinosaur; she wished, secretly, she could have had an iguanodon as a pet.

Interest lost much of its unconsciousness. For the first time it demanded expression; into her rough drawings she poured crudely of the spirit that she felt. Once or twice that mythical time "when I'm big" had seemed a little nearer, or rather another period was in sight when she would start her work, whatever it might be. A palaeontologist, perhaps; and yet, interesting as fossils were, there was something about them, a slight and cramping aridness, as though her imagination was

DEVELOPMENT

being squeezed into a dark hole, too small for its bursting wings. There was something in her that could not be poured into the minutest tracing of a browsing triceratops. At this psychological moment her father gave her a volume of tales of the great artists, their real lives.

It had never occurred to Nancy that art had an actual existence. She had touched statues, she had seen pictures, she had no idea how they were made; like books, they were fashioned of mystery. She had supposed the artist a child; then, with a single day, a painter. The intervening period of apprenticeship she had ignored. Much more than the actual pictures, the lives of these men appealed to her, how they learnt and fought and conquered. As history had made her in some sort a historian, palaeontology a palaeontologist, so with this book came the thought, "If those men could paint such pictures, why could not you?" Nancy seized a pencil, swift as a tide between a narrow strait the passion seized her; from that hour she splashed everywhere with paint. Pictures flung themselves in headlong riot through her mind; straightway from a few words she could see the little street crowded with water-sellers and their lemons, the painted carts, all the South she knew. There was nothing she saw but she wanted to draw it; nothing she knew but she wished to form it to a painting. It seemed so wonderful that the most irksome detail could be made living, that there was no need to seek adventures; the most trivial incidents of her own ordinary life could be a treasury richer than any guessed at in her dreams. She wished to live in the past no longer. Before a week had gone she decided she would be a great artist. True, there were difficulties. She could not draw a straight line, but in her mind she could see wonderful pictures complete to the tiniest detail. All the artists she read about over-came obstacles, so why could not she? And of each story Nancy felt a picture might be made; she longed to pour her own enthusiasm into line of head or body, to create the world of her dreams. But her faces looked mere lumps of paint, and she could not capture even an illusion of movement in the limbs of animal or warrior. Most of the artists had started by learning to draw. Coming to London that winter, Nancy was granted after much entreaty a course of lessons.

The South of France had spoilt travelling for her, with two winters of Nice and the monotonous dullness of Paris. Paris meant long walks looking at the shops. She hated shops; and Nice, though they moved from snowstorms into sunshine, meant restrictions, no ex-citement, nothing to do. It was a land of formalities, and rather than face a third winter there Nancy had enjoyed the novelty of staying at home, too absorbed in drawing to miss even Naples or Syracuse. On a March morning, a bundle of paints under her arm, she came for her first lesson.

It was the usual art class; casts hung round the wall, plaster crumbling to the floor in a white dust

DEVELOPMENT

from some of them, a sick-looking greyhound lay on the platform, and six or seven girls sat talking in front of easels. As the door opened they all bent to their work in seeming enthusiasm, though the one or two farthest away managed to glance up to see the cause of the interruption. Nancy was given a stool and an easel in front of a cast of the head of a bloodhound and told to make a quick drawing of its outline.

As soon as Mr. Baker left the room she started drawing. To her amazement most of the others stopped and began chattering on any subject but art. Nobody took any notice of her, for which she was grateful, and after her first hurried glance round she never raised her head until Mr. Baker came up later. He looked at her drawing, pointed out the worst faults, then tore it in two and told her to start afresh. Nancy was there for six weeks. The smell of the place, the daubs of paint scattered everywhere, the brushes on the floor, the broken bits of charcoal were joys to her, for she felt among them as though she were beginning at last. The other pupils surprised her; except when Mr. Baker was in the room they never worked. Her imagination had pictured them far too intent to utter a sound, except a few words of grateful thanks to their teacher occasionally, or perhaps criticism of each other's work, yet she heard them discuss art but once.

All the time that Nancy sat drawing outlines of a greyhound her head was filled with dreams of the time when she would be a great artist, the time when she

74

would know other artists, have utter freedom and be able to talk about art all day long if she wished. Going home along the grey streets she would smile at the people she passed and think, "You cannot love the sun as much as I do."

Proud as she was of studying at a real Art School, she looked on the other students in a pitying way, firmly convinced painting meant more to her than to any one.

To crown her joy an artist whom her parents knew was asked to tea. Nancy had heard of his pictures, but had hardly dared hope to meet him. To her delight he sat down near her and began talking to the others of the early Italian painters. Nancy listened eagerly; she felt he was wise and very kind. Presently he went up-stairs, was taken to the schoolroom, where Nancy had put out her masterpiece, a large canvas of a basset hound, hoping it would attract his attention. Afraid he would not notice, and again afraid he would, Nancy waited by the door. He came in, walked round, and said, "What a nice airy room this is." Her father pointed out the basset hound, saying Nancy had painted it, so he walked round the table. "Yes, you can see it has got a head from here; she has not got a bad sense of colour, but the drawing is all wrong."

Nancy was far too disappointed to say anything, and all the way downstairs he would talk about some book of travel he happened to see in her bookshelf. As soon as he had gone she rushed upstairs to examine

DEVELOPMENT

her treasure. He might be a great artist, but she was sure he had not bothered to look at it properly just because she was young. There was hidden genius in it. The legs were unsteady but the head was beautiful. Many painters had not encouraged beginners, whose work had later been recognised as great. Nancy felt this must be one of the discouragements to be faced at the start. Perhaps the background was a trifle dark; out came her paints, and she set to work again, more convinced than ever that she had in her the making of a great artist.

Fourteen is old to retain the fancies of childhood, but Nancy had no schoolfellows to laugh them away. Yet a change was stealing over her; she began to know she saw only the outside of things, to weary of it, and wonder what lay beyond. Childhood was ready to slip from her for ever, had she but known it, waiting just a touch to lift its wings. However she loved painting, books, her constant companions, would not be denied. History lessened in interest as desire for expression increased; instead, it was natural to turn to poetry. Sheer enthusiasm for anything rhymed carried her through the *Dunciad,* though the heroic couplet was but harsh music even to her inexperienced ears. Tennyson she tried and hated, Keats was too weak to satisfy her. Art had lit her imagination but not filled it, she could not mould the fancies that panted to escape. Lonely, not for playfellows, but for some one to share her dreams, a wet April morning sent her to search the library, sent her to a worn book on the middle shelf: *The Dramatic Literature of the Age of Elizabeth,* by William Hazlitt. Was it the hint of history which made her take it down, some innate interest in the old cover which made her carry it upstairs? There was a sense of richness in the paper as she turned the leaves, as lines obscure in meaning, strong in music, ebbed into her head. Nancy had come to her own land at last.

She had wanted to find the world. It opened to her in the Illyrian loveliness of the great Elizabethans, teaching her with one hour what life could mean, her own power. Bellario was not raised so "high in thought" as she, meeting with Orlando Friscobaldo, the Duchess of Malfi, Endimion for the first time. The stories conquered her imagination as their music captured her thought. To read some scenes was to taste immortality; to watch the death of Vittoria Corombona, the meeting of Hippolito with "old, mad Orlando," or to listen to the mockery of Bosola until all pride, all courage broke in the one reply,

"I am Duchess of Malfi still."

Palamon and Arcite made "almost wanton" with their captivity because they were together; Caesar bending towards the body of his enemy to call him "conqueror"; the strong, true phrase of Hazlitt, "It is something worth living for to write or even read such poetry as this is or to know that it has been written, or that there have been subjects on which to write it"; this made adventure, this was life. She was to be loyal to drawing yet a few days longer, but in her mind she knew books were stronger than paint. Into the intimate presence of poetry she passed, mute with delight, offering with her opening youth of the same love Endimion swore to Cynthia, "Whom have I wondered at but thee?"

As she walked down the grey street that evening a professed knight of literature, two passing, muttered, "How ugly the roads are." Ugly, could anything be ugly? Nancy wondered. And as if in answer to her challenge the street put forth new beauty, an April sunset fringed the edges of the roofs with gold, transforming them into towers, turrets, and a thousand fanciful shapes; the lamps just lit glimmered like a line of newly blossomed daffodils; the distance was dark with night, an intense blue, full of mysteries. Midway an insolent scarlet pillar-box flung its colour through the blackness, answering Nancy's spirit,—she felt she could dare the world.

As soon as the light was put out and she was alone she travelled each night to a new land. It was more magical than riding with Roger, or sailing with Cortez, because there was mingled with it the slightest touch of reality. She could never be a sailor, she could never be a boy, but she could be an artist, she could be a writer. It was a strange exultant region; she feared if she breathed it might vanish, if she moved she might wake and find it gone, yet every morning she woke to a fresh treasury of knowledge, of things to do and to learn. True, there were inexplicable mysteries, truths that seemed covered with a haze of carnation and faint gold, delicate as a moth's wing when she approached them; but she was content to lie there dreaming, knowing now and then the haze would lift and something more would be added to her knowledge. She was full of an overwhelming gratitude that such a gift was allowed her. All life seemed hers to do what she would with it; obstacles were as nothing if she could express something of what she saw, something of what she felt. The equal of all workers, for had she not begun her work, these few exultant hours were to be a beacon in the bitter days that followed; vision of a loveliness never quite to pass.

People marvelled at her strange silence. "What is the matter with you?" they would ask, smiling. Inarticulate, Nancy desired more and more to be left alone with her dreams. Although in actual knowledge ahead of most girls of her age, possessing at fifteen the intellect of a woman of twenty, her feelings were those of a child of seven, truant with imagination, unmingled with reality.

"We are going back to the country and on Saturday you are going to Downwood School, as a day girl. You shall go and see Miss Sampson to-morrow. She will be very kind to you, and you are sure to enjoy school very much."

DEVELOPMENT

Nancy could not realise at first what the words meant. Something in the tone of the voice made her uneasy. "But I want to go back to the Art School," she faltered.

"Not just for the present, perhaps you can go when you are a bit older."

An ominous fear was stealing over her; still her head, full of plans and hope, could not understand. At last the truth in all its shattering agony burst upon her.

The nightmare of the following days drew to a close. She waited in sickening dread the beginning of the term. She had desired reality—it came, in a numbing, tragic blankness. From the delicate bloom of peach the spirit of childhood flushed to the tenderness of a wild rose, it was ready to be one with dream. Unconsciously she clung to its wings, but the hurricane of life was abroad with desolation, trenchant with destruction that a later June might blossom. April, April, no use to call April; at the first touch of sordidness the spirit of childhood, amorous of dream, passed, in a flight away.

BOOK II

BONDAGE

"Young? why do you
Make youth stand for an imputation?"
                                    Thomas Middleton

CHAPTER I

TRAGIC REALITY

SATURDAY morning.

May, in mockery, painted the skies her most radiant blue, the sun set the bees humming in the ivy, and all along the garden path golden-hearted tulips lifted their exultant scarlet heads—but nothing might comfort her. She walked out silently, though inwardly she raged like a caged animal, shaken with that wild anger which only children feel, suddenly deprived of their freedom for some reason they cannot understand. At nine o'clock she was left at Downwood. It was one of the coldest, bleakest places she had seen, with open windows, worn-out carpets, and a mass of white paint inside, and outside a long weedy lawn and a few flower-pots. Her first impression was the incessant noise. Girls seemed everywhere, all in white blouses and blue skirts, their hair tied back with an enormous bow. Miss Sampson met her, took her into the library, and told her to wait. Books with torn covers lined the room, and Miss Sampson's little black dog lay in the only arm-chair. Nancy walked over to it and waited,

DEVELOPMENT

instinctively feeling that a dog was better than being alone with a lot of noisy girls. Never, never would she speak to any one of them, for she knew that was the reason she was snatched from her dreams and freedom and sent to school. Dreams! At the bare thought of them blind impotent rage swept over her, the rage that only children feel, utterly helpless, dragged down by gigantic forces they cannot understand. Vaguely she wondered if this was what loneliness meant. Through the window the hills shone in the sun, and all the happy afternoons she had spent up there among the bee orchids came back to her. Why had she never realised her happiness then?

Miss Sampson came in and called her; whatever she had to face she would meet as Hannibal would have wished, so, flinging her head back, she followed her into the school hall.

A good many girls sat writing at small desks. All who dared stared at her. "Sit down, dear," said Miss Sampson, pointing to a vacant desk, "and write me a nice essay on the Sea Power of the Age of Elizabeth."

Fresh from Hakluyt, Nancy began pages on the subject as soon as Miss Sampson left the room, but after a minute all the girls turned on her.

"What's your name?" asked the girl next to her.

"Nancy," she answered involuntarily.

"How old are you?"

"Fifteen."

TRAGIC REALITY

"Where were you at school last?" This from the back row.

It was too much, the reality of school burst too miserably upon her. Nancy drew herself together with all the dignity and defiance she possessed and burst out with "I have never been to school before; I do not approve of schools, and I do not intend to remain here."

Nobody answered, but some one in the back row muttered to her neighbour "Funny fish." Odious expression. Nancy wrote on, till presently the oldest girl there turned round and asked her, quite kindly, if she had travelled much.

"I know Europe pretty well," Nancy answered, unsuspectingly falling into the trap, unaware that this truthful answer would label her as conceited and extraordinary until she left the school. If one has travelled it is the rule at school apparently never to mention it. All the girls questioned Nancy at once, but she refused to answer, saying she wished to get on with her essay, and applied herself to the English seamen with enthusiasm. She longed for solitude, anything to free her from being questioned by this rabble. After a time a bell rang and most of the girls left. Nancy wrote on, and a mistress began giving a class at the other end of the room. Against her will Nancy listened. She had heard so much about classes, yet she had never seen one; she was interested in spite of herself, until she sud-

DEVELOPMENT

denly realised that she also would be taught in a class, she, who two short weeks before had scorned the world in the glory of her new-discovered life. Another bell rang, they trooped out and she was left alone. Nancy hoped she would be forgotten, for a moment she even dreamed of climbing through the open window and running away, but stopped in time, remembering she would not know where to go. After a few minutes Miss Sampson returned and called her. "Lessons always finish at eleven o'clock on Saturdays, so you may go home now. I will introduce you to Marjorie, and she will show you the way out; remember you must be here punctually on Monday."

Nancy followed her guide through a medley of girls to the back of the house. "There is the gate," she said and hurried away, glad to be rid of Nancy.

She might not even use the front entrance, but must keep to the school door. It was typical of the whole existence, Nancy reflected bitterly, but at least she was free till Monday, free for thirty-six whole hours.

She hurried home and begged, implored to be taken away. There was a vague hope something might happen which would prevent her from going back, and Monday seemed very distant; she thought she had never realised what a long time a day really was before. Whatever happened they could not take her dreams away, and in them she tried to forget the coming reality. That evening she sat in her room, full of a fierce delight that her thoughts were her own, hoping, wondering. She realised this was an end of painting; besides, she knew and felt so much now beyond her power of expression in paint. How should she draw the despair of the morning? These and a hundred other thoughts rushed through her, the sharp burden of her inarticulate emotion forced itself to expression. Taking up pen and paper she began a poem. No one but herself could understand it when it was finished, but in her eyes it was wonderful. Time after time she read it, feeling when she showed it, all would realise she was a poet, the absurdity of sending her to school. Perhaps there would be apologies for the torture of the morning? With the terror of school taken away, how she would appreciate home and the hills; if it were possible even her dreams would seem lovelier. For an hour she thought of the excitement there would be when the verses were shown, and came down feeling writers and painters were the most wonderful people in the world. After dinner, sweet with anticipation of expected triumph, she showed the poem. To please her, all made valiant effort to understand it. Nobody was impressed. Months later Nancy herself was to laugh at the crudeness of the verses; at the time she only raged, raged, raged like a wild animal, the last hope of escape vanished, full of fears and feelings she could not understand. Till she went to bed she was silent, then Hannibal himself could not have soothed her. Sunday passed, all too quickly. She felt incapable of making

DEVELOPMENT

any effort to save herself; nothing made any difference. It was the blank horror of waking on Monday that was so terrible. She tried to make the walk to Downwood last as long as possible, but it seemed only a minute before Miss Sampson met her, and said, "I am going to put you in the Fourth Form, so you will begin nicely in the middle of the school."

"I won't stay here long," Nancy answered defiantly.

Miss Sampson wisely took no notice and led her to the Fourth, a room next the School Hall, and gave her a seat between two other new girls. The carpet on the floor was very worn, there were three rows of battered ink-stained desks, two photographs of Rome, and an open bookcase. The door opened, a mistress came in, put some books on the desk in front of her, and Nancy's first day began.

The lesson was French. One by one, beginning from the back of the room, each stumbled through a paragraph of a simple book, pausing, to her amazement, to inquire the meaning of every other word. Nancy's relations had told her so often how she would miss her lack of formal education if ever she were sent to school, she had imagined the classes would require a constant concentration of all her knowledge. As it was, she felt free to watch the form while Mademoiselle chalked explanations on the blackboard. Nancy had never been so near girls of her own age before. For the first time the spirit of the crowd—an oppressed thing in turn oppressing, judge of outward aspect only, blind to the finer shades, with the strength of the sloth, the ferocity of a brute—weighed her and weighed her distrustfully. The glare of many faces, weary and uniform in expression, was about her, pressed her down. Surely this was the feeling out of which was born the many-headed dragon of myth? From the mire of crushed individuality and dream, surrendered as the price of a comfortable mediocrity, she could discern the eyes lifted in a piteous helplessness, an unconscious hunger of loveliness, with the brooding heaviness of dinosaur or mastodon. Pity—that was a gift of the future; for the moment, as the class ended, Nancy rose with the rest in the same spirit that an Athenian follower of Nikias, learned in art, faced the ruder Syracuse who had enslaved him, his body compelled to obedience, his soul freer than ever.

The morning was a nightmare. Nancy was given books, lessons, one or two girls spoke to her, but for the most part she was left alone. Lunch was a new ordeal. Being a day-girl, she had no set place, but was left standing helplessly in a corner, until a mistress made room for her at the edge of a table. Then came a walk, two by two. A girl of nine or ten was made to walk with Nancy. She stood away from the others until they were ready to start, then they walked silently up the hill. She did not know what to say to the small child, and as soon as they left the road and were allowed to walk as they liked, the infant ran on and joined another group. Nancy walked alone with her

DEVELOPMENT

hands in her pockets, pretending she was a boy. At six she was free to go home, but as she was leaving, Miss Sampson called her and gave her a straw hat with a school hatband. Nancy carried the badge of servitude home under her coat. It was a fitting end to the day.

The week dragged on, lessons began at nine, in the afternoon there were games or a walk, then preparation until supper. Rumours concerning her travels had spread, how, she knew not, before her arrival. Her utter ignorance of school convention set every girl in turn either to question or to jeer. Their language was peculiar, for a long time she could not understand the slang they used. Irritated rather than afraid, for each she had an answer, stinging and defiant. The first days over, most dubbed her "queer" and left her alone.

It was the afternoon she dreaded most. At the beginning of the second week they forced her to play tennis. She could not play and hated games. The school method of making her an enthusiast was to put three children from the Second Form, who made fun of her, and herself into a court, where if a ball were hit it must go into the bushes. There they had to play or rather knock the ball about for two whole hours and a quarter without stopping. The agony of those wasted hours. Now and again a mistress (watching no child should rest from a game they knew not how to play) would shout from the terrace, "Run, Nancy, run, do you expect the ball to come to you?" Then the whole school would turn on her with a shrill unanimous laughter. In the distance the chimney-pots of home peered about the trees, and old ladies passing said one to another, "How happy the dear girls look."

The games mistress quarrelled with Nancy from the start. She was pretty and knew it, half the school adored her, and she lived on flattery. For her sake games, however dull, became the fashion. Nancy refused both to adore or to admit the supremacy of games—result, trouble—and resented drill keenly. If it had been real drill even, it might have been tolerated, but to parade the School Hall every morning doing the same absurd antics while Miss Andrews praised her favourite adherents was intolerable. Lunch, also, was a dreaded hour, for having no set place she wandered from table to table, having to submit to the usual questioning from a different girl each day. She spent the minutes looking forward to the evenings and to Saturday and Sunday, when she tried to forget the miseries and humiliations of the week.

To add to her troubles Miss Sampson insisted on her joining the Downwood drawing and sketching classes, though she wished to keep her art free from any taint of school. Rebellion seemed vain, and by this time she had become as much of a machine as was possible to her, for she tried not to think at Downwood. It hurt too much. All the other girls at the class were older than she was, and drew according to the convention of Mrs. Marks, the visiting art mistress to several schools. The lessons were given on a Friday,

DEVELOPMENT

and there was a great rush to get ready and a long journey by 'bus, train, and on foot before the fields were reached where painting was to begin. Nobody took any notice of Nancy, for which she was grateful, but the smell of the paints alone brought back the Art Class, a time that seemed to have faded into a distance, remote as the beginning of history, though in reality but a few short weeks before.

"Now you, Nancy, can sit here and draw the cows grazing over there," said Mrs. Marks in a fussy voice, when she had settled all the others at their work after a little gossip with each. Although the work was quite unsuited to her capacity for drawing Nancy selected one, a lovely brown-red colour with white spots, and began. Unhappily cows are not in the habit of standing still, and before long the entire class was convulsed with laughter while she chased the cow. Every time she sat down the cow moved on. All the way back in the train the class made fun of her, miserably huddled in the corner covered with paint acquired in the chase, even with yellow streaks of it on her face, and when she got back to the school girls came rushing up, asking if she were trying to paint a tiger. For days reference was made to it whenever she appeared; for some of the girls had heard, although Nancy had said nothing, that she had been at an art school and wished to be an artist. They had expected a genius and were disappointed. In an ordinary way Nancy would probably have laughed herself, but she was hardly in a mood by this time to be made fun of, especially over art. The feelings she was obliged to keep pent up within her during the day turned to a sullen hatred of the school, the girls, and their absurd conventions. The whole week she dreaded Friday, but happily they went to another field to paint. As she left Downwood hurriedly after they returned, Miss Sampson called her back. "I want you to stay and have tea with me to-day." Nancy obeyed as if it were an order rather than an honour. Miss Sampson tried to be very kind to her, and something in her encouraging way of speaking made Nancy hope wildly for a moment that she might be sympathetic. She could not bring herself to say much, but murmured some incoherent words about her love of Art—surely she would understand.

"I think you are much too young to study art seriously, dear," Miss Sampson answered. "Won't you have a piece of cake?"

To Nancy it seemed as though the whole world had conspired to crush every hope and aspiration out of her. The last few weeks had dulled her into a machine, but that one sentence roused every passion of her nature. Instead of slinking home ashamed and with her head down she strode out of the gate, defiant, with more of her own spirit than she had felt since the day she went to school. The more people discouraged her the more enthusiastic she would become. She went home singing to herself a little song, "They can't take my thoughts from me, and my dreams are my own."

DEVELOPMENT

But when night came, defiance faded with the sun, and alone in the silence she hungered for a childhood that had for ever gone.

After a week or two, even Saturdays were denied her. To accustom her to school ways of thought Miss Sampson arranged she should take a girl home with her to tea. Nancy refused to ask any one, so Miss Sampson called Eleanor, a girl in her own form, with wavy hair and a worried expression, and told her to get ready. Nancy often wondered afterwards who was the more unhappy as they walked down the hill together. She was torn between determination to say nothing and some instinctive feeling that she ought to be polite, for it was not Eleanor's fault she was with her. Eleanor, in fact, was very nervous, and would never have come if she could have avoided it. They walked home, and at last Nancy asked her if she liked dogs.

"I have got one at home," she replied.

"I want one," said Nancy, and relapsed into half-timid, half-defiant silence.

It was a painful afternoon. To Nancy it seemed almost a desecration of home that a schoolgirl should set foot inside the garden. She had nothing to say, for she was averse to speaking of art before a stranger, and Eleanor, willing enough to talk of the conventional interests of Downwood, was bewildered by the inscrutable silence of this alien child, who had no hesitation in opposing Miss Sampson herself. Both were very re-

94

lieved when Eleanor got back to the Downwood gate. It had been a dismal experiment.

Half-term drew near. Nancy hardly cared what happened now, except for occasional gusts of rebellious rage. She never spoke if she could avoid it, and though perhaps by nature the other girls did not mean to be unkind, all made fun of her, particularly of her reading, of her thirst for knowledge, which refused to be bound by the conventional limits of acquiring marks. She interrupted classes to argue a point of view; generally she was "queer." When they provoked her beyond bearing, she would compose long verses of defiance and contempt in French, turn and hurl them at her tormentors, who slunk off, abashed and alarmed by the strange sounds, like a herd of savages. A habit of standing with folded arms earned her the name of "Napoleon." One morning she arrived more rebellious than usual to find they had to go to some missionary service at church.

"I think I have to walk with you; we always walk to church in age," she heard a girl say to her as they clustered outside the back gate, and, turning, saw Doreen, one of the other new girls who sat next her in class. She liked her boyish face and her laughter much more than the rest of the girls, whom she dubbed the "Pack," but kept her rule of silence until Doreen asked her where she lived. Her voice was kind and rich with a quaint accent, so Nancy smiled back and asked her where she came from.

DEVELOPMENT

"Penzance," she answered; "do you know Corn-wall at all?" Penzance, the Cornish sound of the name reminded Nancy of summer days amid the brown rocks and blue open water, of watching the fishing smacks roll to sea, her vanished freedom. She smiled at Doreen and said, "I know Penzance and South Cornwall quite well."

All the way to church and back they talked of sail-ing, animals, and Cornish things. Now Nancy knew why she liked her voice so much with its slight Cornish accent. Doreen told her of the Scillies where she spent each summer, of fishing and her love of the sea. "She is a sailor, not silly like the others," thought Nancy. Suddenly brave as they turned the corner by the school, she looked up at her; "Will you come to tea with me on Saturday?" she asked.

The term dragged to an end. Prize Day passed, the holidays, and with them the hope she might never go back, approached. Miss Sampson allowed her to leave a day earlier than the others; being a day-girl she had no packing to do. A girl passing as this permission was given, said to her afterwards, "You are lucky, I envy you."

There was nothing to be said, only Nancy hoped the girl would never feel as she felt. It was a lesson to her not to envy other people.

"Everybody hates it their first term," said a young mistress, flattering herself that a few stock sentences scattered here and there showed her interest in the girls. "I am never coming back," Nancy retorted fiercely, and went in search of Doreen to say good-bye. She hoped she would see Doreen again even if she left. Perhaps in the holidays she would write some great poem, then of course there could be no question of her going back to Downwood, and when it was published and everybody recognised her genius, she would come up to the school and take Doreen out, because she had never laughed at her, and all the other girls would be sorry they had jeered at her drawings. Filled with these pleasing thoughts she found Doreen, got her address, and said good-bye. Miss Sampson met her as she got her hat, kissed her, and told her she had done very well for a first term. Unreconciled and unhappy, Nancy walked out of the front door with her head up and hurried home, to lock her hat, all that could remind her of school, away in a cupboard out of sight. The curious sensation of impotence came over her again. "I can't go back, I can't go back," she kept repeating to herself, ashamed of school, of its narrowness, its pettiness, its taunts.

Out of the tragic reality towards her banished dreams she came to her beloved books, where for a time there was forgetfulness.

CHAPTER II

A CAPTIVE YEAR

I

WASTE. The dreary voice of a mistress made the French she read a mockery. Eyes, dulled and unquestioning, followed unnecessary explanations on the blackboard; scribbled notes, copied rules, to which they would never refer. Not a girl was idle, joyfully idle; not a mind was interested; not a thought was alert. The class was heavy with an air that numbed all eagerness. Outside the sun shone. No one cared.

Nancy gave up the pretence of listening, ashamed that she was there. She had been sent as a boarder with the autumn term, as resentful as ever of captivity. It was the arid monotony of school that was so terrible; there could be no expansion, no growth. It was not so much that the same subject was taught at the same hour each day as the lack of interest in the teaching, the dreary wastes of their so-called education. The wisdom of school parlance showed a different face, withered, resentful of her scholars to that learning, denied of Fortunatus, who, twin with beauty, Nancy followed in pursuit.

Every hour at Downwood was arranged with mechanical regularity. A bell woke the girls in the morning, another summoned them to breakfast, prayers, and a lecture on their faults. They filed into the dining-room two by two, each bowing and saying "Bon jour" to Miss Sampson, who scrutinised them from the staircase, till Nancy shook with fear that she might laugh at the solemn line of nervous bobbing heads and muttered salutations. Lessons, games, and preparation made up the day, followed at seven by supper. Even then they were not free, but unless they had singing class or were sent to their form rooms to talk broken French and German, which happened once a week, they were herded together in the drawing-room and forced to do fancy-work in silence. Privacy or free time was unknown. Sunday was a blankness of reiterated church and hymns.

The general ignorance of the girls appalled Nancy. They had not heard of the Thirty Years' War, the French Revolution to them was a mere name, outside of England modern Europe just a myth. Yet it was a school that prided itself upon intellectual achievement; in examinations they had always had success. But it was these very examinations that were the ruin of true learning, that instilled in the minds of these children for ever a certain narrowness, wearying them of knowledge. School that was (as Miss Sampson told them daily from the platform) "a preparation for life" made mockery of life.

"You will translate ten lines of *Britannicus,* beginning at the top of page 18. The books must be in by Thursday." The mistress rose.

Stung to madness Nancy looked down the long line of wasted paper, wasted effort, wasted lives.

II

Sicily and Egypt had been poor training for an English winter, for the rigorous severities inseparable from school. Trying to those reared among it, nobody there understood the physical torture it was to her to stand about the draughty corridors to answer to her name, to sit in a classroom frozen to an immobility that made the thought of moving torment, while a westerly gale blew in through the cracks of ill-fitting windows. The thickest jersey could not prevent this sensation of an unrelieved and sunless bleakness with no refuge of warmth anywhere except at night in bed.

"Good-night, girls." The shrill voice of Miss Evesham, a snapping off of light, the closing and opening of doors, drew nearer down the corridor. Nancy thrust her book hurriedly away, waited a little timorously the resented intrusion, shivered as a hurricane and the sharp lines of a stiff blouse blew through the door together, and with eyes wide open in the darkness listened till the heavy tread resounding on the crumbling plaster passed the three steps and away into the distance. Secure from interference Nancy stole out of bed, and began, with due care for silence, the preparations which insured some measure of warmth against the Arctic night, spreading her coats and garments, nestwise, till she could slide back beneath the blankets, and taste the luxury of warmness for the first time since waking. The day was at an end. Life might begin.

It was cold lying there in the darkness, trying to forget the poverty of the day in thought. Only an hour to dream and the shadow of waking never absent from the minutes; mornings barren of knowledge, barren of joy. She was sick for warmth, for a little physical loveliness; her intellect expanding preyed on her, starved and desirous of learning. Soon, nature intervening, she would sleep, forget (save for overwhelming moments of a poignant sweetness when homesickness for her own land, her South of almond blossom, came over her) the realisation of a mournful present, empty where all had been so full. Made of a sudden so poor she turned increasingly to poetry, become a sanctuary against the onslaughts of the day. It was to the Elizabethans, the fragments that she knew of them, that she came perhaps most frequently; to the sentence, quoted of Hazlitt from *Philaster,* "'Tis not a life. 'Tis but a piece of childhood thrown away." The thought of life as a fragment of epic infancy seemed to her fashioned of the essence of that beauty which is also truth, a

DEVELOPMENT

strict reality; and then the plaintive sadness "thrown away" taking a tinge of her present feeling as the ruins of her own childhood seemed to smoulder behind her, useless, crushed.

One by one she saw her companions of the class-room, remembered some fragment of their idle chatter, some desire expressed in the day. Their nights were not lit by the music of Beaumont or of Webster; for them there was no oblivion in books. To Nancy it seemed terrible that they had no sweetness, neither a reserve of strength to lighten the burden of intolerable days or galling rule. Helpless as a herd of deer they huddled together at injustice, staring with frightened eyes, with muttered words. True, they had mocked her, had denied she would ever write; in spite of this, resentful as ever that she had come to Downwood, Nancy at her loneliest moments pitied them the poverty of their monotonous restricted thought.

III

The holidays came again but Nancy was too unsettled for any work. Until her term of bondage was at end, even at home she felt the taint of school breathe on all old desires. She longed for solitude with an almost passionate intentness; desirous of expression she became more inarticulate than ever. With neither new nor old for company she fretted in an idleness she might not fill, turning as often as she could to books, the one refuge that never yet had failed her.

The Elizabethans led her to Spenser, to the *Faerie Queene.* Making no attempt to read from cover to cover she explored the six books, choosing adventures that seemed to her of interest, neglecting the rest. She could not help identifying herself with Sir Calidore and Downwood with the Blatant Beast, nor, as she read, was her heart barren of hope that this present monster by her might be recaptured, and if not imprisoned, deprived at least of its sting.

Marlowe was explored, Webster only in fragments, for the strength of the seventeenth century Downwood mistranslated "coarseness" and therefore banished half literature from its shelves.

But school had robbed her of unconsciousness and some refuge was inevitable against the pressure of existence; something to dull its sharpness, some life that was not life. Elizabethan vitality became too strong for this period of silence; she dared not live in that world for long together at Downwood; reading the plays existence ceased, the reaction of awakening was too acute. She needed sheer dreamfulness and found it in the tales, half truth, half myth, of a romantic forgotten world.

She detected at once the essential falseness in Mallory, plunged into earlier ages to turn with Sir Gawain on adventures, to come with him to the hall of Bernlak de Hautdesert, to follow him through the snow till he met the Green Knight. A summer voyage to Norway and Denmark led her to translations of Vigfusson, the quaint Icelandic history of the "Burnt Nyal" saga, the Laxdale stories, English Beowulf, and Havelock the Dane. She read fragments of the *Roman de la Rose*; she was captured at once by the *Earthly Paradise* of William Morris, by his earlier poetry and his prose.

The boyhood of Michael, one long imagining even as she had dreamed, Rhodope, strong, her face set to seaward, Jehane in the moonlight, a land of forests, poplar, and red apple, cool water slipping about a carven boat, had just that note of a fanciful or rather a past reality that fitted this period of sundering, of transition between her infancy and youth. The temper of Morris fitted hers, his poems full of movement and colour, blent with the magic of history to make "a strange tale of an empty day." Even drill was tolerable when one was "east of the sun and west of the moon." Would that she also could ride through the summer weather, ride with hands roughened by a sword hilt, actually to win or be defeated instead of this interminable waiting—actual combat instead of the unceasing mental struggle against the sordidness of school. The remembrance of past Aprils might be crushed, but the spirit that drove Goldilocks forth from the farm, in his holiday scarlet raiment, saved her from sliding into any silent acquiescence of the customs of the girls.

A CAPTIVE YEAR

"Swerve to the left and out at his head," therein lay her desire.

IV

The one break in the intense monotony of school were its quarrels. "Landmarks of each term," as Doreen called them, they were disturbances born of the spirit of the school, petty happenings magnified to tragic events. Technically, until it had come before Miss Sampson, no incident could claim to be a "row," between girls it was just a "quarrel," or, when the "ladies of the staff" were involved, a "fuss."

The term had begun badly, with storm and weather impossible for even the dreary crawl two by two down the front. A feeling of unrest spread from form to form. The excitement of Half Term passed. Sunday ended with hurricane of wind and hail.

The Sixth was ever a cheerless room; opening on to the garden, gusts of wind blew up and under the ugly linoleum. The hills were hidden by a mist of grey lines. Cold, fugitive raindrops battered the cracks of the door.

Disturbance was not unusual in the Sixth. The dozen girls it contained formed separate parties of twos and threes. Oblivious of the angry voices, Nancy sat down to read.

She had scarcely turned a page before she realised that this was no ordinary happening, but a big, possibly a historic occasion. The history of Downwood was written in its "rows." The head girl, an embodiment of pitiless monotony, colourless and hard, was ominously full of the "welfare of the school." She was not a good head girl and knew it. She had no individual character but was heavy with hypocrisy. Downwood rightly regarded her of no account. Stung by her own impotence and near to leaving, the moment was ripe for a convulsive attempt to show the power that slipped so easily into the fingers of younger, more vigorous girls. It had fallen to Lydia to provide an opportunity.

Lydia refined the sentimentality of a schoolgirl to the quintessence of unneeded emotion. She had a weak heavy face like an elephant mourning for its trunk, and three pocket-handkerchiefs. She was already hysterical.

It took Nancy some moments to unravel the excitement. Lydia's friend of the moment was a girl in the Lower Fifth. She had been ill, had missed a history class. Permission had been given for Lydia to help her prepare the missed lesson. They had been found on the ledge when they should have been at drill, working at it. The head girl had ordered them to drill, they had refused. In a fit of anger she had gone to Miss Sampson. Such seemed to be the substance of the story.

Conscious now the moment of anger was past that such action had merely shown her weakness, the head girl was trying, savagely, to recover a measure of dignity by an address copied from Miss Sampson's speech at the beginning of each term. About two girls listened to her. Lydia was enjoying herself. It was an understood thing nobody was reported for missing drill, and with the injustice she had risen from obscurity to being the momentary heroine of half the Upper School. She took out a fourth pocket-handkerchief and sobbed violently. Girls who the day before had passed her unnoticed, flattered and consoled her. The stately Sixth threatened to rival the Third in noise. "Anyhow," as Nancy remarked during a lull, "what is the good of going to drill with Pussy?" Pussy was the nickname she had given to the Games Mistress, who walked both with the airs and with the footstep of a cat. The name had become popular at Downwood, and to Nancy's annoyance she found herself famous for a chance remark, instead of the epic she believed would make her immortal.

The head girl looked up, growing angrier each minute. "If you are not careful I shall report you as well." Veritable battle raged. The noises fell to a sudden silence as the door opened unexpectedly.

"Miss Sampson wishes the Sixth Form to go to her in the drawing-room."

Recklessness died away as they crowded up the stairs. The drawing-room was the court of justice where offenders were tried. Out of the windows a mass of short trees, rank foliage that never obscured the hills, and hedges heavy in their trimness, were visible. The room was hung with prints, crowded with cushions, removed by the head girl whenever the school-girls occupied the chairs. The air was full of a pitiful striving after beauty, most barren of success, and on a week-day was never without the sound of music, practised by girls lifeless and uninspired. Miss Sampson entered, already wearied by the two other rows she had settled that morning.

"Sit down, girls." The invitation was unwelcome, for it meant a long lecture and the rare half-hour of leisure the wet weather had brought would be lost.

"I am grieved," began Miss Sampson earnestly, "I am grieved that it should be necessary for me to treat the Sixth Form as I would the Lower School. If some child from the Third is reported to me her foolishness is excusable, but I look to you in the higher forms to set an example to the rest." There was an audible sob from Lydia. "Why do you go to drill?" Miss Sampson tapped the ground impatiently with her foot, aware how triumphantly she impressed her knowledge and her power upon the girls. "Because it is good for us," stammered the girl nearest to her. "Partly." No answer was perfect for Miss Sampson until her own explanation was added. "Drill teaches you not only to be obedient and erect in body but to be erect in mind as well. I want every Downwood girl, both in her holidays and in the term, to look up not only literally but in her lessons, above all in her friendships. . . ."

From frequent repetitions Nancy knew the speech by heart. She dared not look out of the window, but it was safe enough to think if one fixed one's eyes on the pattern in the carpet. She dreamed regretfully of the book she had been reading before Miss Sampson summoned them, no school book but one out of her own store.

"To bear disappointments with a smile, to be cheerful and contented no matter what the circumstances. . . ."

Miss Sampson's eyes grew as weary as her voice. But Nancy was murmuring to herself joyously, triumphantly:

> Hence all you vain delights,
> As short as are the nights
>   Wherein you spend your folly!
> There's nought in this life sweet,
> If man were wise to see't,
>   But only melancholy;
>   O sweetest melancholy!

Yes, pain was better than contentment if it meant poetry. (In her heart she believed poetry meant joy.) Better solitude than to share a lifeless acquiescence, the colourless dreams of this multitude about her; better to bear their mockery than accept what passed for pleasure with these girls. These lines of Fletcher's brought her strength each time she repeated them, denial as they were of all that Downwood taught.

"Before you go I will say one word to you about opportunity. . . ." It was an exquisite pleasure to

DEVELOPMENT

Miss Sampson to define the word. Nancy smiled. She passed her days desiring the chance that the school denied. "Work." "You come to school to learn." Vague phrases floated past her ears. She wanted knowledge, loved it, longed for it. But Downwood had nothing to teach her, only the books she discovered and read for herself. "Opportunity." The irony of it all. Her mind drifted back to Fletcher—

> How the pale Phoebe, hunting in a grove,
> First saw the boy Endimion, from whose eyes
> She took eternal fire that never dies;
> How she conveyed him softly in a sleep,
> His temples bound with poppy, to the steep
> Head of old Latmus, where she stoops each night,
> Gilding the mountains with her brother's light,
> To kiss her sweetest.

School could not last for ever and with freedom must come loveliness, some realisation of this Elizabethan beauty, even in a modern world.

Downwood broke upon her thoughts.

"For life," Miss Sampson said, "is only a continuation of school." Dull faces answered this with silence. There was no movement, no revolt. Nancy stared at the faces, stared at the room, pierced by a subtle fear. What if the books had lied, what if this were the truth, suppose there was no escape?

Dumb with fear she rose as the others rose. Miss Sampson kissed each solemnly as they passed.

A CAPTIVE YEAR

V

The hot sun smote the geraniums by the gravel path until they seemed to fade. Only a noise of bees in the ivy and a scratching of pens marred the unbroken stillness. Through the open windows Nancy stared over the bent heads of her companions to the hills, immense and quivering in the luminous heat. In an hour a bell would break the silence, there would be turmoil, shouting, a herding into the garden, but for the moment there was forgetfulness; antiquity had returned.

"C'était à Mégara, faubourg de Carthage, dans les jardins d'Hamilcar."

A stab of pain—the unwilling grief of an exile—pointed the familiar names. Sick for an old happiness Nancy dared not speak of childhood, yet was it ever absent from her thought? Hope was no longer fresh with dawn; she lived on the memory of her former dreams. All day, from rising until sleeping, she kept a difficult way among the rules she hated, turned as if up a river, ignorant of the shallows, while her heart hungered for the sea. And out of this alien world to a new loneliness, *Salammbô* had summoned her with its subtle words.

Her own memories of the South crumbled their colour into the richness of each phrase. This was reality—the leaders in their bronze greaves, "sous un voile de pourpre à franges d'or," the feasting in the garden—rather than the broken inkpots, the battered desks. And each word was pain because she was so far from Carthage, and each word was joy because it restored her to a forceful world that was not sordid as the school was sordid, nor weak as these girls were weak.

In the light of flames and torches and unsheathed steel Salammbô pleaded with the Mercenaries in all the dialects of the South.

The fetters of her present bondage were broken as she dreamed, but it was bitter to read instead of feel, to imagine only where her life had been so rich. School would pass, liberty would come, but would it restore her to a life wilder than the torches, sweeter than carved ivory and frail Tyrian glass? What would her freedom bring?

Dawn rose over Carthage. Not daring to read more Nancy put the book away.

A bell rang. Flying plaits and shrill voices surged in tumult to the lawn. "Why are you not in the garden?" Nancy looked up stupidly. Outside the younger girls were already at drill. Round and round the dull tread of fifty rubber soles beat the grey asphalt, up and down they marched in futility of aimless movement, the head girl in front, her head up like a pyramid no rain shall soften, no sun shall kindle to burning. A rush of girls swept Nancy outside on to the path. Her dream snapt.

It was Downwood that was a lie.

"The last term." There was a gasp of relief whenever it was mentioned, even from those who would be sentimental the last day and cry. Every window in the School Hall was open to let in the sunshine. There was a general air of Saturday, a day of fussy trifles, about the impatient girls. Nancy listened to the whispered plans around her, vaguely curious as to what passed for happiness in the minds of her companions, but the talk never reached beyond the transient interests of holidays and school. Miss Sampson rushed in late, as was her custom. Prayers over, she came a little forward, an ominous sign.

"I have already spoken twice this term about the cloakroom being left in disorder. I want every Downwood girl to be punctual and tidy, to have a place for everything. Will the two girls nearest the door fetch the basket of shoes I have collected and give them to Miss Andrews for distribution? If another pair is found out of place this term, sweets will be stopped for a week. You are given a place in which to put your shoes, it is pure laziness not to keep them there." A pause. "Have any of you seen my fountain pen? I have mislaid it for two days."

Miss Sampson gave out the letters while the basket was being fetched. Nancy watched the smaller girls go up for them very pitifully, knowing they had four or five years' imprisonment before them. The narrowness of school weighed heavily upon her. What was Miss Sampson but a tyrant, well-meaning, yes, but holding arbitrary rules, and with a body-guard, the mistresses, who carried out her laws and her commands in no impartial spirit? The first quality a child appreciates is justice, but in a school there can be no appeal. Downwood was a dust-heap of dead individualities. The girls filed out, face after listless face. It was unbearable to think that these would leave and others take their place, to be ground to the same pattern by the same machine, and nobody moved, nothing was done to alter or to improve. Could not people see that teaching was an art and an inspiration, not the mere matter of a useless degree? It was a wonder there was any childhood left.

Even the "ladies of the staff," what were they but overgrown schoolgirls, living so long at school that they became school, their minds bounded by its restrictions, fettered by its jealousies, unable to lift beyond the boundaries of each term? Like the girls they had their lights put out, only an hour later. They had to be in to meals. The girls went home, but if they left they merely changed from the tyranny of one school to that of another, they neither grew up nor lived.

Nancy, staring out of the window of the classroom, beheld the tragedy of it all; tragedy of the underpaid mistress grown old and cast aside for youth and a modern degree, tragedy of the sensitive child whose slightest slip from accepted custom met with a cruel derision, tragedy of the eager intellect denied expansion, tragedy of the brain forced and exhausted for the credit of the school. Eyes amorous of beauty, hearts desirous of freedom,—all crushed, stamped into acquiescence to the pattern of the school.

This was Education. This was what people worshipped.

VII

Prize Day came with its artificial absurdities that seemed to Nancy more incongruous than ever. The morning was a nightmare of clamour and fretful orders, distribution of red carnations, the "school flower." Why they had a school flower, what it represented, not even the "ladies of the staff," to whom Nancy appealed for information, knew. The head girl came round with a basket and doled them out, collecting threepence in exchange. Then they were forgotten for another year.

"When the bell rings after the distribution, every girl will pick up her own chair and march with it straight to the School Hall." Over and over Miss Evesham reiterated the order, as though by mere force of repetition she could prevent mistakes. For this one hour she lived; measuring her life by Prize Days, the other months of the year were preparation. Seeking a disordered flower, a badly tied bow, her eyes moved up and down the lines, with that mixture of hard anxiety

DEVELOPMENT

and kindliness an enthusiast displays to his machine; should the parts get out of order they must be petted or scolded till they work again, each form moulded to its stereotyped pattern. In Miss Evesham's vision there was no room for any excrescences of individuality.

Row on row of girls, dressed in white, with the absurd carnation, trooped across the lawn. Nancy wanted to scream with laughter at the stupidity of it all, at the anxious mistresses and parents herded in front, looking so obviously unhappy. The platform, with its flowers, the staff, the table of prizes, reminded her of a prehistoric gathering of a tribe to pronounce justice. A hot sense of shame came over her that she was here, and helpless, in the midst of such inanity.

Eleanor, forgetful of the dreariness of the terms, thought in a sentimental misery, evoked by the occasion, of all these faces, that she as a schoolgirl would never see again. Actually, the names of many of the babies were unknown to her, but sentiment obliterates such matters, and, for the moment, Eleanor was near weeping that even the wooden chair would never be hers any more.

Doreen hoped the distribution would not take long. It was an episode of dullness. Miss Evesham worried at the long speech. All the girls had filed in correctly. It was marching out they got so careless; last year there had been three mistakes. Waiting was so trying. They were always so slow to see the signal to get up. The prizes on the table dwindled. From her place

A CAPTIVE YEAR

in the centre of the platform Miss Sampson hoped the girls had made a good impression.

The table was empty of books, the bell rang, the girls stood up. Frantic signs; they filed up the steps, one long line of moving chairs, past Miss Evesham, a smile on her lips for the watching parents, hardness in her eyes for the two girls already at fault. Her life might have depended on the way they kept in line. Nancy gave a wicked flourish to her chair as she passed. Two more days, then freedom. Helpless with mirth, she regained the Sixth. A small girl passed, visibly excited. Uneven groups of parents moved into the School Hall. A squeak of violins announced the concert had begun. Nancy picked a Milton out of the row of battered school books; she needed something impersonal and very cold, some abstract contemplation to restore the dignity of life within her mind.

VIII

The last night came! Nancy piled her books in a heap in the dining-room, a leaving custom which reduced many of the girls to tears. Even Eleanor, now the actual moment had come, forgot the discomforts, the narrowness, the walks, and needed consolation; besides, it was a tradition to be gloomy the last day. A little group of the elder girls hung together, besought mistresses to write to them, whom, a week before, they had hoped never to see again. They were afraid.

117

DEVELOPMENT

School had taught them, had bound their thoughts by rules, had manufactured dreams for them, had given them a language. They had surrendered their individuality. Now they were leaving and Downwood offered in exchange an invitation to next Prize Day and a Latin motto no one understood.

Actual liberation would come only with the morrow, but as the lights snapped out, with her mind already almost free of school, Nancy went to bed. Had she gained anything by her stay at Downwood, was it utter waste of these two years? As regards knowledge, yes. She had come speaking French and German fluently, with a good accent. Much of this she had forgotten, and the insane rule which compelled eighty girls (many of whom knew scarcely a dozen words of a foreign language) to speak French all day had ruined all trace of accent by force of constant hearing of the English words with French terminations which this rule produced. She had read books—in the time she was supposed to be doing something else—but not as many as she would have read at home. She was disgusted with the sordid pettiness of school life, at the narrow hypocrisies among the girls. She could not help feeling Downwood must be relieved to be rid of her, of her disturbing theories, her lack of reverence for authority. School had wasted two years of her life. There was a touch of bitterness about even the hours of the last night.

She woke up happily and hurried down to breakfast. The school hat was packed in her case. She and Eleanor were leaving a little earlier than the others; they said good-bye and fought their way through the crowd at the library door. Miss Sampson was kissing Eleanor, near to weeping, then she turned. Nancy stared into the eyes that could control her life no longer, a little sorrowful for all the years wasted on a bad system and a wrong ideal.

"Good-bye, Miss Sampson." "Good-bye, Nancy." The girls, helpless and afraid of homecoming, with no beginning of term to steady them, huddled in the passage. Nancy looked at them for the first time with an immense pity. There was no beauty in their lives. Then she strode down the hill without once turning her head.

BOOK III

TRANSITION

"But beauty is set apart,
beauty is cast by the sea,
a barren rock,
beauty is set about
with wrecks of ships,
upon our coast, death keeps
the shallows—death waits
clutching toward us
from the deeps."

H.D.

CHAPTER I

MIRAGE

I

NANCY leaned on the rail, watching the horizon, eager for Syracuse. It was too late for almond-blossom, but there was snow on Etna and the South itself to welcome her—the South, after six years.

The past few months had been a space of disillusion. Childhood had shivered into a thousand pieces that May morning she had entered school, and instead of starting afresh Nancy had wasted time trying to find and fit together the broken pieces. She seemed to have slipped back a whole age. The wonder and imagination she had treasured were gone and knowledge had not come to fill their place. She had lost her early facility of writing verse; become critical, nothing she attempted satisfied her. That she would have had to lose her childhood some time never occurred to Nancy. In the usual way she would have lost it imperceptibly; as it was, she could date it back to the violent shock of school, and had not learnt enough to know that this was a period through which it was inevitable for her to pass. At Downwood she had shut herself up in a world of her own, away from taunts and all unpleasant thoughts, and there this refuge of silence had been a necessity, but she could not, with leaving school, revert to infancy, and the friends, the life she had dreamed seemed mythical as ever though the months of bondage had passed. With the growing realisation that to escape from one prison might not mean to have the world at her own disposal, she yielded herself more and more to the true intimacy of books, beyond the limits of childish experience, painfully groping a way to a harder knowledge.

Adventure half forgotten, Nancy had left England with no enthusiasm, nine months after her return from school. She could not care at first, but as the familiar names slipped by, the familiar colours, the hills that she had last seen dusty with almond-blossom; a mirage of her childhood drew perilously close, and as night came, in southern loveliness, in a blue that shamed the waves that curve on delicate curve moved ever towards the shore, her heart beat quicker for even the hint in wind and sea that they were near the home of her early dreams.

II

Amid the rattle of anchor chains, people frantically inquiring if Eryx were a general, or trying to mend

MIRAGE

their ignorance of Gylippus by a five minutes' perusal of the guide-book, noise, shouting, late one April afternoon Nancy landed at Syracuse. To her it was no strange place to stare, to wonder at, and leave; it was home, the haunt of her childhood, to be taken simply and quite naturally. School had robbed her of happiness; the South would give it back to her. Rich with memories she moved forward with the throng towards the centre of the town.

"Of course you could not appreciate or remember the South when you were here before, you were too young."

The stinging words Nancy was impotent to refute rang in her ears. Appreciate! She had had the South in her heart ever since she was seven. Remember! Why, she could take them to the very corner of the ruined amphitheatre where ten years before she had rebuilt the whole city with a bit of mosaic and a few pieces of marble, while they, for all their guidebooks, could not picture a single building. At every step another impression of a crowded childhood greeted her. She turned from the look in their eyes. "I made you," the South taunted, "and what have you brought me?" A few lines of verse, dreams—was that all the six years had wrought? Oh, those wasted years at Downwood, the desecration, the shame of school.

She was bitterly homesick for her childhood. She felt sundered from it as though it were whole ages away, as though she could never have been the child

DEVELOPMENT

she remembered playing with heroes in a heroic land. There were the familiar orange trees, but the dreams themselves had vanished for ever. Sometimes under the almond boughs one would brush her cheek, but they were hers no longer and there was nothing to take their place. "You were too young to understand," they told her, while she thought of a far-away figure that had been Carthaginian, Syracusan, and Greek by turn on that very hillside, and raged that she could not bring other children to learn of beauty in the same dream way, instead of being flung into the ignorant atmosphere of school, to ape the narrow thought of a schoolgirl of sixteen.

"How fascinating this atmosphere is," chattered the girl at her side. "I love those little green shutters and those babies; how typical they are of the South." (She never looked at children at home.) "Nancy, you don't realise how wonderfully romantic it all is. I don't believe you appreciate travelling at all."

Nancy, lost in dreams, was silent, and suddenly round the curve of the road came a herd of shaggy goats, sweeping her back ten years. To her they had always been a part of Sicily, one of her earliest memories. Her companion shrank back shivering as they passed.

"What a desecration! Get away from them; they spoil the atmosphere."

"They are the South," Nancy answered simply.

MIRAGE

III

Childhood had failed her, the South had failed her; what was left? Infancy (unwitting of companionship) school had rendered impossible of recapture, but reality offered only a friendship of harsh chattering, unconsidered mirth. Her hope, her dreams, shaped to a definite longing for something to fill her loneliness, give her knowledge; to a thought that only a book of her own making would admit her to the friendships she desired. She grew each week more desirous of silence, natural, when what to her was joy, a riotous sweetness, became meaningless words, uncomprehended emotions, to the girls about her, for whom Corfu, history, metre, were chaotic obscurity, "interesting," but out of their way. This indifference of others assured Nancy in her belief she was a poet; expression broke to lines of echoed verse and worse thought.

A poppy sail burned on an umber ship, the golden oars of a Greek rower were birds on a space of silver; pansies, rich with dream and purple, were truant about the shore. In dangerous and defiant ridges visible Albanian hills curved scimitar-wise in the blue May morning. An eager strength breathing about the air brought renewal of her old wish to go to sea. Greece was a tranquillity, an interlude of loveliness, which made her eyes afraid. Poems breathed among the darkness of the cypress trees; the islands drifting out to sea were magical as song. For the moment she lost trust in the future; ahead of this present all was obscure. Bewilderment slipped gradually away; childhood was not so poignant in its memories. But glad as her eyes were with beauty, the spirit of the South was fugitive, a mirage that never waited for her soul.

From Corcyra, rich with scarlet poppy, pointed cypress, they came to Delphi, austere and desolate in a precipice above the silver olive trees; to Delos, where in an ivory stillness broken statues kept a pristine splendour above Ionian water, crushed to a blue of porcelain, the porcelain that hid the grass with fragments, quiet as the banded lizards, inscrutable as the sun. Athens was explored and Aegina on the hill where, between the magical leaves, waves were a ragged violet as they climbed the slope. Rhodes was denied her, it was too far south; but before they turned northwards and home the approach of June found them anchored one morning in the bay of Crete.

IV

A noisy throng threatened the silence of the tiny room, one blazoned volume of Minoan centuries. The haft of a broken dagger, the rough pottery of a rounded vase, held no speech intelligible to their eyes. Crete was a place to see, forget, or associate with the warmness of the day, some happening of the journey. One or two would have lingered; travellers, to whom the spirit of

MIRAGE

antiquity was not utterly inaudible. They were dragged away by the clamour of the crowd. Happy with a knowledge rent from map and history book, Nancy paused alone before the pictured life of Crete.

Minoan civilisation held her with vivid interest. Had not the islands been the home of sailors? Had not the Cretan ships linked Mycenae and further Greece with Egypt, with the East? Her early knowledge of the Nile, of Phoenician history, helped her to spell from painted vase and moulded weapon the tale of the rise of Knossos, the sack of the palace, conquest, the end of the island dominion. Why had she no friend with full knowledge of the early history of the South? Mycenaean discoveries were not more wonderful than this.

The last straggler vanished. Solitary, before the frescoes of the bull ring and the Cupbearer, Nancy recovered antiquity.

Knossos was not desolate, but vivid with life and heat. Tall scarlet poppies grew by the narrow path. Peasants in mediaeval jerkins flung the umber earth aside with their spades, in warm heaps. An April noon at Carthage had seemed the heart of stillness, but here the place burned. One could see the luminous quiver of the air.

"Let's hurry and get on board again. I know I shall get sunstroke." The throng murmured, querulous with heat.

Nancy strode deliberately into the hottest sunlight,

DEVELOPMENT

drinking a life too strong that flamed her soul to wildness, flushed her with dripping gold. Earth was warm,
the air was warm; she was mad with the colour and
the light. The woods called her, and the hills; strength
was abroad in them, and in strength was happiness.
Oh to strip herself free of fear, to escape; to know the
darkness of the boughs, the broken warmth of poppies. Life waited for her in the hills, no mirage, but
truth, eager for her to call, eager to be held. "Come,
Nancy; you are keeping everybody." Escape—but
could recapture be eluded? The throng clambered into
their carriages. "Come, Nancy." She turned, an unwilling prisoner to civilisation.

V

Give me freedom in your woods, Knossos of the sea; the loveliness
of flowers, the loveliness of honey.
You were beautiful as snow that lifts, a white narcissus, on Mount
Ida. O frail shell, stained with dawn, you were lovely as the
moon.
Sun wrought you and foam, the crushed hearts of crocuses—
rhythms of gold light across a marble of white lilies.
Watcher of the woods, watcher of the sea, Life, wild as an iris bud,
crusted your jars with dreams.

The youths knew your strength, Knossos of the sea; the hot edges
of hill above the cypress boughs.
The wild goats on the grass slope stiffened with fear, leapt upward.
The bronze head of a javelin smashed on a grey rock. Loose

MIRAGE

stones, scarred earth—was a spear, the wind, as swift as a Cretan? Wild flight, wild limbs—the hunters passed.

Girls loved you for beauty, Crete, heavy with orchards; for the pool of violets, dark as sleep, crushed by their sun-browned limbs.

Noon blossomed in your hands, spilled in cups of gold and onyx; your nights were ivory petals carved of dawn on a white rose.

You were a wild pear amorous of sunrise: were you not afraid to give of your loveliness to the North?

Could you have kept your dreams for the wood cyclamen; could you have lost them in the reeds, Knossos, you had lived.

But the North snapt the agate hilts of your daggers with a touch. Their eyes hardened with evil as they lifted the gold jars. While your merchants traded with far isles they cried "To Crete."

The waves were shrill with the invading oars of darkened ships.

O sea flower, where was the wind that it left their sails unrent? Surf of Crete, where was your strength that their anchors tore the sand?

For the last time, Knossos, you were beautiful with sleep.

The wood gave no warning: you were abandoned by the moon.

A twig cracked in the darkness. The watchers laughed: "Some hunter has lost his way from the hills." A torch flashed: "It is a beacon to guide in the fisher ships."

They poised their spears in the shelter of the orchards. The archers crept forward. A wild goat, stiff with a sudden arrow, Knossos woke.

You shattered under their javelins, Crete of the open water, as under a heavy sandal crush the coral-tinted shells.

Your loveliness was sullied by no fear. Death was swift.

The stem of your beauty snapt. Life wept to watch you perish by the sea.

Torches fired the wood. The spearsmen clutched gold. Sun-

DEVELOPMENT

coloured porcelain splintered into dust. Fragments of onyx, fragments of agate, littered the torn earth.

The sharp scent of burning cypresses was sweeter to the archers than reaped grass.

Bough of wild pear, you were smitten by the wind.

You were desolate, as Carthage shall be desolate, and Troy.

In far islands they hung your daggers on the wall; they poured wine from your honey-tinted jars.

In far islands loveliness trembled into leaf, bitter with seed from your dreams.

Give me freedom in your woods, Knossos of the sea; I know Life rests with the wind, not an arrow's length from your hills.

For here is a wild hive plundered of its honey; here are thin poppies dead with the pressure of his limbs.

I am all wildness: where the shade dusts the hollows with black mulberries, let me thrust my hands in the earth and feel your strength.

Your spirit is not perished from the woodland nor from the parched cliffs.

Knossos of the scarlet poppies, Knossos of the sea, bring me to the ledges where Life rests.

CHAPTER II

"VERS LIBRE"

"I WANT to read Verhaeren." Nancy was finishing a French lesson in a vain attempt to recapture the accent lost at school. To an enthusiastic admirer of the Elizabethans with their richness and their freedom, the perpetual Alexandrine was wearying in its monotony. Quite by chance she had just read an article hinting at some new form, at "vers libre," with vague mention of Verhaeren, de Régnier and others. "Vers libre!" The very words seemed full of possibilities.

Madame exhaled horror, petrified and rigid with it—no dragon could have turned her more successfully to stone. "Young girls cannot read Verhaeren." She shivered as though something secret and terrifying had been revealed to her.

"Why not?" inquired Nancy, unabashed. She had not known Madame so careful of her morals before.

"Les Flamandes."

"But why not?" she persisted. "Les Flamandes." Nancy had no intention of yielding.

"I could not be responsible if you read it."

133

DEVELOPMENT

"But he wrote other books. I could read those."

The agitated eyes made last appeal. "He has no ideals. I will bring you a nice book of Francois Coppée; he is poetic, and you like poetry."

"I hate Coppée. I want Verhaeren."

"You cannot read Verhaeren." Horror was breaking into rage. "He writes 'vers libre.'"

"That is what I want to study."

Perhaps Madame knew that if Nancy wished a thing she usually fought till she got it; perhaps she thought to give her first *Les Villes tentaculaires,* one of the most difficult of modern books for a child of eighteen to understand, would be to turn her against this hated, this perturbing "vers libre" for ever. Two days later *Les Villes tentaculaires* arrived.

True it was that Nancy could not understand it at first. It was the spirit of Verhaeren rather than his actual poems that she loved. Here was something strong, new, impetuous, with much of the vigour of the sea winds he praised, something answering to impalpable sensations she felt herself, undeveloped, but assuredly there. Reading him, adventures seemed possible after all. She demanded more of Verhaeren, more of "vers libre."

"Tout la mer va vers la ville."

Much as she loved the past, Nancy could not help seeing loveliness in modernity as well. She had always felt an inexplicable beauty in the side of trade that is poetry; in the docks with their hint of wind and vigor-

ous sea. The dirtiest collier took on regal colour in her
sailor heart; sleep never came so eagerly as on a boat,
or in a train shaken by the powerful rhythm of the
engine, and it was this precise spirit that breathed
through Verhaeren; like the Elizabethans, he treated
things grandly. With him there could be no quiescence,
no tranquillity; he got hold of one, forced one to follow. Others sang for themselves; he sang for humanity.

Perhaps it was his power of making poetry out of
anything, perhaps it was that, in a slighter way, Nancy
could not escape the vision of the pitiful waste of
earth; or was it because they shared belief in a confident future? but Verhaeren, and through him other
modern French poets, gave her a sensation of reality
as contrasted with utter vision and utter dream, the
one word which had never before entered her vocabulary—Life. They gifted her with discontent. She
looked towards actual fulfilment of her hopes.

At least her days were spent in the company of
poets, if actual speech were ever to be rare. Mallarmé
was difficult; it was hard to read meaning into his music, though in a subtle way—as a wind threatens the
plum-blue tranquillity of night, then perishes unawak-
ened—she was conscious of his influence. Henri de
Régnier with his cadences, vital and breathing of the
resin of forest branches and the salt petals of sea
flowers, haunted her mind for days.

Rhyme had already begun to grate harshly on an
ear that daily grew more sensitive to curve of rhythm

DEVELOPMENT

or subtlety of phrase. Words were, of themselves, loveliness; of themselves, colour. But it was the modernity of many of these writers, their fondness of experiment, that made them not alone a technical revelation but brought a new and vital element of wideness into her vision. Swept away by the vividness of the poems, from books that led her outwards to the world, fretting against the narrowness that jarred on either hand, she longed to pull the universe to pieces and build it up again in her own way. With all her training grounded in the past, her feelings beat their wings towards the future.

Development placed Nancy far in front of school companions. She saw while they were wondering, but it was hard to be a discoverer and have no one to echo her enthusiasm. Her thought became derision, her vitality a wretched violence, without a friend. She wanted speech, constant association, with minds that possessed all the vigour and the wideness of this poetry. Surely the immensity of her appreciation should gain them for a friend? But there were only schoolgirls to chatter of Downwood and their newer classes, they, and to tramp the windy streets and catch hint of Verhaeren, an answering audacity, in the storm, in the hail.

Oh to be a boy and have the world. What was the use of existence to a woman, what compensation could there be for loss of freedom? It maddened her to think that as a boy she could have gone to sea, shaped her own experience. A man has liberty, the disposal of his life so largely in his hands, but a girl—she had no wish to write books woven of pretty pictures seen from a narrow window; roughness and adventure, these formed her desire. To possess the intellect, the hopes, the ambitions of a man, unsoftened by any feminine attribute, to have these sheathed in convention, impossible to break without hurt to those she had no wish to hurt, to feel so thoroughly unlike a girl—this was the tragedy.

She was shaken by a craving for colour, for friendship; for something to still the hunger of her starving brain and fill it with expression. Perhaps it was experience she needed—she wanted to live, but knew not how to start. She tried reasoning, patience, to be calm; but the sudden sight of a wild-rose sky, a line of a poem, a single dream, and all the foundations of her citadel of reason crumbled into foam. Stung with the thousand trifles of an ordinary day, choked with her own inarticulate verse, taut on a thread of wavering hope, she trusted the absolute certainty behind her doubts that all these differing elements would mingle in her making, shape her eventual writing, be absorbed and form her mind.

Rain, sharp silver slanting lines beating down the street, crystal breaking a dull transparence of wet slate. The grey and flooded road mirrored the separate trees, an etching on the water. There might be ever an illusion of freedom in the hurricane and knowledge;

DEVELOPMENT

there was always knowledge. Flaubert, de Régnier, Verhaeren, lines, thoughts, vitality, surged through her in a single enthusiasm. Oh, that she might help to part the universe from narrowness, to pour beauty and a splendid tolerance within the reach of all. To them nothing was impossible. Surely to personal liberty she might at last attain.

The park was deserted; long silver lines of rain hung on the branches, a forest of icicles. Cold drops trickled down her collar, a wet draggling skirt made impediment at each step. Would she were out in a boy's suit, free and joyous and careless as a boy is.

A wilder wind snowed the ground with leaves. An orange leaf bounded by, a runaway hoop, rolling over and over the wet gravel. They made a tapestry of brown and scarlet on the water; they drifted on the slanting gale. "Le vent." Mightily shouting, it burst between the trees. The glorious vigour of the forces of the world thundered through the hurricane. Knowledge: there was always knowledge. Wisdom spelt conquest. She would force everything into her brain, absorb it and pour it back in riches to the earth. Tempestuous conflict there might be, but sometime, sometime, freedom should be hers. "Le vent." Rhythm of rain and beating wind. Whatever might befall, space, storm and air kept for ever immortality.

Night was near. The reflected lamps shone, distant crocuses waving in the Serpentine as the wind blew lightly across the surface of the black and shimmering water. She turned towards the darkness of the streets. The lamps hung lemon-wise between a silver mist; light fell in lemon ripples on the sombre pavement. She passed into a tranquil blankness of warm light, uneasy in its silence.

The years must bring her freedom and achievement.

CHAPTER III

BARRIERS

HER book had come. Nancy turned the pages without excitement, almost without interest. Weary of having her ambitions treated as a passing whim, weary for friendship; she had arranged for the best of her verses to be published at her own expense. They had seemed so beautiful when she sent the manuscript away, but in the months that had elapsed before it returned to her, a bound and printed volume, the vital impulses of "vers libre" had discovered and cut away much of the stagnation, due to Downwood, from her mind. She saw now that her rhythms were but echoes, that her thoughts had no strength. And here was a newspaper praising some of the verses; how dull it was and false.

Was this all that life meant? A veritable wresting of expression from a soul not yet articulate; even with printing the consciousness of failure. Were the years to fill only with fresh hopes, the making of one book to be succeeded by another book, each inevitable with disillusion? Was it true what people told her, that she sought a reality that had never known existence?

BARRIERS

She closed the volume. Another hope had gone.

Everybody wanted to read Nancy's verses; nobody wanted to buy them. Older people smiled at her as though she were a spoilt child given a new toy, and watched to see her tire of it. Reviews came; they were read in a quiet, impersonal way.

Monday brought "It is somewhat of a disappointment that the South should have inspired such aimless versifying. The author should remember that the light of the celestial flame needs no aid of coloured glass. Possibly the sense of rhythm may one day win a place among the minorities." Tuesday retaliated with "This tiny book of verse contains more of the true gold of poetry than many a weightier and more pretentious volume. Unlike much modern verse, all that is attempted is well within the scope of the poet, and some of the smaller poems are exquisite, clearly-cut gems. The rich-worded pictures are finer than mere description, and have behind them much of the haunting quality of true song." Wednesday stated that it was "a gathering of bright and cheery verse." (Whoever had written that, had either never troubled to read the verses through, or had given her the notice intended for somebody else.) "There is much tunefulness in this little book," or "Many charming lines occur among these verse," became the stereotyped opening for those too lazy or unwilling to condemn. One detected the influence of Tennyson, whom she hated; another, trace of Arnold and Poe, whom she had never read.

DEVELOPMENT

The longest verses in the volume she had based on the wish, felt so often, to escape into roughness; to feel the sharp sand crunch, frost-wise, between the soft dust never fingered by the sea and the smooth wet surface covered by the tide; to be free and out on the open water, and the realisation that this would mean cessation of intellectual growth, that poetry might be lived there but never written. In her verse she had traced this in an imaginary poet. Two critics solemnly ascribed it as an ode to ———, a writer of whom she had never even heard.

Letters came. "Ever so many thanks, dear, for your book of pretty verses, which I shall always treasure. In the future, doubtless, you will do better work, but there is just one point," etc. "I think the verses are simply charming" was a variant on "Thank you so much for your charming book of verse." All ended with paragraphs of advice that, followed, would have ensured her complete silence; existence took its way precisely as before, except that people coming to the house felt bound to inquire "Have you written anything lately?" and to add hastily they were afraid they did not understand poetry.

Months passed; Nancy was tormented by a desire for expression keener than ever and the sense that until she had some knowledge of actual life she would write nothing that was vital, nothing that was true. Better silence than to sit weaving into words pretty echoes of her favourite poets or her own immature dreams,

BARRIERS

untested of reality. Yet had she been a boy it would have been so easy to obtain experience; it was this accident of being a girl that doubled her difficulties, dragged her back at every step.

Sometime she would be free, sometime opportunity would come and she would assert her right to freedom; meantime there was nothing but to read and dream and tramp miles in the rain and the wind, longing for liberty.

To speak to other girls seemed as unreal to her as ever; she felt it was better to be alone as regards intimate friendship than to wear gloves every day and be polite. It was not only that none of them cared for literature or history or that she was, as people called her, "shy"; it was rather the dread, so deep a root of her nature, of the insincerity of such meetings, of her inability to see life from the accepted point of view. Then to go out meant her best clothes, and in them she felt as awkward as a child trying to make mud pies in a clean pinafore. So she was forced to dream in silence, to seize a hint of adventure sailing among the Scillonian islands, or on a rare expedition alone with Eleanor to a mountain cottage in Wales. But to live roughly for a few weeks only made the return to civilisation seem more incongruous; made it harder to understand the strangers she was forced to meet occasionally, full of an existence she ignored.

"And so, dear child, you paint." Nancy was startled from meditation by the restless remark. "No;

DEVELOPMENT

I write." "Wonderful! After dinner you must show me your book. Is it a novel?" "No; poems." "How interesting. What a magnificent picture that is in the corner," and Mrs. North turned her head to the other side of the table with a swift rush that threatened to shake her hair, of a wonderful unnatural red, from just the precision of artificiality she affected.

The book was fetched. Mrs. North turned the pages with the rapid motion so characteristic of her, reading not a word.

"Wonderful, dear child, wonderful!" Her eye caught the name, inscribed beneath the verses, of the place where Nancy had written them.

"Palermo," Mrs. North chattered. "Palermo. A charming place. I once spent a winter there. I met such nice people at the hotel." She laid the book aside. "Child, you will be a great poet, and we have need of poets. Oh, what a beautiful vase that is!" She jumped up and rushed round the drawing-room, murmuring before each ornament, "Wonderful, too wonderful!"

Nancy resented her intrusion. Outside, the experience of meeting her might have been amusing, but there was no place for her abbreviations, her sharp rushes in the quietness of the room. Roughness Nancy could pardon, but insincerity jarred her spirit; it was an evil thing.

Mrs. North leaned from the tapestry chair. "This house is too wonderful. You know, I always say to my friends, if I could live in a beautiful room I should never feel wicked any more." Sighing, her eyes hinted how inexpressibly wicked she was.

Nancy turned away, looked to the figure poised on a cream shell, white and beautiful above the rose and ivory of the lit room, looked, eager for silence. Would the evening never end? "I adore the country," Mrs. North was murmuring as she rose to leave. Nancy knew that meant some uncomfortable seaside hotel. "You must come and see my daughter to-morrow. Just a schoolroom tea, dear child; but you won't mind, will you?"

Nancy stared helplessly, unable to think of an excuse before Mrs. North had left the room.

Confident the following afternoon that it was only "a schoolroom tea," quite unafraid, Nancy rang the bell. To her horror she was shown into a room full of people, girls predominating, all with an air of mingled indifference and restraint. For a moment the old feeling of first entering Downwood came back to her, but before she had time to think she was sitting on a sofa nearly buried in cushions between two girls, one fair, one dark, and both equally uninteresting. The room was one of those comfortless places supposed to be furnished in an artistic style with nothing cheerful about it, peculiar chairs, and a bookcase full of sentimental novels. Every one moved and spoke with such exaggerated politeness that they seemed to ooze artificiality. Nancy shivered miserably in her corner. How absurd it all was.

DEVELOPMENT

At length the fair girl leaned forward and murmured to the dark one, "I have just come from a lecture on some French poets."

"How interesting, Miss Chester," the other replied; and Nancy, supposing she had better say something, and hoping the girl was not as dull as she looked, turned and asked, "Are you fond of French poetry?"

Miss Chester, placing her arms and legs with slow expressionless movement in another carefully chosen position, smiled at her. "No; are you?"

"Yes."

"How splendid!"

There was an awkward silence. Mrs. North, a plate of cakes in each hand, rushed up, knelt on one knee before them, and chattered. Nancy supposed it must be the latest fashionable attitude, for the position was repeated before each group in the room.

"And did you like Wales, dear?" Mrs. North was back in front of them again. "I think it was too brave of you to go up there all alone."

There was a look of interest in Miss Chester's eyes.

"It was great fun," Nancy answered.

"How well you look, dear. Climbing must be good for the complexion," and Mrs. North was away on another of her rushes.

"Do you live in Wales?" asked Miss Chester.

"No. A friend had a cottage there among the mountains and I stayed with her."

BARRIERS

"How splendid! I suppose you knew a lot of people?" This from the dark girl.

"No; we were quite alone."

"Wasn't it very dull?"

"No; it was so wild. We were right among the hills, and we climbed a bit."

"But what did you do there when it rained?" Miss Chester was as interested as her languid movements would allow.

"Put on our oilers."

"How splendid!"

"Didn't you catch cold?" The dark girl was actually curious.

"Of course not. Besides, there is always such a sense of adventure in the rain."

"A friend asked me to her cottage once," sighed the dark girl. "She kept four servants, and I should have enjoyed it for the week-end, but I was not allowed to go."

Nancy smiled, incapable of answer. "Still, I'm having a good time, you know." She got as confidential as formality would allow. The good time, as far as Nancy could make out, consisted of a series of interminably dull lunches and teas and in never being allowed outside the house alone.

"Did you have much trouble with your servants?" Miss Chester interrupted.

"We did not have any servants."

DEVELOPMENT

"Oh; you were in an hotel?"

"No; my friend had a cottage."

"But how did you live?" The tone was very bewildered.

"In the kitchen."

Both withdrew as though Nancy were either insane or unfit for their company. They looked at each other. Then Miss Chester's training reasserted itself. "How splendid!"

Eager to escape, Nancy rose. "To live on intimate terms with one's frying-pan is a solemn experience," she assured them as she left.

Nancy passed from the dreary afternoon into the windy street. It was an hour she jerked herself from dream, hungry to touch reality. It was people she wanted to write about, and people baffled her. Yet she understood them, felt their hearts in some instinctive phrase, surprised in a chance gesture whole strands of their intimate life. Perhaps these monotonous years had blurred the freshness of those with whom she came in contact. They awakened no answering vitality, but spilled black words on white paper, barren and dulled with the dregs of remembered bondage. She looked beyond the lamps to the indigo darkness invading the trees, angrily aware of her need of life to sting her into expression.

O to weave all this into a poem, to listen and to learn, until the strange incessant noises, the lemon lamps and the scarlet, blended with darkness and with dream. Outside was so much beauty, and inside—she had by heart what would happen. She dreaded to go indoors, to go up and down the staircase, to wonder how many times she had climbed it, how many times she had come down to emptiness, dreaming the same desire. She remembered when she had at first discovered poetry and had come up softly, hardly daring to move lest in its very fragileness it should vanish; then as it grew clearer she had come up triumphantly because there was so much joy in her heart. Downwood had followed, solitude; and she was no nearer to her wish. Expression to her meant life. She was willing to fail, prepared to fail, but to choke with poems she could not utter was intolerable with anguish. She sought, and could discover no ultimate escape.

So the years passed, and hope was hard to keep.

CHAPTER IV

SALT WATER

POEMS, breathed by the sun into material form, the Scillies rose from the summer depths of blue and iridescent marble. There was little of earth about the islands; even the hills had the curve of a wave; on the western rocks white sand rifted through the grass. The sleepiest July, stirring amid the clover, could never rid the air of a strong and pleasant saltness; while the ice-plants, breaking in flames of rose between the colder stones, had much about them of the sea anemones. A miniature continent, many-regioned, set, circle-wise, about a space of water ever an intimate reflection of the outer tide, each island was so separate, so individual in atmosphere, that an ocean might have divided one from another rather than an iris pool.

Untouched by any spirit of historical antiquity they breathed freshness; as though, a bubble on the lips of the sea, each had been blown to reality that morning; so new in colour it was strange they neither drifted nor took flight, seagull-wise, beyond the horizon, yet full of a primaeval oldness as if, with no intervening dream, Phoenician merchants might return to trade and fill the harbour with their anchored ships.

Nancy plunged her shrimping net into the sedge, swayed back and forth by the tide as grass is moved with a windy day. Fern-fringed seaweed, glistening with pods, trailed amber about the edges of the rocks. Water whirled past her, stilled into pools; weed and sea flower, strange in shape and colour, hid the shelving sand floor with their roots. In the slow heavy push of the net she came near to the heart of the sea, glad with the very stinging of its salt. Now a crab was lifted, tearing at the mesh with tough brown claws; now shrimps and jelly-fish silted into the bottom of the bag. Gulls, whiter than sea-froth, drifted towards a wave with pointed wings. Spray broke about the further islands. All was movement, all was life.

Salt water and the sun began to burn away her silence. She must write; an imperious need of expression was upon her. She was torn from dream only to feel desire flood back upon herself. What was there but her own development she could fit with words, days of epic infancy, childhood broken by a frozen bondage—this solitude of years among her books, with wavering hope for company, it might be ended by adventure? The books she longed to write must still be put aside lest she should mar them with immaturity. It was false to write of emotions her mind had not experienced. She must see, she must know, before creation were possible. Yet it was hard to stay for a future that was

DEVELOPMENT

so slow of waking; hard to return to Scilly, summer after summer, and mark another year as barren of achievement.

Thin sand shifted about her feet as she climbed beyond the shore to the first hollow rough with bracken and a clump of heather. The evening, at least, would bring her a new experience, for if the weather held they would go by moonlight to scratch for lances on Pellistree beach. She emptied her basket on to the nearest rock. It was something to feel the sun, to watch the sea.

The lance hooks jangled in the darkness. Nancy followed the others up the road, knowing she was a boy. A clock had long ago struck ten in the clear Scillonian air. The black stems of scattered masts were lit by gold buds. It was an hour of childhood recaptured and fulfilled. The moon was hidden; no one spoke.

It was strange to feel the short clover underfoot, to tread on sleeping flowers. Moths were blown from shadow to shadow, white rhythms of orchard petals till their wings touched earth. The sense of night, new, lovely, intangible, made mystery of the hedge. Even the air filled with a sudden richness, the scent of slumbering grass.

The whole island seemed to have changed its shape with a single hour. Sleeping birds in the darkness, rocks drifted into the water beyond the open bay. Far in the distance a light flickered and was still over sand colourless in its coldness, neither white nor faded gold, rather tinged as a star struggling between the crinkled edges of a cloud.

Nancy stepped over the chill pebbles of the beach, waded along a thread of pools, plunged her lance hook firmly in the sand. Tiny phosphorescent stars were flung burning on to the cold shore, a sudden shiver of silver missed her hands. It was her first adventure with night; a strange, a wonderful experience, full of the mingled dream and reality she desired.

A trail of seaweed fell across her feet with sudden warmth. A lance quivered in her sandy fingers; the bay flashed with the silver of leaping fish. The baskets filled. Out on the boulders which kept no thought of earth Nancy touched the freshness of the sea, elemental, sharp as it had been to the fisher folk who, before history, tore shells from the rocks and plunder from the sedge.

Her own hands were thick with oil, crusted with salt and sand. The tide turned. Water surged over the crumbling stones. She stood erect, looking seawards for a last time before they left the beach. Gold heart of a white and open rose, the moon rifted the petals of the clouds.

Hugh Town was asleep when they returned. The clock struck three in an air heavy with peacefulness. There was no wind; no ripples broke the silence of the waves. Hot with rebellion Nancy opened the window of her room, reluctant to leave night, loved for the first time, eager to touch the darkness, to keep the softness of it near her face. In an hour dawn would rise; iris morning would chisel the hills with gold. What waste it was to sleep.

Even the flowers were too delicate for her mood. She needed to plunge her lips into the salt, to grip tough roots with her hands, rock. Strength, she longed for strength, might of wind, surge of clamorous surf. All the wildness of her spirit night liberated with a touch. She stood; all eagerness, all longing, just to smell tar, to feel rope, not to watch but to battle with the waves. Yet the door was locked; she could only wait at the window, desolate with lost adventure, desolate with a boyishness that might never put to sea, denied the secrets of the wind and dawn a sailor has by heart.

Clouds drew over the moon. The islands slept.

Sunset carved the eastern islands out of grape-blue darkness with a gold knife. For a last moment, on the rose-red stone-crop of Ganilly, day remembered noon. Black seals dived for fish in a purity of green water left by the sand beneath. The distant mainland and the distant waves deepened with night.

Nancy stared out seawards as though adventure waited her at the horizon. She was living a dream near to the immortality she loved. It was evil to think of beauty as tainted by any transience, but wind, if it stilled, passed into another wind, the sea slept and

SALT WATER

knew not death. Evening was ready to flower above the ridges of the water, drop after drop of honey, light spilled into the foam. Between the islands, almost beyond sight, the swift, beautiful outline of a ship followed the swifter day.

The wildness of the hour took Nancy's heart in its strong grasp. She stared at the mainland, rigid with rebellion. Winter, desolate hours she fought to keep even dream; how had she failed that she must face them year after arid year? It was only her ignorance that kept her from expression; always to watch, never to feel. She needed a future that would hold no sting, no bondage; to slip free of the old hours and all their fetters, to kick aside existence and clutch life. What was strength that she should fear it, what was roughness? It was better to know the beauty in bitterness than to freeze into a tranquility that had turned away from truth.

Cold water tossed seawards beyond the black drifters, beyond the harbour wall. Nancy shook the water from her oilskins; spray burst over the bows of the launch. All she had known of liberty, all she had read, lands of wide grass, rough hills, open beaches, the wildness that was freedom, sharpened her desire. With a sudden moment even the islands were too small for her. It was there, out there, she longed to be, out at the horizon—following the wind until her spirit broke beyond morning, in the great hunger for a new world that is the impulse of all discovery.

DEVELOPMENT

She felt a sailor as they landed on the rough stones of a harbour that was a link between the dark, unconquered life of the drifter cabins and the stone cottages of the dwellers by the shore. Seamen passed up and down, with ropes in their hands or nets; the spirit of the sea about their salt-encrusted clothes. It was a page torn living from some book of old adventure; never free of the smell of fish, of ships, of tar, all the queer sea-scents that pierced Nancy with a strange, a sudden longing for a world she could never know. She looked once to the single scarlet flower the sky lifted above the waves, then turned; angry her joy should be as transient as light, hurt that she might never make achievement of a dream. Yet truth lived, the truth that was adventure, the truth sailors surprised at dawn when morning opened over the far coasts of the world.

Why was she born with a boy's heart when she might not go to sea?

CHAPTER V

THE COLOUR OF WORDS

EVER since Nancy could remember, all words, as she heard or read them, appeared to her as colour. It was as natural as breathing, so thoroughly an element of her mind that it was only by accident she discovered, at fifteen, they were printed symbols to the multitude, and to speak of them as gold or crimson merely provoked derision. It was not until nine years later that she found she was simply a colour hearer and that, while it was not common to every one, as she had at first imagined, it was not confined to the few, but was, in one form or another, fairly prevalent.

It was impossible to think of the alphabet as colourless. Often she questioned people, "What do words mean to you; how do you see them?" Yet this was useless; despite proof and reasoning her thought compelled her to credit all minds with this sense of colour audition.

Natural objects apart, which kept their actual hue, the initial letter gave the word its colour, but there were exceptions to this rule. Contrary to the French examples in the books she read, vowels were indecisive; it was the consonants that made a page as vivid as a sunset. Seven letters were white, C, G, Q, S, T, O, and U; three of the others were black, D, E, and I. W was crimson; H, M, and Y were various shades of gold and primrose. B changed from raspberry to umber, N was the rich tint of a red squirrel, F and J were a deeper brown. Other letters brought blue, as sharp as a broken wave, as dark as Alpine gentian. R was rose; A and P seemed too weak to be definite and varied with different words, though with names of places or people A was occasionally iris-blue or scarlet.

Often the consonants would mingle to form some complex colour, purple or a lazuli dusted over with frost. The wind, blown between the trees, was sharp with blue or silver; surf brought her petals, as she closed her eyes and listened, the white petals of narcissus. Heavy sounds were thick umber or grey; the singing of birds was the transparent surface of a deep, just-rippled pool.

Music was no joy to her but an indefinite blur of notes. It retarded thought and offered no emotion in its place. Usually it was some dark shade powdered over with silver, but very high or very clear notes were daffodils, bending from their stems. Swift notes were silver, occasionally blue. It was a curious point that she never cared for green and seldom saw it in a spoken phrase, yet it was visible in music and was slightly irritating in effect.

THE COLOUR OF WORDS

Silence she dreaded; she liked to sleep with sounds waking outside the window. Even work was easier in London with the stir and rumble of traffic just perceptible to her ears. Stillness could have a paralysing effect upon her mind; was, of itself, sufficient to bring fear. Not that she disdained quietness, but she liked to have it set about with movement, wind rifting the trees or the distant passage of wheels. Nothing calmed her so much as to lie on a boat and feel the heavy beat of the engines swinging under her limbs. A swift burst of thunder could send her mad for joy.

Nancy desired the right of the Elizabethans to forge new words; English grew impoverished and demanded freshness. She liked to feel the exact colour of an impression had been recaptured in a phrase, but to translate form and motion always by comparison was foolish. It was absurd to dismiss in a score of terms the uncounted lights and shadows visible at dawn, the fragile ridges of the dented hills. There was nothing to express scent; apple blossom in an April evening, tar and salt about a harbour's edge, wild thyme, meadow clover—smell and fragrance had to serve for all. The language of movement spoke to the eyes alone. The circular swing of a wind-touched leaf, the rhythm of a bird's flight, muscles that bent and lifted with each gesture—these were unremembered because they might not be portrayed. Some words possessed a sense of substance. To say "shrill" or "audible" was to feel, in thought, a thin narcissus petal; to speak of "clamor-

ous" or "mulberry" was to touch an apricot ripe with
bloom. But more terms were needed to describe actual
texture; short, simple words to express the grades between rough and smooth.

So much beauty was obscured by an ugly term.
Flowers, especially, were gifted with unimaginative
titles until it often seemed that the more beautiful the
blossom the clumsier was its name. Could any mind
sensitive to sound use "geranium" or "begonia," and
why must the wallflowers lack a word to bring their
reds, the richness of their browns, before the mind?
Gillyflower might serve for a bronze petal striped with
yellow, but it was too thin, too colourless, for the wilder roots of a steep hillside.

Nancy had no care for the origin of a phrase provided that its sound and its meaning were both beautiful. Speech should be strong as a sea wind or delicate
as pear blossom; it was the mediocrities of either that
jarred. Just to remember some words was to touch a
flower: "adventure," a blue so lovely only the rain-
flushed petals of the iris offered it to the eyes; "amorous," crimson pressure of a peach against its kernel,
bitter with life; "cinnamon," more beautiful than the
colour it described; "Illyria," which brought sleep and
the dreams of Endimion within its hands. To speak
of "ivory" and "orchard" was to touch the wings of
beauty; she had a fondness for three syllables, "fugitive," "unpossible," "immortal"; for "honey," which
gave her richness; for "almond," which gave her the

THE COLOUR OF WORDS

South. She sought for vivid and original expression of a colour as another might have hunted for a moth or a rare shell. The sudden use of an unexpected word would lighten a whole morning; remembered lines could stab into enthusiasm the most ordinary day.

It was the rhythm of words which gave them their emotion. The more sensitive her ears became to the curve and pause of a cadence the less able was Nancy to read rhyme or any definite metre. Syllables had a movement and a spirit of their own; to force them into a crude jingle of regular beats was to mar their loveliness, rob them of life. Certain lines could wake in her moods she seldom otherwise experienced; strange, unconnected phrases which lingered in her mind for no apparent reason. She had only to read or to remember

Salt Cleopatra, soften thy waned lips,

and for a brief moment triumph cut her from existence; she was prouder than one to whom a lost battle has promised swift, inevitable death.

Some rhythms of themselves brought loneliness, the bitterness of wisdom:

Ainsi mourut la fille d'Hamilcar pour avoir touché au manteau de Tanit.

To think of this freed a pride in her that was mingled with irony rather than with joy.

DEVELOPMENT

All courage, all despair broke through this rhythm:

> Your white flesh covered with salt
> As with myrrh and burnt iris;

and to cry this cadence:

> Shall I hurl myself from here,
> Shall I leap and be nearer you,
> Shall I drop, beloved, beloved,
> Ankle against ankle?
> Would you pity me, O white breast?

was to stand (however desolate the day) on a wide beach and to be burnt by light, by the wildness of the sea salt and the wind.

Not all writers could free this sense in her, nor was it usually dependent on the meaning of the phrase. Shakespeare, Webster, and Flaubert could madden her with their rhythms; Massinger and Ford left her perfectly unmoved. To read the prose of Lodge, of Lyly, or of Middleton was to lie on grass and wild clover and plunge one's hands deeper and deeper into red earth and sweet herbs.

Nancy could find little to interest her in contemporary literature. In France a period of immense richness had passed away, almost before her eyes. The strength, the clarity and truth of half a century of vision had ebbed into the mere cleverness of Romains, the mere brilliancy of Fort. America was hopeful; there was, at least, a sense of vitality abroad, but it was promise, not achievement. England was dull with echoes of just dead age, or too troubled by transition to remember beauty. Nancy read book after book to find they were only lumps of unwrought material, a long preparation for something which never happened, heavy, blunted, barren of definite aim. The "romantic" volumes set out to be wicked, and drowned themselves in a mire of untrue psychology and false emotion. The realists photographed the time, but somehow managed to omit the spirit. There was no mingling of irony with loveliness; the unpleasant truths of existence were blurred with a false perspective or were never faced at all. Discouragement marched in the train of this futility, and from these pages of degenerate weakness Nancy turned with relief to *Tom Jones*.

There was a root of power and firm, exacting observation about Fielding that was very satisfying; he was, contrary to apprehension, the reverse of dull, but, pleasant as the books were to read in a leisurely, haphazard fashion, there clung about them too much of the atmosphere of a century that had never held her captive as antiquity had done. The world of *Joseph Andrews* was not a world she envied, and amusing as it might be to read of Sophia or Amelia, their company would have caused her the profoundest irritation.

In moods when the impulse for freedom and self-expression was strong upon her Nancy read the Elizabethans. The roots of all things interested her, and

DEVELOPMENT

Middleton, Lyly, and Marston gave her the inside of an age. To open *A Mad World, My Masters, A Fair Quarrel, Eastward Ho,* was to step back three centuries and actually enter the Elizabethan world. The side of her nature which resented the impossibilities of Fletcher, however beautiful the poetry, was not disquieted with Moll, the Roaring Girl.

It was indeed a mad world she read of, curious mingling of a very ferocity of strength with the "light-colour summer stuff" out of which Euphues, Campaspe, and Rosalynde were fashioned. To listen to Bellario, to meet Orlando Friscobaldo, to watch Endimion waken with the moon, was to breathe the air of adventure, to surprise adventure itself, to plunge into a morning when poetry was common to existence, to be free of this twitter-light of stumbling prose. The mere assuming of a boy's apparel, so favourite a device of the period, enchanted her never-dormant desire of unrestricted freedom. Be a girl and there were always barriers. Nancy liked to dream they were no more when the actual jar of their existence most oppressed her thought. Yet she loved truth too much not to remember the cruel reality of such adventure (pictured in *More Dissemblers besides Women*) as well as the exultant moments passed with *Philaster* and *Cymbeline.*

Her intimacy with Bellario and Bellafront, with all that Imogen ever spoke, made friendship in this modern world difficult of achievement. They brought her a wideness of vision strange to this later age; she admit-

164

ted them to secret imaginings of her own, unbreathed even to dream. Her ears came to recognise in their accents an unrecaptured immortality, to need this and sorrow for it should it cease to break her thought.

She admired the strength of Wycherley, his clarity and his truth, but with the Restoration a certain heaviness crept into literature; she missed the freshness and vitality of *Father Hubburd's Tales* or *The Anatomy of Wit.* All that was strong and beautiful seemed to have died with the Elizabethans, or to exist in this later English only imperfectly and in fragments.

Nancy turned to England for her poetry, to France for much of her prose. Almost from infancy she had divided her literary allegiance between the two countries, knowing that a mood which defied translation in the one language might find perfect expression of its beauty in the other. The Alexandrine, the definite French metres, wearied her ears and were tinged with a formality quite alien to the power and richness of the English spirit which had kept a semblance of *vers libre* alive throughout the centuries, despite Chaucer's betrayal of cadence to a foreign invasion of rhyme. But English prose (the Elizabethans apart) was apt to be heavy, slow of rhythm and emotion, blurred both of vision and of form. The clarity, precision of outline, and psychological mastery which she desired seemed only to be realised in French.

It was Flaubert who commanded her enthusiasm; *Salammbô* that exposed much of her dream of Car-

thage, *Bouvard et Pécuchet* with the splendid cruelty of
its vision, a cruelty that brought no torment to the
nerves. All the richness, all the power of antiquity were
in his hands. He was alone. He gave nothing; he expected nothing. His was the pitiless mind of an early
leader who would bend the world to his power. It was
an accident of circumstance he hewed his way, not by
the slaughter of men, the burning of slaves, but by the
javelin points of his words.

How strong he was—the walls of inscrutable
Egypt at speech with the tranquil stars. The mob
might howl about him, jackal-wise, but the sand,
scratched with their footsteps, only made his silence
seem more beautiful. In a time that was a dumbness
of rejected beauty Nancy came to him for shelter from
an unjust, a brutal, and a bitter world.

Yet there were days when Flaubert was too cruel
for her, days when to read the Elizabethans was a
mockery, and in these moods Remy de Gourment
could amuse her thought. It was impossible to be intimate with his books at once. At first Nancy even mis-
understood his mind a little; it seemed pure intellect
that, unsatisfied and untired, recoiled, ravenous, and
devoured his own spirit. Then as she learnt more and
read him more she came to understand his bitterness
was but the sheath for his pity, for a weariness of
knowledge too keen to be ever shared.

"Rose aux yeux noirs, miroir de ton néant, fais-nous croire au mystère, fleur hypocrite, fleur du silence."

"Marguerite, Balsamine, Amarante, je vous préfère aux plus sérieux enchantements, fleurs trépassées, fleurs de jadis."

Crumbled beauty, beauty that was a torment to read, spines of beauty that brought her the disdainful eyes of some imagined Caliph, burdened with orient empires until he crushed them into dust, crying, "Of what worth are these?"—the music of his phrases troubled her almost to weeping. Colour was so subtle in his hands, he spoke of it in a new language; in a line a gesture lived, or the fragrance of the fields, definite and beautiful. He compelled imagination to obedience; he never forgot reality was the calyx of his dream. His prose was poetry; strong as a bough of apple blossom, frail as a wild rose. The wind of his elusive rhythms troubled her emotions until they spilled the pungence of a June meadow about the dreariness of her thought. He understood and did not stab to fresh endurance; the loneliness of his wisdom, too subtle for any sympathy, forgave her the despair of moments she cried out only for peace. Almost alone of poets he offered tenderness, a tenderness wrought of truth that was sweet as a snapt flower.

Certainly these French poets stimulated thought. It was not only their wisdom which gave to Nancy a new consciousness of strength, but their courage and their power to see both truth and beauty unmisted by illusion. To read them was a constant lesson in clarity and restraint.

Maupassant she admired, but he missed true achievement. He was rigid with a bitterness that had neither the wisdom nor the loveliness of Flaubert to redeem it. One had only to compare the best of his stories with a page of *Bouvard et Pécuchet* to note the margin between intellect and brain. Yet it was good to feel his coldness cut the mire of this hypocritical existence and bare the essential facts.

Huysmans was a disappointment. She read *À Rebours* only to shrink back from the evil of its weakness. There was no sanity about it, no truth; phrase and thought were blurred and filled her instinctively with dread. *À Vau l'Eau* was better. It was, at least, uncompromising in its realism—hatred had hardened it—but she was not tempted to any further exploration.

Stendhal had no sense of beauty, but he held her mind. There was a curious illusion of reality about his work; it was less a book than a document, some analytical brain editing an unpublished diary that smelt of dust on the front page but was otherwise as vital as the modern hands of its discoverer.

Gautier she enjoyed, yet his prose was over ripe with sweetness; rather it was a richness that was unrestrained by thought. She turned to *Mademoiselle de Maupin* hopeful of boyishness, but the psychology, subtle as it was, had blent with it such unpossible imaginings, the whole seemed a little false. As a poet his rhythms were too rigid for her ears.

Rimbaud promised to be interesting, but she could give him no enthusiasm. She was sensitive to Mallarmé, never to Baudelaire.

Henri de Régnier's novels satisfied a sense of forceful richness untasted otherwise save in Elizabethan books. *Le Bon Plaisir* might have been a comedy of Middleton's blent with a modern irony and retold. His prose had all the quality of poetry, was often more emotional than his verse. To read his books was not to see so much as to touch; he evoked the substance of an object, amber, pears, the plum wrought of warm agate M. de Breot chose from the heavy basket. She had her favourite passages: all of *La Double Maîtresse,* the realisation, in Justin and Jérôme de Pocancy, of the unrelentant brutality of earth, the crust of coarseness and crude colour, the fish scales, the rough soil, that are the elements of strength. Yet, although he expressed the blunt, quick tragedies of the body rather than the protracted, sensitive torment of the nerves, his books were no mere outward portrayal of beauty; under the flesh, burnt with noon, so vivid with life, was a kernel of trenchant analysis and vision.

The intervals of her reading Nancy filled with her own manuscript, wrought neither of imagination nor remembered stories but of the one experience she knew from end to end—herself. Utterly careless of what is misnamed of the multitude "success," she was

DEVELOPMENT

eager for expression, to frame in words her belief in freedom, her own need of truth. She wished to tear from every language all it might hold of beauty; to fill her imagination with every colour she could wrest from books or life. It was intolerable to write of any mood she had not personally experienced; she fought for knowledge, fought, and groped for it in the dark. Work was difficult in an unbroken isolation which fettered thought and plundered her of dream, yet, sharp as it was to wait for life, there were days she forgot rebellion and was glad of her solitude, the solitude which had taught her the loneliness, the transience, and the loveliness of words.

CHAPTER VI

VISUAL IMAGINATION

THERE is existence. There is life. Existence is transient. Life is eternal. Existence begins with birth and ends with death. Life is immortality touched and tasted—the gift of a rare moment. Existence is earth. Life is the root and leaf—flower of dream opening from the calyx of reality.

The aim of the artist is expression. The expression of life is art.

But no art is possible without freedom; fear and ignorance are the negation of life. To be free is to choose a world and dwell in it uninfluenced by sentiment or circumstance.

There is doom of days of fear and emptiness. There is beauty, wise and young and with the eyes of sleep. And between them there is a bridge—the bridge of visual imagination.

The eyes look outward on to an actual world, the world of existence. The eyes look inward and see a world as vital and as clear, the world of dream.

DEVELOPMENT

When the world of existence merges into the world of dream, the eyes look on the world of life.

Illusion is to reflect, for the point of a second, the world of dream upon the world of existence. Vision is to project the world of dream beyond the eyes until the actual world is obscured.

To dream is to draw pictures across the black curtain of the mind. A thought occurs, a wish, and is immediately translated into a picture. Wish joins wish—picture fits into picture. The result, whether experienced in a sleeping or a waking state, forms a dream.

Life is a constant effort to dwell in the actual world familiar to these pictures. Dreams are the hieroglyphics by which the mind expresses its true thoughts.

All roots open from childhood—beauty, knowledge, adventure—but they are useless to the artist until they are blended with experience. Experience is personal contact with the elements of life.

An artist must be rough to brutality, sensitive as a poppy leaf is to light, for to know the precise moment in which to pass from coarseness into beauty is the root of art. He must be free of the literature of all nations. He must see the same problems, the same thoughts, through the eyes of each different race.

The desire of the spirit is immortality. Cessation of growth means cessation of life.

Visual imagination is a gift of the child and the artist. It is the root of the creative impulse, the vitality

VISUAL IMAGINATION

of appreciation, a half of the ingredients of dream. It gives the power to live not one life but many lives, a share in the immortal beauty of the past life of the earth.

It is rare to find children who are not able to see "pictures," though with maturity these tend to fade and to disappear. Yet in a few cases their colour deepens with each month, grows hard of outline. They become the shells from which poet or painter pours the eventual expression of his mind.

A photograph is the impression formed on the mind of the actual world. A picture is the image traced by imagination or by accident on the brain.

The inside of the head seems as a row of cells—a hive, open in the middle and dark. A line of a poem, an adventure, a new thought, opens one cell, many cells, and frees the pictures they contain. The liberated impressions drift across the head.

Pictures are of three kinds. Unconscious—when they pass through the mind without conscious effort to evoke or to retain them. Conscious—when by effort of will these pictures are retained and made clear to the point of reality. Visual—when images unconnected with the imagination appear for a moment, vivid with light and movement, as if centred in the lids of the eyes.

A figure seen in a conscious picture could be recognised at any future period. A figure seen in an unconscious picture would be definite in outline, but the details (colour of eyes and hair) might not be very clear.

Colour and line are dependent in an unconscious picture on association, in a conscious picture on choice.

The pictures of a child are usually unconscious or visual. Only an artist of some degree of development has the gift of conscious vision.

In actual life thousands of photographs are impressed upon the mind. Some are retained, some are thrown away. During some process of selection (imperfectly understood at present) certain details from many pictures slip back towards the eyes. The result is a visual picture.

"A bright blue sea beats against an island of brown rocks. Foam is flung high between the sharp points of pinnacles. Sea-birds—gulls and cormorants—fly overhead or perch on the flatter stones. It is no island known in actual life, but the shape is too vivid ever to be forgotten. The sea surges and withdraws again with shrill, incessant movement. The light on the waves is visible as the sun catches them, and again they darken as they surge forward into hollows."

Such was an image which occurred after a day had been spent fishing between many small islands. A changing series of impressions had passed before the eyes which had retained at will certain photographs which the mind desired to keep. But of the many rejected impressions some had silted away from forgetfulness and re-lived a moment in the centre of the eyelids.

In duration a visual picture comes midway between conscious and unconscious images. It may last from a second to several seconds. It may appear, vanish, and appear again. It is common in childhood and detached both from imagination and from thought. Usually it occurs just before sleep (not invariably), and of all three kinds is by far the most intense in colour and in movement.

Unconscious pictures are the images, vague in outline but definite to the mind, that a child sees, turning the pages of a story-book, or that make some line of a picture or a poem the gate to the artist of another world. They are as swift and as natural as breath, and to some minds the inevitable accompaniment of each thought.

A conscious picture can last as long as the mind and eyes can endure the rigid concentration. It is the image built by an artist, eager to create a desired world.

"The sea—blue and intense as a wood hyacinth— sweeps beyond Carthage to the south. A ship moves out of the harbour, her prow pointed toward the sunset, a dark Libyan pulling at the ropes that free her purple sail. A string of camels print the dust with silent footstep; a war elephant with slow, defiant movement strips the leaves from a wayside shrub. Another ship, low in the water with Sicilian grain, breaks into the circle of the bay. A Numidian gallops past toward the date-palms and the desert; the rich African sunlight burns the city to a flame of gold."

The mirage of antiquity grows sharp until the body almost feels the sun and the eyes, so hungry for colour in a grey land, are appeased. But the strain across the eyelids is so painful that the image, with a few minutes, is allowed to slip from sight.

It is only when a picture is "felt" as well as "seen" that artistic expression results.

There are days that are immortal; hours the bird-heart of freedom deigns to shelter an instant in a human mind. That these be untainted of any evil existence—night upon flowers—scatters over the memory leaves of sleep. But let some poem be read or some adventure be achieved. As the light falls they open out of the darkness—for the wind dies and the sunset; it is only these hours that live.

There was existence; there was also life. But in this present time it was hard to capture the reality of dream. Modernity was evil with weakness and repression; a swamp that sucked breath back out of the light. The intellect of modern France had lost its sharpness, exhausted by half a century of expression. What was England but a wallpaper of rigid pattern in art, in education, and in life? It was true a convention of revolt existed, but with the first test the rebels slunk back into the horde. They made an artificiality of freedom.

VISUAL IMAGINATION

False realities were stamped—pink buds or decayed leaves—upon the acquiescent paper of their minds. Even Downwood, even the schools, were but loose bolts in an engine rusted to breaking-point. Fresh paint only made the corruption seem more hideous. And trying to face truth, trying to grasp it, Nancy knew that there was strife about her and ahead of her—a fight, with death as the prize. But she must know and write. She must achieve and express freedom. There must be no pity for an ugly world; pity that was so easy and so wrong. It was better to die for beauty than to exist for lies. And the horde—so ready to stab at any unguarded moment—could not plunder her of Carthage, could not blur the islands from her mind. As long as winds breathed and dawn flowered there was her own South to welcome her, the South itself to answer her "Beauty lives."

THE END

The author has in preparation a second volume to be entitled *Adventure,* in which the story of *Development* will be continued.

TWO SELVES

"This is a continuation of *Development*
published some three years ago."

Copyrighted by the author
Published by
Contact Publishing Co.
12, rue de l'Odéon
Paris-France

Editor's Note: The original manuscript of *Two Selves* has occasional incon-
sistencies of presentation of punctuation which the editor has judged to be
errors in the type rather than modernist textual practice. These errors have
been corrected in this current edition.

TWO SELVES

Bryher

TABLE OF CONTENTS

———

CHAPTER I

TWO SELVES

TWO selves. Jammed against each other, disjointed and ill-fitting. An obedient Nancy with heavy plaits tied over two ears that answered "yes, no, yes, no," according as the wind blew. A boy, a brain, that planned adventures and sought wisdom. Two personalities uneasy by their juxtaposition. As happy together as if a sharp sword were thrust into a golf bag for a sheath.

It had happened eighteen months before, this division. Just as she had left Downwood. A queer feeling across the head. As if something had hit her very hard . . . so hard one felt no pain . . . only a numbness. As if the active section of her mind had been smashed by a heavy fist.

She wanted to go away and forget everyone she had known. Get to a cottage in Cornwall and live there by herself. Make a new world in a book. Start afresh. She had asked for this. But people scolded her at such a request. "We have given up our lives for you," they had said. "It was for your own sake you were sent to school." They had been so upset she had insisted no further. She hated hurting people's feelings. It was terrible of them to have given up their lives for her. Only she had not wished them to do it.

She wanted to be free.

But school had paralyzed her. As she left its doors some long deferred consciousness of terror broke . . . perhaps she would never be able to make a decision, act of her own initiative again.

Two selves. The one complete enough, chaffed by every restriction, planning to reform the world, planning to reform schools, planning to know and experience everything there was to know and experience. But the other self . . . blown apart with every wind . . . it was painfully inadequate a covering.

She had no words to make them understand. "If you are so eager to learn you had better go to college." But college was void of wisdom. Wisdom was not only books . . . it was something . . . "you know when it comes" she had pleaded.

It was the only way to escape. A way to be hidden in silence. But wisdom was not easy to find and the road there broke off, got lost in other tangles.

A black pekingese trotted past with a red rosebud caught in his silky hair. The plane trees shook into leaf; hyacinths spiked the sharp green lawn. A bulldog scrunched under the low park railing to leave audacious paw marks over the dewy grass. People passed; people laughed; people sat and watched the riders.

Nancy would have liked a dog to follow her; a bulldog or a griffon perhaps, something with completely flattened nose, utterly useless, utterly artistic, a heavy frog-like, bee-like creature, with soft fantastic tulips tangled in his collar. She hated sporting kinds with their smug strength, their over-obvious utility. Hated their owners with their inevitable sentence, "I like a dog to be a dog," their continuous sneer at any sensitive intelligence. Anyway she could not have an animal so why watch the French bull with his furred out collar and his soft black muzzle. She could not have a friend.

Yet none of the faces passing would have urged her to a sentence could she have stopped them and have spoken. The accent of their voices, the chance phrases she caught, repelled her. If she had friendship ever it would be immediate, inevitable. There would be no recognition of each other. Simply a placing together of two lives.

How busy the park was with faces and with flowers. Parchment buds tipped the chestnut trees and waited to be unrolled. The sky flowered into a myriad forget-me-nots between the sharp green leaves. Girls in dresses the colour of the hyacinths leaned above the stiff blue cones. Borders of white and red daisies merged softly into grass.

"I thought Mr. Gavin very nice."

"I didn't like him much."

"Why, Nancy, he seemed so interested in you."

TWO SELVES

"Can't help that. He has no right to treat his children the way he does."

"But he talked all lunch time about his son. I thought it was splendid of him to be so wrapt up in them."

"That's just the trouble." (Fool to get on dangerous ground.) "Why doesn't he leave them alone? It's cruel. Cruel to bribe that boy of his with a cycle, not to drink or smoke till he's twenty five. Before the child realizes what he is being asked to do. It's inviting him to be a liar or an idiot."

"I think myself it's a pity to tie the boy. But you're too violent in your statements. And he is fond of the children."

"That's no excuse for bribing a child of ten to give up liberty of action at eighteen."

"I suppose you will say next that we are too interested in you . . ."

Why must they take every sentence as a personal matter . . . never any detachment? It was awful to think about, the impotence of youth. Never to be able to express an opinion without their being hurt. If only one had a friend. Eleanor was interested but she knew no more than one's self. Doreen only cared about fishing. Miss Sampson about the tone of the school.

"It's all those books you read."

Queer how everyone despised intellect . . . as a shame . . . something to be hidden. The weight and smell of a word. What was it in the Futurist manifesto?

TWO SELVES

There was something right about that. Something new. Everything new was laughed at. If one read history that was all that happened. A chain of people laughing at a new idea, fighting it, accepting it and fighting the idea again that grew to take its place. The young and the old. Couldn't people *see* how rotten English education was? Parents were too lazy to see. They were afraid of a better education. Afraid of what it might make their sons say to them. Afraid of the independence it might give their daughters. She wanted to talk out that Futurist manifesto with somebody. Talk it out intelligently, without laughter. How far is it possible to indicate the weight and smell of a word? Colour. She had always seen words as colour. They laughed. Her aunt would laugh. Doreen would laugh. It was not the laughter that mattered but the boring re-iteration of it. Whenever she spoke. "If only you would have human interests. If only you had a sense of humour." So tedious never to hear but the one opinion, the one scale of remarks.

Vers libre. She must throw her old note books away. It was a hard discipline. Without rhyme one had to create. Create an experience. She had no experiences. Rhyme blurred over one's faults. Rhyme covered up one's incapacity. Rhyme was a trick, a perversion of rhythm.

Vers libre had ruled England until Chaucer's time. Those fool Italian metres had kicked it out. Old English poetry was all unrhymed. Anyone could find

187

rhymes with or without a rhyming dictionary. It was just patience and memory. But only a poet could make a sound, a colour. Only a poet could forego repeating a past age.

She must remember to throw her old note books away.

Always somebody wanted her. Just as she began to work. She must try to do as they wished. She hated hurting people. She must write out phrases in a note-book and learn them, to say to Millicent the next time she came to call. Something that would interest Milli-cent. But Millicent seemed to care for nothing. She said "yes", and "no", and "really", and the headlines of the papers over and over . . . one could write down . . . Nancy had written down . . . all the answers to all the phrases exactly as Millicent would say them.

But people were so kind. If only they would not be kind. Not give her presents nor ask (trying to be interested) if she had written another book yet or how far she had got in hieroglyphics.

Everywhere it pressed on her; a ramification of people being kind and never any freedom.

"I know there's colour somewhere," she would say suddenly. And immediately, inevitably, there would come the tag about wanting the moon.

There was no doubt but that she was most ungrateful.

TWO SELVES

At fifteen she could have gone ahead. Nothing had frightened her then. Not even making a fool of herself. Now liberty seemed bound up with hurting people. She had wanted to go to an Art School; she could have talked to strangers readily. Even at school she had felt anger and not fear. But now, it was a queer numb apathy. A terror of going even through strange doors.

There was a world somewhere. That was the worst of it. Just as she reasoned, uprooting root and mood, that this was her life and that it was no good upsetting people, a glimpse, tag of a life, of another world, got to her.

But Downwood was a memory two years old and her soul was no further.

CHAPTER II

LEOPARD GOLD

"BEHOLDING Joseph's beauty, her knife cut the hand that held the pomegranate." Professor Foster's even voice read out the unfamiliar words, translating as he went from Arabic to English.

"How very stupid of her," commented Miss Leyton, the Egyptologist, leaning back against the arm of her chair. "Let us hope she was not unduly affected by the sequel."

"It is, of course, a later exaggeration." Professor Foster could not miss the opportunity to compare, co-relate. "You do not find it in the Jewish version. And . . . by the way . . . I think we had better omit the next two lines. Mark on your copies please, two lines passed over. The licence of the East is well enough in its place but really there is no need to drag it into a lesson."

The thin youth opposite Nancy blushed. He bent eagerly over his notebook and scribbled hastily the Arabic equivalent of some Swahili phrases. He had already been in Africa a year and was back in London simply to pass a Consular examination.

LEOPARD GOLD

"Very little one can choose for class reading," the Professor commented. "Except religious tracts and Miss Leyton insists on something entertaining. Though think what an opportunity you miss," he turned towards her, "of discussing with some Moslem elder the intricacies of Koranic lore on your next expedition up the Nile. No, no, Miss Leyton," he broke across a stream of gutteral dialect, "you must not use your donkey boy Arabic here. We are not an excavating party but a class of serious students."

He smiled as he took up their papers from the table, scrawled over with uncertain Arabic characters and corrected in red ink. The wide bookcase lined room faced on to the quiet Kensington street, alive with sparrows. A few bare boughs showed through the window; the tiny court beyond the house was full of fallen leaves. But the winter had been broken with these familiar if unmemorized phrases that had all the grit of sand in their sound, the silent padding of camels and the flash of hoopoe wings. A sentence splashed and fell like the black and white kingfishers darting from one side to the other of the Nile. Even the conjugation of a verb brought back the gold caravans of far off days that met and parted at Kom Ombo.

The student who spoke Swahili read through his exercise, a pencil in his hand, a notebook before him. His seriousness was a blank despairing thing: the language was linked simply to more pay, a better opening, somewhere in a land that had already given him fever and harsh journeys. Miss Leyton, her black feathered hat perched on the back of her head, her black and white coat pressed against the chair like a chessboard waiting to be unfolded, was as abstracted as was Nancy. Arabic to both was less a practical matter than an attempt to answer a question, find a new path forward.

For learning opened paths. As if one's mind were a ship sailing from island to island. Finding anchorage in one language, fogs and mist in another. White sand and bays of coral and crushed shell as some new science leapt from the surf to greet one. Building a city with new words; gathering what one pleased of wisdom that was strong and sweet as sea wind, or red peaches.

"So the Arabian Nights has fascinated you," someone had said, hearing of the lessons. "Charming fairy tales. You want to read them in the original, I suppose." But that intrigue and embroidery of tales was of another's fashion. Nancy had hardly glanced at the book. What held her, what kept her, were the dark nights, the leopard gold. Horses and stars. Battle chants. The sinewy tense split of words like steel. Turquoise and silver and cornelian. Night and the moon whispering jackals forth.

"You have another six weeks," Professor Foster said, shutting the grammar book. "Ground yourself in the first ten chapters and you ought to do all right.

LEOPARD GOLD

Now you want to catch your train, I expect" he looked up at the clock, "we are a little late."

"Thank you." The youth rose. Professor Foster followed him into the hall to explain once more some complicated phrase. Miss Leyton looked up swiftly. It was the first time that she and Nancy had been alone together. "Why don't you train as an archæologist?" she enquired.

"I should like to. But then I saw them find a carved duck near Karnak. In a basket of sand. So it's natural I should be interested. We were out there two winters."

"I go out alternate years. Right into the desert where no tourists come 'Digging.'" "You could train as an assistant. Why don't you take it up seriously?"

"Perhaps I could, sometime. I spoke Arabic when I was out there but having no practice in England, I've forgotten every word of it. And I used to know some hieroglyphics."

Professor Foster came back into the room and began to read Miss Leyton's paper. Nancy stared at the books in front of her. It would be fun to ride over the sand again and watch children empty baskets, gather carvings and uncover paintings and papyrus. But was excavation any answer to her questions? Everyone would be sure to find reasons against her being an archæologist. She must be sure before she insisted or even asked about it, that it was really what she desired.

TWO SELVES

Miss Leyton and Professor Foster went back to the East as a sailor returns to the sea. Nancy relearned Arabic because it seemed absurd to have forgotten it. She seemed to have known the East before she had known the West. No doubt it was those early winters spent riding about the Pyramids that made the indigo robed Egyptians seem less strange than the omnibus that jolted down the street, and olive and orange-flower more familiar than the buttercups. The books too that she had read before she was twelve. Travels in the desert, translations of the Arab historians, Antar, Bedawin battle chants. It irritated her to hear Professor Foster explain an Arab custom. Everyone must know about it, she felt; everyone must know about the East. Perhaps this was the sensation that the Downwood girls had experienced, when they blamed her for not understanding their slang. It had been native to them as the smell of Egypt and the palm trees and the camels were native to her, so familiar that she longed for the unfamiliarity of the West.

Two selves again that split her. The Mediterranean self. And the self that wanted to find the day after tomorrow in a new and unexplored continent.

"You heard," said Professor Foster to gain time, as he glanced in half-concealed despair at Nancy's paper. "You heard about the new Persian classes."

"I saw the prospectus," Miss Leyton answered, "what about them?"

"They began yesterday." The Professor smiled decorously. He and Miss Leyton were brothers in arms as far as their profession went.

"I trust there was a good attendance," Miss Leyton straightened her hat in anticipation of some gossip. Her face was old, always had been old, but there was humour in the eyes set almost like claws in the wide cheeks.

"Well, the authorities insisted on some formal inauguration. The Persian Legation, several members of the Foreign Office. Oh and a Lord somebody or other who was interested in Omar Khayyam and gave money towards establishing the courses. They visited the classroom with an address to the students."

"Well!"

"There was one student. Going out to Tabriz for some Oil Company. All those gentlemen in the room, addressing him. On the beauty of Persian poetry. The necessity of Persian for a proper appreciation of the East. He has written I understand, to say he prefers to continue his studies elsewhere. He was a little shy, I'm afraid. And it was his first lesson."

They laughed. With the protection of the mirth about him, Professor Foster took up Nancy's paper. "Why do you find these grammatical forms so difficult?" he asked, holding it up a mass of red corrections. Nancy had no answer. "Our time is up so I cannot go over this in detail but I have written the sentences out at the bottom of the page and perhaps if you copied them several times you would not confuse the Nominative and Accusative so much. And both please," he smiled at Miss Leyton, "do exercise number 23 and post it to me not later than Tuesday evening."

A cold wind stormed at their faces as they left the front door and went down the steps. At sea a hurricane must be raging. Nancy was aware of Miss Leyton smiling at her just before they left the shelter of the gate. "If you get into difficulties with your next exercise why not let me help you with it? I know Coptic well and that is very similar." She held out a page torn from her notebook with an address on it. "I'm usually in after six o'clock."

Nancy took the sheet. "It's very kind of you." She put it in her pocket. But she knew she would never go. Miss Leyton might suggest things. Things she would like but that she would not be allowed to do. And, after Downwood, Nancy could not risk refusal of her requests. Better say nothing, do nothing, disassociate herself from all emotion, than face again the fight she had failed in because she had not realized till too late that it was up to her to fight. If she were sure, with her whole mind, that she wanted to be an excavator she would insist. Miss Leyton, with a smile, hurried off the opposite side of the road.

It would be easy enough to be an archæologist. Forget everything but the happiness of living in a different world. But it could not answer the sharp wishes that came when the sea called; when adventure came. Knowledge was a fire more vital than the sunset; heart of the desert, strength of the sea. There was something beyond, the other side, almost nobody got to. Forget—all but the carved duck shining in the sand. Forget—but that would not be life. Why forget till life itself had been found and welcomed?

Nothing of her experience was an answer to her questions. Perhaps the answer was middle age. Then perhaps to every wish would not come the reply "but you are too young." Then perhaps she would have a school. Or a business. Re-make of education a beautiful live experience. Why did they always say "when you are older?" When she was forty she might have lost the will, the energy, to desire or accomplish things.

It was the lack of organization that had made Downwood so terrible. In five days she would have changed the entire school. Just by treating it like a business where time was money and wasted energy spelt inefficient management. She had no patience with their vague idealism. She wanted facts, practical results.

Childhood was a long surrender of one's brain. School robbed one of the knowledge one was born with. Nancy was sick of this immaturity forced on her. She wanted to develop, run a school, have adventures. And all that was offered her was the temptation to drop from the present to the past.

She would not go to see Miss Leyton. It would make her want too much, freedom, and the South.

CHAPTER III

PATCHWORK

"YOU'RE too early," Miss Cape said as Nancy took down her fencing mask. "It will be another ten minutes before they finish."

The room shook with the stamp of feet overhead. Occasionally a word in French rang out above the clatter of the foils. Nancy shifted into her padded jacket. Her legs were free for once. It gave her an incomparable sensation of boldness.

"I know I'm too soon. But it doesn't matter. I don't mind waiting to-day." She enjoyed the chance to sit there; to question Miss Cape, wonder of what world she came and why she seemed more interesting than the Downwood girls or Millicent or Mrs. Lodge. Perhaps it was because she had a job; she taught dancing in the big room beyond the fencing hall and helped the secretary in her spare time. Or was it the quiet decision of her eyes?

Miss Cape sat down in the empty chair. "Had a nice weekend?" she enquired.

PATCHWORK

"It was all right. But I hate the move from one place to another. London the middle of the week and Meades over Sunday. I should like to settle in a place. With my books. Not to have the change, backwards and forwards from the emptiness of the country to the noise of the streets here. I would rather be here. One feels more is happening."

"But the country must be nice now. With the red may out and the laburnum. I get so tired of the dust. There is always such a crowd when I catch the bus in the morning. The day smells of dust and wheels."

The light fell from the window on to Miss Cape's faded hair and neat black dress. "Did you cycle out anywhere last Sunday?" Nancy asked, re-buttoning her jacket collar and gathering together in her mind scraps of Miss Cape's life collected in a dozen leisurely conversations. Upstairs the fencers were resting, for the room was suddenly quiet.

"No. I have not been out on the Common since last autumn when we went to pick blackberries. Since my sister got a job I've had to help with the kitchen. I'm going away though. I wanted to tell you. You might be interested, I thought."

"Going away! Where?"

"To South America. I've got a position at Buenos Aires. With an English lady. Her references are all right and it means double pay and a share of the profits in three years if I can stand the climate."

TWO SELVES

"Shall you like it?"

"Well, there's not much to look forward to, in England, is there?" Miss Cape got up and put a stray pair of shoes away automatically in the large locker. "I shall be thirty soon. And I can't get a higher salary here. I haven't any capital or chance of getting enough capital to start out on my own. What I can earn hardly leaves enough for bus fares when my food is paid for. And when I'm older, what am I going to do?"

There did not seem to be any answer. Miss Cape had mentioned casually before that she never took a holiday because she could not afford the railway tickets. But to go out to South America—alone.

"If I can't stand the climate they will pay my passage back after two years," she continued in a matter of fact voice. "And I can always get some sort of a job, I suppose. I shall learn Spanish out there and that ought to be valuable."

Nancy tried hard to think of something to say. Something helpful. One couldn't put sympathy into words though. There seemed nothing she could do about it. The door banged upstairs. Miss Cape sat down again. "They're leaving," she said, "I can hear the foils being put into the racks."

Nancy picked up her fencing glove and moved clumsily to the door. "I hope you get on all right. You're sure to. But I don't envy you the start."

Miss Cape's eyes lit with adventure. "Oh, whatever happens it won't be . . . what I was brought up with. I

200

shall see you on Thursday, I suppose. I don't leave here for another ten days."

"Bonjour, mademoiselle." The white padded figure of her fencing master swept the épée from the rack and faced her with his black projecting mask, like a penguin huddled on a sandbank. Treacherous impression, as Nancy knew to her cost, for the scarred fencing glove was swifter than her thoughts. There was nothing hunched or stolid once the sword moved but he was waiting now for her to begin. And lose.

"In a duel, Mademoiselle, it is the most impetuous one that is pricked the soonest. And when blades are sharp, mistakes cannot be corrected afterwards."

That was the fun of épée. One fought with it. Foils were dreary; a succession of ordered movements. Foolish like dancing. Like a technical exercise. But épée . . . to hit where you could or pleased . . . that was worth learning. She shifted her grip under the big basket-shaped hilt and stood watching the opposing point.

He tapped her blade, provoking her to begin. The foils clashed, stirred in her a rhythm of bright moods. From her first lesson she had been captive to the sound. *Clash* of steel, *crash* of thunder, *smash* of surf, these were sounds for a boy to love, to listen to and make songs of. She would try a cut-over, for the fun of feeling the sword sweep up, smite down.

Fool. She might have known that his point would catch her that way, as she sprang back.

TWO SELVES

"Not quick enough, not nearly quick enough, for a coupe, Mademoiselle. Your feet must learn to move. And your wrist remember, not your whole arm."

The chase down the room would begin now. She retreating and springing back and making tentative attempts he parried with light touches. All the same if he had not insisted on her doing difficult attacks she doubted if he could have got inside her defence so easily. Not if she were back against the door and could wait her time. She could wait an hour it seemed, her eyes on his wrist. And when he came, shorten and catch him as he swung back. It would be rather fun if the swords were sharpened . . .

"Too heavy. Don't sweep your arm round. You lose time and your opponent realises your intended movement. Fencing, even if you use épée, is fine . . . the point, so. Not a windmill of crashes."

Nancy shrugged her shoulders. She was always rough. Clumsy and rough. Partly it was her temperament and partly the first lessons she had had, with a retired army sergeant whose axiom was: "you've been given a foil to defend yourself with and if you get hurt it's your own look out," who had forbidden fencing gloves as an effeminate luxury and whose instruction consisted of making a foil into as much of a boxing glove as possible.

"Beat and lunge at my wrist. It is not good form any more to kill in a duel. Beat, drop your point and the difficulty is settled. No harm has been done and your opponent is disabled."

Tap, disengage, lunge. Hit the wrist edge. With black glove and white sleeve shifting always before her. One was free as one fenced. Free—out of the world.

"You defend too well," he grumbled, "but your lunge is slower than the passage of a century."

They sat down to rest on opposite sides of the bare room. He took down a foil or two and tested their suppleness. "You can't toss them on this wooden floor," Nancy said, "needs a lawn for that."

"Oh, you know that trick."

"Broken plenty of foils trying it."

"You have been fencing a long time?"

"Ten years. Since I was eight. Just foils at first and not continuously."

"When you want a change I can teach you sword and dagger," he suggested. "I worked out all the old passes. But I should have to get weapons made."

Of course that was the way to fight. Delude your opponent and catch him with the knife as he lunged past you. But it was too romantic somehow. The fencing master annoyed her with his mediæval face, these reminiscences of the Middle Ages. She had learnt fencing simply because "girls couldn't have boxing lessons." What she really wanted was to smash out with both fists and knock somebody over.

"Once, I arranged it for a fencing class, we reconstructed the whole scene from a Dumas novel. I on the lawn and three, no four, of my pupils who burst from the bushes at each side. I had a cloak and backed to a tree. We had worked out every movement and I managed the four easily." He looked grotesque as he spoke, with his mask tilted back over his head like a helmet and the épée over his knees. But there was a desperate sincerity behind his phrases. He believed in his romantic gesture. Yet it sounded false somehow beside Miss Cape, going out alone to Buenos Aires. There was something Elizabethan about that. To go out second class on a three weeks' voyage and turn up in a country where you didn't know the climate. Nancy shook herself. Perhaps she owed sympathy to both of them. But it robbed fencing of its real spirit to turn it into adolescent sword and dagger trifling.

As she stood up, straightening her mask, a straggly white figure with a black leather breast pad marched into the room. He looked surprised to see her.

"This is Major X," said the fencing master jumping abruptly from his chair. "Major X, like yourself, has only just begun épée. Would you like to try a bout together?"

"This is hardly a sport for ladies," remarked the white penguin in a harsh voice half lost in the mask. "I might hurt her," he indicated Nancy with his foil.

"Oh, that's all right," she protested, "I've got double padding inside my jacket. But I'm no good, you know."

PATCHWORK

"Of the Guards," whispered the fencing master as they measured distance. Nancy saluted mechanically. How beastly to be matched against a stranger.

"Begin." She waited quietly. "Do not be afraid." Nancy forgot caution and lunged. To find nothing. To find the tall penguin squinting down his blade at her. She jerked the sword aside just in time.

He lunged. She scratched him on the wrist. "Don't stop," came the order. The major, now angry, beat her down the room. She had to yield to the hammering of his arm. He got through her guard somehow, tapped her on the shoulder.

"Pardon. I trust I did not hurt you. This is no sport for ladies," protested the penguin, polite but contemptuous.

She wanted to say, "that tap? I couldn't feel it if I hadn't on a jacket." But that would be to disparage his fencing and he had got through her guard. She paused, almost ran up under his foil, stabbed viciously at his elbow.

"Touché."

One to her and he had to salute. Then the battering began again. What did the fencing master mean by putting her, barely five feet one, against a giant over six feet? It was ludicrous. Her full lunge scarcely reached his fingers. And fencing was too intimate, too revealing a thing to be done with any stranger. She could just stand the fencing master because he was showing her the tricks of the game. But swords as they

touched betrayed one's personality. Surge of an undesired temperament choked one, flowing in at one's
wrist. Only friends should fight—or enemies one
fenced with to defeat. But strangers, the mob, this heavy
English guardsman with his "pardon," and "sport,"
ugh, one stifled with the rank mob-mind pouring out
of his hilt.

"Seven. Three. That will do for to-night." She was
more skilful but his strength battered down skill. The
superior length of arm. Still she had got him nicely on
the arm and once on the mask as he had tried to force
her defence. She shoved her sword in the rack.

"Good evening." He saluted. "Really I should have
thought hockey was more suitable. Epée (one could
see the heave of his shoulders) epée is not a ladies'
sport."

It was not worth while stopping to argue. "If only
I could box (thought Nancy defiantly) I'd break his
beastly nose." That had been a good hit though, when
she had caught his head. If the fencing master had not
kept shouting them on and she had been very cool and
quiet and the points had been unprotected—he might
now be caressing a neat hole where his black jacket
flapped open instead of making remarks about hockey.
Men were the limit anyway. What good did hockey do
or where did it take one? Fencing was a world leading
to freedom. Men always wanted to keep the best things
to themselves.

The bare hall as she came downstairs was lit by a

PATCHWORK

single light. Miss Cape had gone home. Only the two fencers were left upstairs. She pulled her heavy coat over her fencing breeches and thrust her jacket away. The walls were decorated with photographs of children in white jerseys making a machinery of their arms. The room smelt of varnish and soaped wood. Ropes crossed straightly from side to side—telephone wires transmitting no messages. It was bleak. Like the penguin's mind. One felt the pressure of the classes that had drilled on the yellow floor: actions done over and over with no progress in them, either mental or physical. The acquiescent mediocre mind that demanded only that its children ask no question, burst no environment apart.

Black, black, black. Outside was the night. Shaded over roof tops into plum-violet, heliotrope, with threads of reseda and cinnamon brown. The moon hung over the branches. Flowers, lights, pushed up beyond the park in streets that wound like green paths between them under the clipped box shadows of the pillar rounds. Thin railings rose into daffodil leaves under the yellow trumpets of the lamps. Spring flowers and a sudden face were caught and lost in passing. Life that beat and spilt in colours—the sunset on a dead city. Life was the colour. Existence the city. How did they relate one with the other, with what was spoken round one, round one? With Miss Cape off to Buenos Aires, Eleanor looking for a job, Millicent spending mornings with a dress-maker, Doreen gone home to Cornwall; with the ignorant pressure of a stranger's blade, her own blade leaping . . . how did these currents merge or mingle with each other? Two separate roads that melted in the shadow but ran out clear beyond, separate, where the shop lights flashed and the electric signs were lit. There was no relation— it was a negative meeting in the shadow. Perhaps moonlight on the roadway was an unconscious jest, perhaps the stare of the stars over plane leaves and the single wild white cherry was an inquisitive repetition of her own demand—only there were two worlds separate and related as were her own two selves, actual, not dreams, but worlds or selves to be touched, smelt, tasted and accepted.

Reality of questions and of colour. Days, grey words, battering of mob-mind upon thought.

"Had a good lesson?"

"Splendid. Some major or other came in. I had to have a bout with him."

"I thought they kept you a long time. You won't forget Millicent and Tony and Mr. Pherson are coming to dinner. I've put out your white muslin and as soon as you've got out of those fencing things I'll do your hair."

"Couldn't I have my hair cut short?"

"How can you say such a wicked thing? After all the hours I've spent brushing it is that all you care about me? You ought to be ashamed of yourself."

PATCHWORK

Nancy pulled at the buttons of her coat. She could not see what her hair and her emotions had in common. She ventured another protest. "But it hurts me, this length and length of it. The pins always stick into my ears. And you say I ought to be interested in my personal appearance. I think short hair is pretty. These long plaits look like a cow's tail." She shook one down and wagged it too and fro. To no avail.

"Don't be idiotic. You know people are coming to dinner and it's late as it is. You never try to help me in any way. Now go right upstairs and get your brush and comb."

Nancy did not hurry up the stairs. She had no intention of hurrying. Her personal appearance bored her thoroughly. But the pressure of hairpins could not be ignored. And there was a weak sloppy sort of look about coils and plaits. She had always wanted short hair like a boy's. Quite short hair. That one shoved in a basin, shook and forgot about. That was so short one didn't even have to comb it. It gave more force to any head. A dignity of line to the most mediocre features.

If she could not have her hair short she was not going to worry about her dress being on right. She wouldn't know if it were on right anyhow. But if they had even consented to discuss the matter of the hair she would have *tried* to get the sash tied straight. As it was she would read "Philaster" till the very last minute and hope for the best. Clothes. The agony of clothes.

TWO SELVES

She always felt ashamed in them. Ashamed to have people look at her. Only when she could sit in her fencing breeches and read did she feel at ease. Or on days when nobody ventured into the windswept park and she strode through puddles in oilskins and sou-wester. Then she was not ashamed. But fine days and at dinner when she was dressed in white muslin with coloured ribbons she felt such a hopeless idiot . . . stuff tangling between her legs and no pocket for her handkerchief.

If they had given in about the hair she would have gone to the drawing room early and sat there waiting for Millicent. As it was she would read.

*"It is but giving over of a game
That must be lost."*

Nancy managed to get a look at the menu card as they sat down. A good dinner. Soups with bits of marrow in it and beef. Moments of colour were flashed across the grey. Meal times.

Stupid of people not to be interested in food. Equally stupid were those who favoured French cooking. She loathed French cooking. Why eat if the ingredients had to be disguised? Cutting off all the fat and calling it a name that meant nothing. Making it "dainty." Slopping sauce over it. If she were patriotic about anything it was about food. Roast English beef and mutton; Sussex puddings.

Mr. Pherson was beside her, a quiet little man from

the North of England. You knew beforehand exactly what he was going to say. But he specialised in roses, so that if you kept to gardens you were safe.

She could hardly see Millicent for the carnations, very tall in the glass vases. Tony was opposite her. His short black curly hair, the green eyes bulging from the sallow face, reminded her of a frog. He was said to have given up art for business: possibly (Nancy uncharitably wondered) because he could not face the long drudgery artistic achievement involved. He was said also to hate women. Except widows. They, according to his phrase, were "safe."

"Do you think," Mr. Pherson leaned timorously toward her mother, "that I could get any results at all by planting roses now. We have just acquired a little summer cottage . . ."

"You haven't seen the 'Girl who dropped her Garter?'" shrieked Tony across the table, banging his fist on the cloth. "It's been on six weeks and you mean to say you haven't seen it?" "We all know *why* you like that show," bantered a voice across the rose carnations. "Well, Niette never has done anything better in her life. A real artiste," he turned to help himself to sauce, "and do you know what happened? She told me herself. You know Green the composer used to be in love with her. And they quarreled. He was hard up and wrote those two songs she sings, the only decent music in the piece. A nasty fellow but he can write. He was terribly afraid she'd turn them down. Yet he was scared she'd think he had written them for her. So he sent her a note." Tony coughed the words over his laughter: "Dear Niette, 'I Always Come Back to you in the End' was written six years ago and has only just found a producer. Don't turn it down because I need the money." He ended on a hysterical outburst of mirth. Gulped down his fish and sauce. "Oh, that reminds me, roses. I must send her roses. She's giving a party to-morrow night."

"Niette is sweet, isn't she?" Millicent enquired from the opposite chair. "I met her at a dance. Really pretty, I thought."

"So you advise, in pots." (Mr. Pherson then had kept to his rose garden through all the clamour.) "And you think they would cover the trellis this year if we lined the walk with tubs?"

"A man no longer has these opportunities." Her father was speaking from the head of the table. "Business has grown too vast. The chances that I met with at the beginning of my career do not exist for the modern generation. Except perhaps in South America. The competition is too fierce."

They jarred; this roomful. Tony and Millicent were of a world perhaps. Her mother with her love of fine embroidery and songs and all romantic things linked perhaps on to Tony's circle. Mrs. Hearth at the opposite end and Mr. Pherson might belong together. She herself was rather like her father. People told her so. Said they looked the same way when their wills were crossed or their orders disobeyed. Yet they were, at the end, different.

"This generation," sighed Mrs. Hearth. "You should be thankful Nancy does not want to rush about much. All they care about is pleasure. Their own pleasure. If I had my way I should make them stop at school until they learned their duty to the home where they belong. These pernicious screeching women with their reforms and their ideas are ruining family life." She leaned back happily in her chair and helped herself a second time to the pudding.

But how wonderful it would be if there were no family life.

Being afraid of hurting people was a tyranny worse than that of a school or form of government. Against harshness one could rebel; it was kindness that hindered one. And without rebellion there could be no development.

It was as if Nancy sat, seeing, in a room with the blind. Not with the really blind, but with people blinded by the snow. Because sometimes they saw. Then again when one expected them to see, they were visionless. It was as if her whole being were concentrated into an eye. As if she saw straight through people and actions and conditions. Their falseness; their rightness. It was not her fault that she saw. She had not asked for the gift though she was glad she had it.

People would not believe that she saw. She could

not prove her vision to them. It was perfectly right of
them to require her to prove it. But she could do nothing unless she wrote a book that everyone would read.
Then she could persuade them perhaps, tell them what
she knew, get them to be interested.

"Do you know what it feels like to be mature and
yet be ground down by rules made for the immature?
To be at the mercy of brains less developed than one's
own and to watch them refuse knowledge to seekers
who could use it? To know wisdom almost within hand
grasp and not be able to attain it?"

Mrs. Hearth cut her peach skin into tiny tendrils
with complacent fingers. Tony leaned his arms on the
table shouting another anecdote. Would it matter
whatever one achieved?

Would they care? Would they listen?

Beyond the cream curtains that fell into shell-
blue shadows, the street sounds broke like waves on
summer silence. Through the unfastened windows the
sky flowered into spikes of scented stock between the
roofs. If it had not been for Millicent, Nancy could
have disappeared into imagination. Completely disappeared. Turned off the electricity as it were, fixed her
eyes on the carpet and remembered nothing. But unless she behaved she would be rebuked to-morrow. She
must act out the necessary interest.

It was not that she disliked Millicent but they had
no common meeting ground. The fair round face with

PATCHWORK

curls already slightly tinted faced the window. Lavender ribbons strung a lace bodice and a narrow skirt across the bare round shoulders. Lavender with threads of green. "Millicent lives for dress", Eleanor had said contemptuously. Why shouldn't she if it pleased her? Beauty was all important. But Millicent if she did centre her energy in clothes, did not give one a very happy impression: not the effect even that Eleanor achieved in her rough jersey and corduroy climbing breeches. She looked merely bored, curiously insincere with the heavy powder dabbed too thickly on her cheeks.

It was awkward to see things clearly. Nancy could not join the other girls when they laughed at Millicent for giving up her life to dress. To express beauty in coloured stuffs was not wrong. But the lavender dress was stupid and Millicent and her powder somehow did not match.

Something startling, something really vivid, a hard yellow splashed with blue or scarlet dragons, paint even used as a savage might use it, that would be interesting and right. But that would mean that there was an intellect behind the paint and cloth. And that was what it came to in the end. Had a person a mind, an artist's mind? Otherwise the simple useful clothes were best.

"We are coming to Meades this summer," Millicent put down the blue and gold coffee cup and straightened her curls.

TWO SELVES

"Shall you like that?"

"Oh yes. Don't you think Meades is very attractive?" She spoke with a curious slow mannerism as if she paused an extra beat on every syllable like they taught in a French phonetic class.

"No, I'd rather be in Cornwall. Away from people." Nancy realised too late that she spoke with an unnecessary roughness.

"You're so energetic. I care very little for walking," she toyed with her lace handkerchief. But she looked too young and healthy to be fragile. All her mother's fault. Training her up to be a Restoration countess when she was a fresh stolid little milkmaid. Nancy thought again, ventured another remark.

"Did you like school?"

"Not really. But some of the girls were sweet and I came home every weekend. But it's nicer to be grown up, don't you think?"

"Yes." It was useless to assert that they were less free than school children. Millicent probably had never wanted to be free. Nancy wondered again why she saw both sides; the desire to slide back into the unconsciousness of childhood, the cruel denial of growth to the adolescent mind. Did one brain in a hundred thousand have the courage to achieve full development? At any rate Millicent had missed even the rough indifference to everything that had given Downwood a slight value. Millicent was rather like a pedigree kitten that had never been allowed to lap alone

216

lest it should take a spoonful of milk too little or too much.

"And shall you go to Cornwall?" Millicent asked in turn, in a drawling babble of a sentence.

"Perhaps in June."

They watched the night in silence. From the voices across the room queer phrases drifted. They were talking of another world. "Young girls even . . . " Nancy could not hear exactly what provoked the shocked tones. It was something to do with breaking away from the traditions of a century. "They never answer an invitation by letter, they *telephone*." Mrs. Hearth was very red and flustered . . . "Rushing here and there, no time for ordinary civility." They looked over in her direction. "Reckless, reckless." How the whispering went on. But it did not seem as if Millicent or Eleanor or herself would ever have the chance to be reckless or even rude.

So there was another world. Something that was the heart of this roar of wheels, the black centre of the flowers, the scent of the chestnut spikes. Terribly beautiful; or it would not be so criticised. Where people "did" things. Said what they wanted. Where the rules of this rigid existence that drew its false silence over her, were not observed. Where life was above criticism or law, a vivid breathing thing, like a book, like apple-blossom sweeping the rain-blue sky.

CHAPTER IV

CHERRY PIE

"TO WIN freedom I must write a book." Easy enough to say but words were brittle playthings. And worse than words were thoughts.

"Oh, why do the great winds
Come whispering to me?
My heart's aboard a drifter
That sails the swinging sea."

If she were a boy and at sea she would not be afraid. But how could she get it into verse? How express her mood in poetry or prose either? There was something too authentic and too storm-wracked about her emotions for the right word ever to come. And if the right word did not come it would not be good enough to be printed and if it were not printed she would never get a friend. If she did not get a friend she could never find answers to her questions, never be recognized as an individual, never be free.

It was not glory she wanted. That was all right if

CHERRY PIE

it got thrown in extra. That she could have a try for, later on. What she wanted was a friend. That spoke as the Elizabethans wrote. That brought adventure to her like a flame.

"Why do the great winds . . . " Drifter was a good word. Black. With the thin lines of the Viking ship she had seen at Kristiania. And the sea swung—great heaves of green freckled white. Swung up to the rail of the fishing boats in Scilly. "Swinging sea!" But it wasn't a great poem.

"Bellario. When you ran away what did you do? How did you get your page's clothes to begin with and how did you get out of the house? I know you told your father you were going on a pilgrimage but there must have been servants or something . . . and why were you such a fool as to care about Philaster? It must have been fun . . . the early days . . . were you terribly scared while you waited at the fountain and what flowers did you pick? Cowslips, I think, and cherry pie and primroses. Come, Bellario. I am so tired of dreaming you. I want you to teach me sword play. I can fence, modern fashion. Come and teach me and tell me things . . . do you know how lonely I am with no one to talk to? I can make questions but I can't make answers . . . "

Fool, fool, to cry out against the darkness.

Yet Bellario had run away. All very well to write she had loved Philaster. But how did they know that she had not loved freedom first and run away to gain it?

TWO SELVES

"Dare you be yourself,"
mocked the wind in the cowslips,
"Dare you drop your dress
and the phrases they have taught you,
dare you be yourself,
break your bars and follow me
or shall I find you sleeping still
at dawn?"

And I answered the wind.

"Ou-hu,
were you not able
to find in the stable
threads of lavender,
petals of sweet william,
caught in the leather
straps on the wall.

Birds will be glad
of the hair I threw in the heather;
old hair—old life—
a thing I'm through with.
Ou-hu.

The fox on the lawn
knows that a skirt
peeped into the stable
and breeches came out."

The scent of the garden blundered through the window. Elizabethan flowers. No fear. Not once she had found Philaster and was riding behind him across

CHERRY PIE

Sicily. Breeches and short hair and freedom. Questions answered. What fun, tricking them all. Being one's self.

Garden scents . . .

> *"Cherry pie is for riding*
> *with the wind in my hair,*
> *the firm breath of the wind.*
> *For the hooves of the horses*
> *on the fair green turf."*

How join reality and dream?

Philaster was the limit anyway. That was the only fool thing Bellario did, to be taken in by him. More fun to wait on Arethusa. More fun still to wait upon one's self.

> *"Owls at dawn*
> *can hoot to the starlings*
> *where to find silk,*
> *where to find ribbons*
> *to soften their nests.*

Why was she such a beastly coward? Slip out now while everyone was sleeping. But she would be recaptured, cried over. She hated hurting people's feelings. If only she could make them understand.

Write a book and make them understand.

Write a book. And find she had a friend.

CHAPTER V

BROKEN GLASS

"IT MUST last three years. Don't tell people so, Nancy, or they will laugh at you. But once a gigantic outbreak of this kind is set in motion it cannot stop suddenly. I'm afraid to think, if we could have peace to-morrow, of the re-organization necessary before normal conditions could be resumed. It has thrust civilization back for fifty years and every month it goes on puts us back further."

Her father took up his paper again. There was a sense of oppression about the damp air. Everyone was already saving coal. The empty fireplace looked mournful and the great doors seemed to shut the wrong things out of the room. Her mother was playing patience on the little inlaid table. Doreen, up for a month from Cornwall, was working beads into a belt.

It was late autumn. The air was chill and blue with hint of winter cold. The park was torn with heavy boots of volunteers learning to ride and drill in the Row. The English had taken to war with surprising alacrity. They went about in uniforms, babbling uncouth words.

"People who make wars ought to go out first and be shot," protested her mother vigourously. Doreen picked out a blue bead and matched it with a red.

Nancy just saw chaos; felt a bewildering uneasiness. She had no particular confidence that the Germans would not land. She had heard a little too much of the inside of things to be confident as the mob was confident. Modern warfare was not a decent matching of one sword against another. Europe might topple over and perish in a night.

They had been in the Isle of Wight that August. All the end of July watching and helpless. Could it come? Must it come? Going out into the dark night with a candle stump to read news of the first battle. Watching the shells fall about the bow of the ship that got in the next week and knowing nothing of events, had tried to sail past the mines.

There was something particularly degrading about war. The worst side of everybody leaped automatically to the surface. Patriotism was the easiest disguise that vice had ever had to wear. There was not even the decency of organized conscription but screaming hysterical compulsion—of the wrong people. Everyone knew that the Germans had prepared for war for years. Why had the other nations not made counter-preparations or insisted on disarmament a generation before?

TWO SELVES

"As long as human nature lasts warfare will go on," her father said. But there must be some way out. It was like education. People were too lazy to develop independence in their children. Nations were too lazy to prevent the roots of war.

It was the grotesque optimism of people that killed. Their snarling refusal ever to face facts. "England is sure to win" was the unvarying answer to any query. With the line being forced back and vessels sunk every day. "England is always right," a crowd screamed in London. "Germany can do no wrong," another mob shouted in Berlin. One's ancestors had refused responsibility; had allowed their inaction to plant war. A generation busy with other problems was flung from work into shrapnel, disease and bombs.

"It seems to me most unnecessary," Nancy suggested.

"Unnecessary! If we had not landed troops in France at once we should have become a German province within five years. Germany would have swallowed Europe, country by country. And then turned her attention to America. How would you have liked to have been forced to work in a German factory? For no wages and bad food."

"I should have hated it. Probably the only thing was for us to go to war. But it ought to have been foreseen and prevented. Not now, but years ago."

"We had an idealistic government that cut down our artillery."

BROKEN GLASS

"I know. But if we had a better system of education we might have had a wiser government."

Useless to talk. There was no dispute about one fact. Civilization as her father said, had been put back fifty years if it had not been put back altogether.

Doreen held her belt up to the light, fixed a thread and emptied more beads out on the table. What a beastly sensation it must have been when the Greeks dashed into Troy. Knossos, like England, had been a sea power; Knossos had been burnt in a night. Guns took the purpose out of everything. Guns, arrows, stones. History repeated itself. Was there ever, in the re-iteration of events, progression?

Nancy could hear a footstep on the stairs. Who could be coming to call so late in the evening? The butler flung open the door with a peculiar stately dignity.

"Madam," he announced in his low quiet voice, "the Zeppelins."

Doreen sprang up and made a rush for her coat. Nancy followed her. "Bring my wrap too," shouted her mother. Autumn moonlight shone through the window. They heard the front door open. Nancy paused a moment to snatch up pencil and paper.

"Hurry." They dragged coats out of cupboards. Ran downstairs.

"I would not have missed this for worlds," panted Doreen as they rushed into the street.

People thronged from every door, in evening dresses

under hastily caught up wraps, in aprons, in working overalls. Heads craned into the air. Maids scurried up the basement steps. And the road stretched into a larkspur distance, quiet, too quiet, as if nothing had happened or could ever happen.

"I don't see anything at all," her mother complained, "are you sure, Brown, that it was not one of our own balloons?"

The butler had re-appeared with a case of field glasses. "No, Madam. I saw it myself. A long silver sausage in the sky. It must have passed before you came downstairs." He took the glasses from their case and waited hopefully. Doreen ran up the street towards the park. Nancy thrust her notebook back in her pocket.

The postman dropt the letters in the box as if an air raid were an everyday occurrence. People in thick coats came out with cameras under their arms.

"This is very imprudent" her father suggested, going however further into the middle of the street, "if any shells are fired we might get scratched with shrapnel."

It was very silent. Everyone watched. There was not a motor car nor the sound of any wheels to break the clear November night. It seemed as if a city had stopped breathing, were collected into an intensity of watching, into a petrified forest of heads.

In the blue air something like a shooting star flashed and fell from the sky.

BROKEN GLASS

People tautened. Looked at each other. "The guns." Out by the park a shrill rumble snarled into the night. London itself was swept into the war.

"How jealous they will be at home that I was in the Raid." Doreen looked eagerly over the rail up the street. They had boarded the omnibus long before it turned into the Strand and had got seats well in front on the top.

"I'm awfully glad you were with us. Wonder if we shall see much of the damage though. I should think by this time it will have been cleared away."

"It can't be. Look at the crowd. There must be thousands out. It was a good idea to get the bus the other side of the square. We should have seen nothing on foot."

Very slowly the driver worked his way between the mobs surging over road and pavement. Most of the traffic had been turned off the other way. The seats behind them were filled with people eager to see what had happened the previous night. The air was a thunder of excitement.

The walls were dingy grey. They were so close to them when the bus stopped that they could see the soot grained surface. It was not silver. Not that lovely silver of far roofs on an April evening. The dark clothes of the crowd were unbroken by any colours, white faces pressed forward shouting shrill phrases from side to side of the road.

TWO SELVES

They were proud. They had not been afraid. They also, the onlookers, had waited and joked and watched as boys might linger about a smoke of gorse some dry summer evening on the hills.

Thunder, thunder of excitement. A sparkle of light flashed from an open space. There were ropes drawn, a barrier. Darts of light, broken glass, littered the scratched pavement.

Doreen and Nancy stood on the seat together. Everyone was standing. The omnibus hardly moved. They looked out over a black sea. Over chips of glass spread like tinsel. Damp air poured through the broken windows into offices. Smoke still came from a building up the road. Firemen were at work. Police were holding the crowd back.

Probably it was immoral of them to yield to the excitement. To stand on top of the bus and stare over battered windows and smashed stone. But it was history. Actual touch of an event that had happened, that was done with, but that would be written out in history books when all the wars and quarrelling were at an end. It was wrong to let themselves toss on the wave of this excitement but it was better than sitting in a room reading—of how civilization and all that one believed in had been put back for more years than one was likely to live.

Faint winter sunlight flashed on the heap of glass swept into the gutter, tinsel, debris of a fête that even the wind had no use for. The smoke got into their eyes.

BROKEN GLASS

Someone made a joke about the "sausages." Someone asked when they would come again. Others looked with quiet eyes into bare rooms that here and there had a single cracked pane left. Men were nailing up wooden frames, dusting splinters out of ledges.

It was unreal. It was pre-historic. But in the age of dinosaur and pterodactyl there had been bright tree ferns and clean water. This broken glass—it made everything wrong, into a book one did not like the taste of, into a game that was stupid. And one had no control. It was going on. Rolling on. Dragging everything, everyone, with it. The whole intellectual world was reduced to a chaos of splintered panes. The physical world was battered into dust. War helped nothing. But having started it rolled on. Nothing checked it; nothing brought it to a close.

"Wonder what will happen before the end."

"Funny to think they will read this up at Downwood in another fifty years."

The bus turned into an unfamiliar street. Glass behind one. In front a world they did not know.

CHAPTER VI

PEACH JAM

THE Scillies were a saga come to life; tangle of sea thrift and ice plant floating on the current. Gulls flew up from the white flecked tide; drifters were anchored in the Sound. The water under the quay was dark as basalt or where the stones curved, serpentine. Far away, far as eyesight stretched, waves drifted water lilies over thin white sand.

Eastward it was tropical. Palms grew and bracken shoulder high. Black rabbits scurried in and out of the heavy fronds. Those were the daffodil islands, with chance white upturned bulbs lying out amongst summer daisies.

But westward it was ship-like, wrested from the sea. It was the home of gulls and seals, a breeding place for fish. Waves smashed on rock edges and turned up wrack and beads and queer shaped foreign shells.

But even the islands the war had changed. One had to have a permit now to fish. There were notices up where to shelter should a German cruiser break through the blockade. The Sound was full of motor launches refilling their petrol tanks and taking on fresh supplies.

Doreen and Nancy pushed off the small boat. There was a torpedoed steamer, beached near Tresco, within rowing distance of the town.

"It's hard to think the war has been on almost two years," Doreen said, pulling on her cap. "Seems longer somehow."

"Yes. It will be two years in November since we were in the first Zeppelin raid together. Remember how everyone was shouting then that it could not go on six months?"

"And now bread and sugar cards seem the normal thing. Wonder if we'll get any preserving sugar this summer. We put in for twenty pounds. It's a good year for raspberries."

"We didn't put in for any. We've only got a few canes at Meades and it seemed doubtful if they would allot us any if we did fill up the forms."

They rowed. The water slipped evenly from the oars. A gull perched on a floating board at the harbour mouth shook its wings. Three boys in tattered jerseys fished from the pier end. The torpedoed steamer, close to Tresco, grew larger and more distinct.

"Which way's the wind?" Doreen asked.

"Don't know."

TWO SELVES

"Silly. Look at the gulls. They face it always so the wind doesn't ruff their feathers. Look at them on that wall."

Doreen pulled harder into the open space of the Sound. There were no French crabbers in this year, no fishing boats. Only drifters in from patrol and a couple of motor launches. But these were moored at the quay edge; the space of water between them and the steamer was bare of all but wind.

Nancy tried to get a word for the colour of the water that slid over her oar. It was not silver and it was not green. New words. Half the Elizabethan ones had been forgotten and the Elizabethans had created their own language. Words were hard to make. Absolutely they must express the shade, the feeling. But she must have new phrases. New ways of expression . . . new discoveries . . . new lands.

"Avec les grands oiseaux d'or pâle et d'argent clair,
J'entrerai par la porte ouverte sur la mer."

Strange how Régnier got the sea. One felt its cadences belonged to English, not to French. Yet there was little good sea poetry in English. Some Beowulf stuff of course, but not as much as one expected, and not much, a few phrases apart, in Elizabethan. Just to mention ships did not make a poem. There was the feel of things to get into the words. The shift from one wave to another as the hours of the days shifted, col-

PEACH JAM

our into colour. For the sea was not a simple thing. It was not the boyish gesture of many writers, "grey waves, open haven," sort of business. It was something as soft and grey-green an hour as this, shaded with sound until light and wind merged into the tide, into the roule roule of it, into choppy surging phrases. Until adventure rose, like an island, from the sea.

"Pull your left oar harder, we shall never get there," Doreen scolded. The ship seemed not so far away. They could see the hole as they drew near where the torpedo had burst in. Scoop out of board and iron as if a dinosaur had flung a weighted armoured tail across some brittle leaf. It was netted over now.

"The first day she was here they rowed a boat into her hold," Sam had told them on arrival. "And the fishermen took shrimping nets and fished out cases of jam, peach jam, and sacks of flour. So we netted her up." The old wrecking spirit was anything but dead. They had had white loaves for lunch in place of dark war meal. Fished out flour, no doubt. It had been deemed wiser to ask no questions.

"Want to come up," an officer shouted. "There, I told you they would ask us on board," Doreen whispered as she tied the boat to the stern of the small launch waiting alongside with supplies. "Tow us home, won't you, Sam," she shouted, as they climbed up the gangway to the deck.

The officer was waiting to show them round. It was monotonous lying out in the Sound while the first re-

233

pairs were being made. They followed him past blistered paint and twisted metal. "We had news a submarine was out and we saw her come up, to starboard. Of course we trained the gun on her and fought her for an hour. Zigzagging. All of us with life belts on." He banged on a metal plate, doubled over, cracked as if it were a sheet of tissue paper. "We thought we had her. Then the second one came up on the port side. I saw it coming, the torpedo. We swerved. In time. We could not escape of course but it struck aft of the engines. And the flour caked into a kind of cement and held her. So we're here."

The hold was sloppy with sea water. At the bottom a few casks rolled about in the puddles. A gang of men with strange looking tools were pumping and measuring below them. "Suppose you had white bread for lunch," said the officer grinning. "If we had known visitors were coming we would have baked you a nice cake."

Doreen laughed. "It was awfully thoughtful of you too, only to have peach jam. We're on the Food Control and that means we can't buy any. But Mrs. Hicks has quite re-stocked her cupboard. Terrible wreckers we are. Used to live on ships in the old days. But you have found out all about us by this time."

"Yes. If we had got that net out an hour later we should not have had enough jam left for our own tea. The little boats were around at once . . . said they were salvage people. They were, for their own homes. The

PEACH JAM

harbour authorities got the empty casks . . . if they got anything."

They could watch the sea from the bow, tossing beyond the western rocks. Grey and wide and broken by the wind. With no barrier in front of it till it reached the American coast line. They were outside England in a tiny world where anything might happen and where the ship's gun was pointed outwards, ready to be fired, for as the officer said, "we might get a submarine popping her nose up near us, any moment."

"Are you ready to go?" Sam called up from the launch. Pleats of tangerine, folds of lemon, crept into the apple-green clouds. The outline of St. Martin's was getting indistinct. "Come along, we'd better get back or they'll think a submarine has kidnapped us," Doreen pulled at her sleeve, "thanks so much for showing us round."

"Well, don't say where you've been but think of us at tea time," said the officer, grinning, as he pushed a parcel the steward had just brought him, into their hands.

"Two pots! The islanders are degenerating or you would not have so much left," Doreen called back as they started down the gangway.

"Next time you come we will bake you some hot rolls."

"Next time will be to-morrow if you can keep that promise."

The launch jerked up and down on the short

waves. Their boat was fixed at the stern with a loose rope. Several casks were fixed along the deck, with a basket of tools and a bag of mail. Workmen sat forward, returning to St. Mary's for the night. "Come up by the steering wheel," Doreen said as they jumped on board, "perhaps Sam will let me take her in."

All the green had gone from the water. It was a deep blue broken with drift and with depths of shadow the colour of dark wings. A few cormorants still waited on the rocks. Light spray beat the rail. One remembered nothing. Only the feel of the wind . . . a bodily thing that put the mind to sleep. Far as one looked there was only the sea and one grey wall that jutted out from indefinite hills like a ship.

Doreen clutched her sleeve. "Look."

They passed a man hunched in a tiny boat, towing wood behind him, "know what that means?" Doreen asked.

"No."

"News must have leaked out that another boat has been hit. He has been out after wreckage. They say last week one man towed in a cask of brandy."

At the harbour edge a petrol hose dript into the water. One motor launch had been re-filled. Nobody had thought to turn the oil off while the second boat moved into position. And on the news stand they could just read the headlines of the latest paper: "Will Shortage of Petrol End the War?"

PEACH JAM

Plash . . . plash . . . the weave of sea fern beat with the tide against the sunken steps. A cold light deepened the water but a pilchard shoal, caught in the narrow cove as in a net, thrust silver wedges through the dark blue waves. Fish, weed and sea swooped and turned between the rift of rocks. Far back were a few gulls.

Doreen lay on the point, almost asleep. Nancy sat beside her. It was like a ship this ledge, that jutted out into the current. It seemed to move as the tide swept in and back. A tuft of thrift beyond them swayed in a miniature gale.

"I want to learn a new language. A language means another land conquered. Wish I knew Greek and Arabic and Phœnician. I liked what I knew of Arabic. There was something desert-like about the words. It would be nice to read Homer. And Phœnician . . . a strong language, something one could growl out like a camel."

"If I were a boy and could go to sea. If I could keep watch at night under the sails. I can't put that gull into words. I can't put anything into words till I've learnt adventure. What is the point of going back into the same autumn as last year, thinking the same thoughts, writing nothing?"

To learn. To learn. It was as if one were the gull sweeping in circles, dipping into surf, leaping up . . . like a seaplane . . . rushing over water, soaring, that was what it was when words came to one, experiences, emotions, undeveloped thoughts. In thought was the future. Perhaps wisdom was what the poets meant when they wrote of love . . . one's mind graping, vanquishing a thought, feeling it bend, become part of one. It cut away from war and tedious acts as the bird cut from air and sea.

The wind swept up, the water crackled, the clouds gathered. Towards the west a shell of gold held day an instant longer close to earth.

Doreen stirred, woke up. "Asleep, Nancy?" She poked her with a stalk of grass.

"No, watching for a convoy. It's about the time they pass."

"If only the war would stop."

"It must be awful at Downwood now."

"It's much stricter. Samp has stopped free time altogether except for twenty minutes on Sundays, to write home in. She keeps them knitting."

"Cracked."

"Yes, but that doesn't help the girls who are there. Glad we're free of it. Oh, there's a ship."

They could just make out the line of black vessels at the sky edge. The sullen blue water beat against heavy rocks. It was turning cold. "I wish it were summer always", Doreen continued. "It's hateful to think that we have to go back to the mainland in two more weeks. Sometimes in winter we stay indoors for days on end. It doesn't seem worth while to go out. The grey settles into one and one is just inert."

"Wish I were a boy and could go to sea."

"Oh, I'd rather have a cottage and dogs. On St. Mary's. With a donkey and cart so that I could drive to town on steamer days."

"No, I'd want to get South again."

"Silly. I hate travelling. It's uncomfortable and at the end, where are you? I'd rather breed chows and show them. And go to London once a year."

Spray splashed up. Doreen got up and looked out seaward. "It's cold. We had better start walking back, if you want to go round the long way."

"It's more fun, the long way."

"Yes. And we shall get the sunset over the islands from the top of the hill."

The soft turf smelt of salt. Tufts of camomile and mint crushed under their tread. Everywhere there was sea—stretching out till they turned with no land in sight. Only the shadow of six steamers and slips of white foam where the waves broke on an edge of rock.

Poetry is—walking along cobbled streets with shrimping ahead of one. Gulls. Sand. And sea between the houses a brighter blue than the lobelias. Bright blue like an awning with a white stripe where it meets

TWO SELVES

the sand. Poetry is—walking to the quay side with shrimping ahead of one.

"A good tide."

"The best this month. We ought to get gallons."

Calm weather. Gulls on the roof. Nice to be a gull and fly—free—untrammelled of persons. That one's a black back. Ought to know more about birds. Puffins, cormorants, and the oyster catchers that flap along the sand like toys, black and white toys dangling from a Christmas tree branch.

Blue linen trousers . . . a child's tale. The old man turned down the narrow passage to the shore. "I don't think he's picturesque, Nancy. Some old tramp." But the creased jacket, the face. The seaman of a boy's adventure story. Tar on his sleeves. The street a picture; the walk a poem.

"What's become of Miss Partridge? Does she stick indoors still?" Queer to shut the door on one's self at forty five. Never go out. Not even to the garden. What behind this? "Oh, she's only one of many. In-breeding. Dozens of them on the mainland."

Steamer day. Donkey carts driving in. With the tomatoes. Boat loads of them from St. Agnes and St. Martin's. "Do you know Nancy, it's cheaper to buy tomatoes at Penzance than it is here. And you can't get good ones either though the bulb fields are full of them. They export the lot."

Everyone is in the square, steamer day. Gossip is life on a small island. The worst of it. Islanders ought

PEACH JAM

to be strong, beautiful. Like the sea thrift and the honeysuckle. But they're eaten up with jaundice and liver troubles. Of the body. Of the soul. Those that don't get out, stay in. China or—a small drab papered room with flies on the window.

"Why how are you, Doreen, and when did you come over?"

"A week ago. No, not a sight of a submarine. They wouldn't bother us, you know. Too small."

Biscuit boxes and jars of jam. Magazines, Postcards in a rack. The red curly headed boy held open his string bag. His jersey had faded a sort of lavender. "One pot of jam please, not apple and rhubarb." Cassiderites, the tin islands. Painted prows, chariots. Write a story. A story of a girl who ran away from the wattle huts and shipped on some Phœnician galley as a boy. And got South. "Nancy, look there's a new puppy on the quay."

Veronica hedges. Lavender blue. Gladiolus . . . honeysuckle-yellow and scarlet. Like great tropic birds perched in the meadows. A blue sea under them. Those beautiful shells on Pellistre beach. Cowries, towers of Babel. Poetry is . . . poetry is . . . standing at the quay with shrimping tide ahead of one.

Outside lavender bushes in the tiny gardens washed their scent in with the sea. Outside pilchard nets were spread to dry, the grapes were ripening, the black muzzle of a donkey snuffed the turf. Outside morning crept into the air, the stars faded, the moon slept. Outside were ships; and freedom; and adventure.

Dreams. Anybody vital outgrew dreams. Unless they had reality to back them up. Either life was— the enthusiasm one felt when a new path of wisdom opened, or else a grey existence broken less and less with the gay ribbons of expectant hours. Possibly greyness was the reality but she doubted it. There was the witness of all the poets she had read, historians, palæontologists, that life was actual, definite, as bright as a patterned bowl or the Cretan lily vases. Only the two were separate; life and existence.

She would go to America. Begin a new life. Blot out the old mistakes. Then come back to Europe and start out the right way.

Two selves. Oh, if she could cut away all that was not herself. This encrustation of conformity. But people did not want the truth. Nobody wanted the truth. Not Doreen even or Eleanor. All would try to prevent her from being what she saw. As they tried now to prevent her seeing.

Why should a slip of seaweed or a tuft of thrift or the blue metallic shimmer of a lobster's back, make her feel faint with beauty? As if her breath had been taken out in a long poignant ecstacy? When the same sea-weed or the same tuft was to Doreen just pretty or negligible. Environment, heredity? A thing she was not responsible for, yet desired. For she must keep her spirit sharp; sharp if it cut into herself. Ready against the moment adventure called her forth. That was the one rule; to see, to analyse, if nothing were the truth, if truth varied as it must, try to dig for the root of it. For some night opportunity might swing open the window.

Six years already. A long time to wait.

CHAPTER VII

ELEANOR

"HULLO, Eleanor, what do you make of the war? It's months since I've seen you." Nancy flung over a rug (there was not enough coal to have a fire upstairs) and settled back in her chair under an eiderdown.

"It's smashing us out right enough," Eleanor grumbled. "The men I know are killed or so broken that they are simply lethargic. And as for the women. The old cats have got power into their hands at last. It has put progress back generations."

"Oh, it's awful. What one sees and hears. Patriotism was never one of my vices but I'm through with what they call morality after this. Killing souls with their red tape stupidity and calling it discipline. Gloating over destruction. When all the wreaths and fame in the world won't give back flowers and friends and the taste of food to the dead. Makes me sick."

"I know. When I go to work in the morning the posters make me ashamed. How can people be so vulgar . . . over death?"

Eleanor put her cap on the table and tucked the

rug well around her legs. Outside the roof tops were gradually growing black. There was a sting of snow in the air that crept under the closed window.

"Well, what are you doing now? No good talking war when we do get a few minutes together. Read anything new? I suppose not."

"No time for reading. I'm running a bazaar for the cats. They take the credit and if one tea cup is broken the Committee will consider whether or no they should ask for my resignation. And what do you think Lady Cockle said? 'I rely on you, Miss Lodge, to sell fifty of these tickets to your personal friends.' And I am their paid secretary! I won't ask you to buy one because it's just a filthy waste."

"What's it for?"

"Providing soldiers with portable bath tubs. Two to a division. But look here, I'm in charge of the thing and they have paid fifty guineas for the hall. Then they pay ten guineas for detectives and police on the day itself. And thirty guineas to the caterers. And their own taxi fares. It is not dishonest exactly but they won't at the end make their expenses. They mean well and it shoves them in the limelight. And every single one of them is over forty."

Eleanor pulled the rug a little closer over her knees and went on.

"It isn't as if any of them were young. They tell any attractive girl they meet to go and work in a hospital kitchen. You should have heard them sniff when I told

TWO SELVES

them I could not live on three pounds a week. Told me I ought not to ask for a rise in such serious times. With the bus fares up and no lunch to be had under half a crown."

"What are they going to do?"

"Refer it to the Committee. I have managed until now, living at home. But they ought to pay me enough for my food."

"Surely if they can throw away so much on a bazaar they can give you three pounds ten?"

"A secretary's salary is an item on paper and not an advertisement or even a bath tub. But I'll have to resign if they don't. Did you tell me that you had been trying to drive a motor car?"

"Yes, they wanted a girl to drive at the hospital my aunt is interested in and everyone thought I ought to try. They turned me out of the class though. After fifteen lessons. Said I was a danger not only to myself but to other people. I'm no good at steering."

"Funny, when you can ride."

"I'm afraid of traffic even on foot and in a car . . . I saw what was going to happen so far ahead that when it happened I forgot what thing to push. I almost smashed up one van and two cycles."

"Too imaginative!"

"Too something. They say that to drive one needs an unreasoning type of brain. But I knew from the start I should never learn. But everybody seemed to think I ought to have a job. If only I could look after

246

the hippopotamus at the Zoo or something quiet. But I suppose even the Zoo now is a luxury. If only the war would stop."

"When it *is* over, Nancy, are things going to be much better for us?"

"I suppose not. It is the furthest one can think though just at present. The boundary of one's horizon."

"Nobody is interested in freedom or development any more. There will be no money for years to finance any new schemes of education. As for the liberty of women! After my experience with Lady Cockle I'm beginning to fear that they will only impose fresh shackles. They squash the young more vigorously than the men."

"It's the old, the old in thought, rather than men or women, I imagine. Most of the girls at Downwood for instance, were born old. Whatever their freedom they would not have developed any further. But it is not much of an outlook."

"Look at me." Eleanor pulled the rug up with a jerk. "However good I am at my job there is practically no chance to get any position with more than five hundred a year. At this moment I'm getting a hundred and fifty. A lot you can save on that! I have never met a man yet I wanted to marry. Think of the men one knows . . . self-centered, uneducated . . . the Public School type, who would want their children brought up with the same code as their grandfathers in a totally different age. One might meet a man with whom one could fall in love but it is very doubtful. The other sort of marriage just means being a housekeeper to someone it would be hard even to respect. And everyone sniffs at me for being a secretary. Lots of mother's friends have dropped asking me to tea. It's funny but it's true."

"You might emigrate. Try America."

"No. I was brought up in England and you know I'm not patriotic but I should hate to live out of it. Hate to miss the chestnuts opening and June in the fields. I don't want to go out to another country and to other conditions where I'm not even sure of finding a job. Where I have no memories, no friends."

Eleanor's dark hair curled softly against her grey coat collar. There was something powerful about her. A clarity of decision and action. Wasted because modern England had little or nothing to offer her.

"I hoped the first year I left school, Nancy, that things were going to happen. New schemes, new liberty. I thought I could have got a job where I could have pushed ahead. How I would have worked at it. I'm supposed to have a good job now, as women's positions go. Lots of girls envy me. But you can't put much enthusiasm into correcting Lady Cockle's mistakes and packing up boy scout pamphlets."

"When the war's over if I can get a passport I'm going to America. Then perhaps you'll change your mind about leaving England and come over to join me."

ELEANOR

"But you're not free," Eleanor objected, "will they let you go across?"

"I know I'm not free. That's what I blame Downwood for. If education is to mean anything it should show one the way to independence. You remember those lessons Miss Sampson used to give us on "the way to live." Obey your parents, obey the school, obey everything and everyone but your own self. Instead of teaching us to live all school did was to knock out of us any little impulse toward freedom that we had. One can't know everything at fifteen. I surrendered my will to the beastly worn out traditions of an exhausted world, as personified by Miss Sampson and "the ladies of the staff." If I had followed my own instincts, kicked, screamed, yelled on the floor till they let me go to an art school, I should be working now and of use to other people. As it is, I'm no good to myself or to anybody else."

"But you kept your individuality. Most of us didn't."

"Yes. But I had only two years of it. You had, how many, seven?"

"Sometime you will break out, I think." Eleanor brushed the air out of her eyes and stretched her legs out more comfortably. "And when you do start you will do something out of our sphere altogether."

CHAPTER VIII

SCARLET AND SILVER

SEVEN years. Seven chapters for seven years. Strands of Elizabethan, French and American woven into a rope together. Cherry pie and Bellario, leather and rose leaves, tumble of canyon words, blurring and merging into a background of rain and scarlet as the oyster sky swallowed up bus and pillar box and London night drooped sadly over them all. Hers was the mad terror of a shell washed under the sand. Not out of earshot of the surf. Not out of scent of the sun. Prisoned . . . able to breathe but not free. The soul slowly dying, slowly turning into grey powderous dusk. Seven years of guns booming, stars falling. Seven years waiting for something to happen. Seven years waiting for achievement or for death.

Everything was wrong. The whole scheme of the world seemed disjointed. Why did early impressions cling so? In babyhood one was taught it was wrong to lie. Afterwards this law was reversed. One was punished for thinking the truth. One was forced to be hypocritical. Yet one had an uneasy sensation all the time that a gate would open and something that was beyond the consciousness of the world would catch one lying and reproach one.

Looking back it seemed to Nancy that her life had been rolled up like a flower in her brain at birth. It had simply to unfold itself. She had wanted to be a boy and write a book. To have liberty and adventures. She still wanted the same things in more intense a way. Probably it was the same with all children. All that one needed was to get hold of minds before they were warped by school.

People were so silly. They had not the sense of marmots. They seemed to think that constant denial of a wish improved the soul. It didn't. Always to be forbidden one's own thought meant attrition of the nerves.

She, herself, could escape into her other self. Swing her legs over the chair and shout "to hell with marriage, patriotism, duty, they are lies, lies, lies." (When no one was listening, of course.) And plot out just how she would run a school or a newspaper of her own. But other people couldn't. They had not the richness of her untrammelled childhood in the south to build up a separate self.

Grey houses, grey minds, grey existences. Why grey when primroses were out and the rain itself was silver and the sunset, amber or cinnamon?

TWO SELVES

Nancy walked with anger in her heart. It was not altogether a personal matter. It was personal to the extent that this web crushed her, retarded a development guessed at, dreamed of, but snatched at only in books. Yet beyond this she desired freedom not to be at the mercy of chance but everybody's privilege.

Behind all her desire was an almost Puritan stolidness. It was this that made the conflict hard. Her brain was a gigantic flower gone to seed before her eyes. She could not help the precocity of insight that made her read the inside of people's motives as clearly as if their secret secrets had been tattooed on their cheeks. It was right for them to ask for proof of her ability. But experience blinded her with the red and turquoise of its wings and flashed too far from her hands. Dreams were a poor makeshift for a soul eager to act.

The trees twisted a black lace across the sky with bare soot-covered twigs. They walked quietly, Nancy and her father, between the park benches, carrying a white newspaper (as advised officially) that motor drivers might see them in the darkness.

"When is it going to end?"

"Who knows?"

A long searchlight cut the night, poised on a branch, shifted. Nobody moved in the blackness.

"Tell me when it will end," Nancy said again, "is there no escape out of it?"

SCARLET AND SILVER

She did not expect her question to be answered. It was a formula to be repeated every evening. A sort of purge to the emotions. The searchlight held steadily above the park gates, pointed to the sky.

"Three more days and we shall be in the thick of raid time again. They might come to-night even."

It was like walking through an avenue of plums. Dark, velvet purple plums. Purple and dark. With shifts of tiny stars between the twigs as the light over the park moved. In America there was no war.

"When it ends will they give out passports at once?"

"Not for a long time except for very good reasons."

She had no particular reasons. Telling a line of officials . . . "if I went to America I might write poetry better. If I went to America I might find . . . " They would say she was mad or possibly a spy. Logically she could not blame them.

"How long do you think it would be after the war ends before I could get to America?"

"A year. Longer perhaps. It would depend on the peace terms. If the Germans . . . "

But she could not blame it altogether on the Germans. It had happened half a century before. Nations had worked toward war, rather than away from it. Scraps and incidents had been fitted the wrong way, into a mis-directed morality and education. Obey. Follow the mob and be responsible for nothing. Battles came like that. Because people refused facts, hated independent thought. She could not believe that a German was less sensitive than an Englishman, that he could desire this horror any more than she desired it. But the individual was wrecked, swallowed up in the whole. Dominated by mob law.

"Beastly having this war smash up all you've made," ventured Nancy as they turned the corner. It was like seeing one's manuscripts torn up piece by piece.

"Who knows what will happen?"

Her father had the thing she admired most, a mind. Also a sense of adventure. As a boy he had run away and climbed mountains. He had fenced. He had been to America. But he was perfectly unreasonable as far as Nancy was concerned. Which was very distressing.

When she was a baby he had wanted her to do the things no other children did. They had discussed politics gravely together since Nancy had been four. He had given her her first French lessons, played geography games. Encouraged her to read anything and everything. At fifteen she had demanded independence. "Art or business. I don't care which it is but I want to be free." It seemed the inevitable outcome of her education. "But I have worked all these years to protect you, to look after you and give you an income," he had answered in a bewildered tone, as if she had asked for an aeroplane. "That's all right," Nancy had assured him, "I'd rather do art. There's no money in

that so it would be nice if you would give me an allowance. And in say, six years, I ought to be earning
enough not to need it any more. If you wanted to continue the allowance I should like it awfully. To travel
with."

The family had not seen her point at all. They had
put her straight to school. "To get companionship
with girls of her own age." To learn to drop her curiously personal ideas. And the shock of Downwood
had stunted her; she was growing crooked. Because it
was easier to disassociate herself and live on her own
mind than to smash to liberty through hurting people's
feelings.

"You will let me go to America when the war
ends?"

"Wouldn't you rather go to India? I have always
wanted to see India again. Think of all the interesting
things there are there. And such a nice sea trip out."

"I don't want to go to the East. I want to see the
West. And I want to go alone."

"Girls can't travel about alone."

"Yes, they can. Why shouldn't they?"

"Never mind why they shouldn't. Perhaps, if you
really want to go to America so much, I can find somebody to take you."

"I have to go alone or with somebody I choose.
Otherwise I might as well stay in England."

"Why not wait to discuss your trip until the war is

over? I wish there was not so much moonlight. It's too light this evening to be safe."

If you hated war, hated it from the beginning, you could stand a year of it. You could stand two years. Afterwards it grew into an apathy, a nightmare, a selfishness. Afterwards the only thing that mattered was that you, yourself, had not had butter for tea. The world resolved itself into a ration ticket. You had no soul left because you did not even hate war. You only plotted how you could get an extra ration of butter or of coal.

Youth. Youth must have been this world of colour and light into which she had dreamed the dive, years, years before. One did not dream any longer. Not of intangible things. Youth was doubtless a state of mind harnessed to a possibility of action. Neither Nancy nor any of her school-fellows had known it.

But America. America was something to hold on to. If she went there she would not pretend. She would not say she liked things she hated; or the other way round. She would not feel afraid in America. It would be so new, so different. They did not despise girls so much. They saw things a fresh way. The poems they wrote . . .

> "*I saw the first pear*
> *As it fell—*
> *The honey-seeking, golden-banded,*

SCARLET AND SILVER

The yellow swarm
Was not more fleet than I
(Spare us from loveliness)"

like those early days in Scilly when they had cut honey-
comb into slices and held it up to the sun to watch the
red light fall through amber and adventure had made
the air almost too poignant to breathe . . .

"Be in me as the eternal moods
  Of the bleak wind, and not
As transient things are—
  Gaiety of flowers."

Strong satisfying music. Something primeval about the
rhythm and force . . . all this Georgian stuff was rotten. Nothing to it, either thought or form. Not even
good Tennyson. The Elizabethans were all right. Some
French stuff was all right. But now—(now one had
breathed war)—one needed something fierce and authentic—set down because you felt it that way. Not
echoes. Not moralizing when one felt no experience
back of the poet. Not any more

"My lady on a parlfrey grey,
Waved to a page across the bay."

Or

"The moorland shepherd with his wrinkled face
And solemn eyes, fronting a thousand hills,
Spoke, searchingly of earth's felicities."

257

TWO SELVES

Oh, America was different. It hadn't had a war anyway. Nor gone without butter and fires.

A tremendous bang broke the air to fragments.

Not the cold drag down the stairs and those hours of waiting again. If one were going to be killed why not be killed in comfort. Fields of flowers and a tumbling sea. Just as one was warm. She turned over.

"Miss Nancy!" A figure shook her. "Wake up, Miss Nancy." Alice, the maid, stood beside her, with a dustpan converted into a helmet on her head. She trembled so that she could hardly hold the gas mask in her hand. "They've come again, Miss Nancy, and everybody but us is downstairs. Here's your coat all ready and I've got your blanket."

Peonies ... tiger rain ... new wonderful words. But she could not keep Alice shivering any longer. Even as it was the lights were out as they began to grope their way down the staircase.

In the dining room the family yawned and tried to rake up the ashes of the fire. "I'll go to the smoking room and see if I can discover anything before settling," Nancy suggested. It was horribly cold and being the last arrival the arm chairs were already filled with figures, half asleep.

Outside it was light. Ominously light. At regular intervals the park guns boomed and barked. Nothing else appeared to be happening. Nancy counted up the raids she had been in. This made the fifth. Everyone said it was all right until you were near a bomb. If you got near . . . within a street . . . and escaped alive, you went to Somerset or the Welsh hills the next morning and shivered at every noise you heard for months.

Something seemed to burst the window into leaping tigers. Nancy jumped for the door. Only a shell bursting in the sky streets away. She ventured back cautiously. There was still nothing but a blue cloud over the roof tops. It was not pleasant, really it was not, waiting for things to burst. Then a whirring . . . whirring of aeroplane wings . . . not in the distance . . . overhead. Shrill sharp snap of the nearest gun and the white brilliance of the searchlights.

She ran for the dining room. That had been adjudged the safest place. "They're just over us but I can't see anything," she shouted.

"Quiet, quiet, you'll wake your brother up" she was reproved. "They're trying for Buckingham Palace."

"They're not really overhead but they're nearer than they've been before."

"Doesn't Alice make you laugh with her dust pan helmet and her gas mask? As if either would do you any good if we got hit."

"Poor thing. She's awfully nervous. Next time this happens let's all stay in our beds. I'm sure we run much more risk coming down to this cold room" . . .

"But you might not be killed outright if we were hit."

"When is this beastly war going to end anyway? Hear that?"

TWO SELVES

There was a crash in the sky, almost next door it seemed. (In reality it was a mile away.) The shell bursts flicked across the room like lightning. There was no excitement about it, only a cold uneasiness.

The shots ceased gradually, coughed one by one in the distance.

"The park guns have stopped. Could we go back to bed?"

"If you want. But the 'All clear' hasn't gone yet."

"It never does till they've chased the planes to the coast. Nancy, rations or no rations, go and get us some biscuits. I suppose we can't ask the maids to leave the cellar yet. Though what good it would do them to be in the cellar if the house came down, I don't know."

"Well, they think it is safer."

"We shall have the whole place down with influenza. I suppose now you don't know where the biscuits are kept?"

"I'll find them." Nancy crept cautiously down the stairs guided by a murmur of voices from the basement. "It's all right, Alice," she called, "they've gone." But Alice, furtively handing her a plate of biscuits (it was asking for trouble to eat in such a state of national emergency) declined to come further up than the first stair. "It's just like them Huns to fool us out of shelter and then come back again. I'll wait here, Miss Nancy, if you don't mind, till I hear the Boy Scouts, bless'em, come round on their bicycles."

SCARLET AND SILVER

"Wonder if much damage has been done" Nancy questioned as she regained the dining room.

"The papers won't say anyhow. They're thinking out the headlines or perhaps they keep a stock of them. 'The greater London area was visited by hostile aircraft last night. One bomb was dropped in a garden causing inconsiderable damage. The behaviour of the population was notable for it's calm.'"

"Don't blame the papers. The censor won't let them say anything."

"Nice scene at the Tube tonight, I expect."

"And I suppose we shall never know what damage has been done. Not till the war has been over a generation and then it will be in a footnote to some Army publication that nobody will read."

"The historian of a hundred years to come will know more about the beastly mess than we do."

"That's inevitable. Let's risk going to bed."

The blankets were disarranged. It was two o'clock. The "All clear" signals had started in the street, below. Making more noise (as everybody said) than the actual raid. Nobody would know how much damage had been done. Not unless one of the maids had a relative in the district where the bombs dropped. Then it would be sure to be exaggerated. All war was an exaggeration and a deceit.

The waste of it all. The impotence of all.

How had the war started anyway?

CHAPTER IX

REBELLION

IT WAS queer, the stillness. It crept over the room like a fog. The tension of waiting for a word to burst it, made it hard to bear. It soughed in waves and beyond them, thin, electric, came the rumble of wheels that linked hope up to life. When the wheels ceased the silence pricked needle points into bare flesh.

"I'm falling. Falling into an abyss." But that was just speech because the shock of the fall never happened. There was never the unconsciousness that must wait at the bottom of the cliff.

"When I'm grown up I shall be free." But there was no freedom. Only an invisible but actual clutch of circumstance that wove grey chains back and forth across her limbs and mind, a chain . . . no being a cabin boy, no mirade of release happening, no great book, no liberty, no friend, no hope.

"I do like Mallarmé. I can't help what people write. If he is old-fashioned. Idumenée is beautiful and lines from the "Faune." It is like that purple-blue flushed with wine colour of ripe plums, like the gold plums where the skin tears. If only somebody would speak to me about these things. I want someone with a mind. And Régnier. Julie with her feet among the rose leaves. And 'fleur hypocrite, fleur du silence.' Words, like flowers, brushing across my brain."

It was her own fault for making no move but how could she explain her world? It would be terrible if they did not understand. They would not understand. Terrible if she had to fight. That evening, seven years before, "I must go to an art school." "You are too young to paint. We want you to have companionship of your own age." If she said she wanted freedom people might come in from the street and lock her up.

Escape. How was one to escape? The girl round the corner had tried to get away. They had shut her up. With two nurses. Told her friends she was ill. The illusion of liberty had been stript from her. She was shut away because she wanted to be free.

One heard these things even if one did not go about. One knew, bafflingly, inevitably, the chances against one.

Escape. Romance. To go down the street thinking one's own thoughts . . . a romance impossible. "Yes, it would be nice to go to tea with Mrs. Hearth. No, the country is pleasanter now than London." Lies, all lies. No rescue. No hope. Oh, God, no hope. Beauty written in the sunset. Do you see that cloud there, like ripe grapes? The girl in the next street kept in her bedroom with two nurses, because she wanted to be free.

TWO SELVES

"I'm living in a prison. How long my sentence. Have I not earned my release?" Say that to people and see what would happen. Tears. Threats. "How can you be so ungrateful?" If only people would not care about one. Not be kind. Hell, life was awful.

It was not that one hated . . . it was not . . . it was only that one was twenty three and wanted to think one's own thoughts. They might guess if one thought one's mind out in the street. If she faced the thing she was afraid people might come in from the street and shut her up. If she went out one night alone would they follow, say she was mad, ill, drunk and shut her up?

Marriage. Girls married to escape. But she hated men. And to cut the knot that way was playing the game wrong. It was to create the same situations over again. And when people married they had children. That was awful. Awful to drag a child into the world to fight one's beastly fights over again. Better die first, any day.

If she had been a boy life would have lain at her feet.

It was not the year that was so long; it was the hour. These indefinite days when nothing happened, were they youth? She waited opportunity but would it ever be granted her? Why was she forced to desire unconsciousness when her spirit cried for consciousness? The hour . . . the hour so long.

REBELLION

"All I have known of youth, all I may ever know, I bring. Are my dreams, life, as nothing in your eyes? I have given you my strength, my wishes, my desire. It was for you I watched dawn rise, for you. It was for you I learnt. I wait as the wind waits that shakes in the pines."

The prayer of her loneliness must call a heart from the street to keep her from despair.

"You are younger than any future."

Not a sound tore the tense longing of her imprisoned thought.

"No more, no more." Yet her mind would not break. Why was she denied madness, unconscious madness? She listened. Her ears strained till to feel was simply to hear. A step on the stair. Yet the door never opened.

"Grant me adventure or grant me death."

Her flesh shrank from the myriad points of the silence. If only her mind would snap. "Adventure . . . death . . . "

Life made no answer.

265

CHAPTER X

SNOW AND APPLE FLOWERS

IT BURST like a flame, the South. In the midst of the snow with a pale primrose moon shivering over the crackling trees. Snowflakes pushed like buds out of the twigs. Branches bent like birds, shook themselves, sprang up free.

She had to do something or die. Die mentally. Which meant gradual disintegration of all forces, intellectual, physical. Something that everyone disapproved of, something that linked the present to that early continuous development, before school, war and a thousand tiny barriers had divided her spirit into a dozen diverse strands.

It burst like a flame, the South. A chariot that swept her from the world into the real world.

For something somewhere had gone wrong. The mechanism was out of gear. She must trace to the root end what had happened. Trace—recover the South.

It was those early years she had picked up olives and anemones. They had been balanced; full. Unsplit. Great blue-purple anemones at Syracuse; Carthaginian poppies. Egypt. Rich, like a vase of many colours breaking one into the other with the symmetry of tides; a vase, a body, waiting for something, perfect but waiting something, a vase painted over with many pictures, many ages, waiting to be lifted, used. Egypt, Syracuse, Carthage, Naples . . . black soil and black olives, gold sand and golden reeds, beautiful, near, friends, but lacking something, not the one thing in all the South, the lover, the answer one waited.

It had come, the lover, the spirit, latest known of all lands, beautiful as a many coloured flower, a shell, the sea, the heart of a white gull,—Greece.

The day she had crossed the boundary line years before, down even in her cabin, she knew she had come home.

"Why the excitement," Eleanor asked, flinging her hat and suitcase on to a chair. "What discovery is it that you have to tell me about?"

"Greek."

"Only that! I was sure you'd get to it sooner or later but somehow I expected—that you would start off with Chinese."

"It was those fool translations put me off. Beasts of pedants translating Greek into rhyme. Like slashing a Persian carpet up for advertising rags. I read a translation of Euripides once and it put me off Greek for years. There was one bit,

TWO SELVES

"Oh for a deep and dewy spring
With runlets cold to draw and drink!"

I'm actually quoting, and it went on lines and lines of
it till it ended at the most tragic moment,

"And rest me by the brink."

Just made me laugh. I looked the lines up in the original the other day and found eleven words shoved in
that Euripides knew nothing about, just for the sake
of the rhyme. I would like to have the professor who
wrote it up for infringement of copyright or libel or
something. Gives a false impression of the language.
Now in H.D.'s translation of the same thing, the English and the Greek words count up precisely the
same, and you get the picture and the rhythm . . . a
wonderful archaic chant."

"It's nice for you that you have time to learn it."
Nancy had surmised vaguely that Eleanor would be
jealous but she could not help it. She had to learn . . .
had to learn.

"It's wonderful. Adventure itself. All the fun of an
Eastern language and it says what you've thought
about. That sea world where gulls are; my South, none
of the sloppy reed Pan-business of Victorian poets.
In Theocritus there's a line, 'Pan has wrath at his
nostrils.' Can't you smell it, can't you see great bull-
nostrils, snuffing nuts and being furious it wasn't a
fat kid? It's strong, it's right. Sharp, like something

268

SNOW AND APPLE FLOWERS

carved. Hesiod . . . I like Hesiod. He writes about seals, those blue-black seals we see in Scilly. Homer's all I thought he was and more."

"But how can you read those things? You can't have had more than ten lessons."

"With a translation. A plain English or better, a French translation on one side. I cut out declensions and verb endings and learn words. Sometimes a word is an island in itself. There's one . . . I found it looking through the dictionary . . . that's a statue. It means the bend of an elbow and the throw of a javelin."

"But what are you going to do with it?"

"I look over the dictionary for hours . . . building the past. It must be some race memory; I feel as if I had known the words before. Did you never want to throw a javelin? I remember when I was little I spent hours working out the way. I never got it. You should not just throw it; there were rules. I could not get at what they were. A rotten age when you're asked to play tennis instead of hurling darts."

"It's a rotten age all right," Eleanor agreed. "Old cats and young men. Sometimes I wonder which is worst. The women who are consistent in their policy, who have always been old, always against improvement, always sour. Married ones as well as the old maids. Yet somehow I wonder if the men aren't worst."

"I'm sure they are."

"Sometimes an old woman will do a tender thing. She has her emotion in the trifles she does. But the men. It isn't even as if they had chosen to fight. They were conscripted—by public opinion which is stronger than law. They went because they had to and they came back as if they owned the world. Lots of them haven't even been fired on. Yet they're everything. Like games in a school. Remember how Miss Sampson used to tell us "we play games to learn to be unselfish" and how the most selfish, good for nothing people at Downwood were always in the hockey team."

"Yes, she discouraged fencing where you have to think, because it was too individualistic."

"I've heard my brothers say, it takes the Public School athlete to show a complete disregard of other people's feelings. And the men who come back from the war are like that. They want to destroy progress because that would mean there would be no more wars. They were full of enthusiasm at fifteen but they come back at twenty five, unsettled, bored, without the practical sense our fathers have, without their sense of work. They want women to amuse and feed them. As for the rest of us, the sooner we drown ourselves in the Thames the better."

"I know."

"To think," continued Eleanor, her lips sneering, "that once I thought there was hope."

"It's wrong, Eleanor. And I know that Greek is valueless. But I must have some beauty or I'll die, from a mental point of view. I often think of the Thames but there's just one chance that if I could get away and be free I could make new schools. It's adventure, Greek, and I must keep adventure to believe in."

"Even if you could you would only turn out girls with new ideas into a decayed and stagnant world."

"They would make it over fresh. Re-paint it."

"Idealism."

"No, facts. If you get right down to the roots its all heredity and education. The war was due to lack of thought and it's being carried on the haphazard way a sick baby smashes plates."

"Well, you can't change it. Not in time anyhow for us to benefit."

Eleanor had gone. They had waited together at the corner till the bus came. She had disappeared a little scornfully, among the crowd of people. And Nancy had crossed alone into the park.

London had its own loveliness. Just at the corner where the park merged into streets and the lamps, the daffodil lamps, hung over squares of white. One could only say it once, "daffodil lamps." In one poem or one piece of prose. But always, always to Nancy they were daffodils. Except those Serpentine lights seen from a far distance. They, in the water, were crocuses. Tiny grapes of sky, tiny purple bunches, pressed between the leaves. The railings were dark. The searchlight held and darkened and flashed forth, piercing, monotonous, like a lighthouse sweeping the sea—or the leaves.

It was not the girls themselves. It was what they

stood for. Doreen had gipsy eyes; she knew the sea. Eleanor had force; audacious but attractive. Yet neither of them had—at the end—a meaning. They were not dead; and they were not alive.

You had to be true to something. Call it truth. Call it poetry. Science even or love. The same in the end. Many ways. Truth was perhaps the best word. If people got between one and one's vision one had to cut them out.

Know it all a new way. That hard blue water under the sharp rocks . . . in Greece. Harden one's vision as Greece hardened waves.

Disassociated beauty. It was all she had gathered together. Letting the wrong people twist her from herself.

"I want to be free." Nancy had pictured the conversation over and over again. "I want to be free. It's not that I'm not grateful for all you've done for me but I can't help wanting to use my brain. If I don't go away I can't develop. I don't want to hurt your feelings. Surely you must see that I don't want to hurt your feelings. But I want to live by myself."

"But how are you not free?" She knew that would be the astonished answer. "What have you ever been forbidden to do?"

"It's the thousand things too unimportant to mention. But that make a barrier. Keeping quiet when Mrs. Hearth talks rot about charities. Not cutting my hair short. I know they don't matter—really—but suddenly they affect one's mind. One can't think clear."

"But Mr. Brown said he would take you on his committee for furthering Red Cross work."

"But I can't do work I don't believe in. I want to write. I have never been my real self to you. You don't know me. You can't know me. I have been silent about the things I cared about. Because I knew you hated me to be rough and independent. I tried not to show that my head was a flame of enthusiasm when I got that Cretan book . . . I knew you didn't like it. I hate the people I've met. The Downwood girls. If I had gone to an art school I should have made friends, of my own world. It's too late to go now. I can't put myself back to being fifteen again. I can't. I can't. I can't help having wishes. I tried not to write. But if I don't, what is there left?"

She could not say this. Could not hurt people's feelings. Things had gone on too long. She who had loved action was losing the will for it. Everybody's brain was a box turning round and round. Empty box. Revolving. How funny. Finding instead of being heroic, giving in, she was merely a fool.

"It isn't as if I were doing any good. I can't fit in."

"But you're so young."

"It isn't my fault I'm only twenty four. I wish, I wish I were middle-aged. My brain's old. It's getting too old. Too stale."

TWO SELVES

Cycles and cycles of days. Nothing happening. Words beat in her head. She could not say them.

"When the war is over, Nancy, if you really want it very much, perhaps you can have a bulldog puppy." That inevitably happened when one's spirit flamed toward rebellion. "Only I don't know what you are going to do with it when we go away."

"I know that's the difficulty."

"It's the servants now. You cannot trust them even to open the greenhouse, let alone feed an animal."

"But their heads are wonderful. Those French bulldogs. Like a bronze flower with the nose and the soft muzzle."

"To my mind there's nothing like a terrier."

"Oh, but a terrier is just a dog. And a French bull, a good one, is a carving, an orchid. Something a sculptor might have spent nights making."

"Exotic creatures. But they say they are safe with children. I wonder though what makes you have such queer tastes."

"Sorry."

"Don't stare like that. You can be very irritating. I'm sure I don't know why. I've done my best to bring you up like a human being, though sometimes I think all my work has been in vain. Mrs Brown said the other day that you looked right through her. You didn't seem to see her at all. Just looked through her and out . . . she didn't know what at. Why are you so thoughtless? Especially in war time. It gives people such a false impression."

"Did she really say I stared through her? What a joke."

"I don't think it's funny at all. Remember everything you do rebounds on your father."

Nancy was about to reply, "why should it?" but checked herself in time. Her mother had something very Restoration, no, it was French about her. She did not believe in conventions really. Why should she try to impose shackles of a world she did not believe in, on Nancy's life?

French with possibly a dash of Flemish. The clear skin, the figure, something warmer than English that was yet the north. As she sat there embroidering a square of cream silk with orchid ribbons she might have been keeping in some remote chateau, a precise and stately court.

"You were very affectionate as a little thing, Nancy. Before all the books you read made you so hard."

Yet it was affection that kept her, sitting on the garden seat, when her heart was across seas, in other worlds. It would all have been different if she had been a boy. They would have understood then her wanting to learn. It was wrong. Her mother ought to have had a daughter with white shoulders and brown glinting hair who matched ribbons and sang songs; who was warm, warm as the young raspberries ripening under the sun. She was terribly sorry; so sorry she could only sit silent and staring at the lawn. The more she felt the less she could speak. They would never understand she had loved them perhaps too much.

But even now she could hear the tide calling her. The nine Minoan periods were beating in her head.

Mrs. Hearth puffed into the garden, sat down on the nearest wicker chair, and took out her knitting.

"Why, Nancy, my dear child, I am surprised to see *you* here."

"The others will be back in a few moments," Nancy answered, ignoring the implication that she ought to have been doing war work. "The news seems better to-day, doesn't it?"

Mrs. Hearth rubbed her face with her handkerchief, settled against the cushions. "Frankly—I had hoped for more. Such a slight advance. Always by inches. But the masses will not realize what discipline is, even yet. I met a man the other day who supplies our army with tinned sardines and he told me it is shocking in the North of England, the way they waste bread. Just thrown down in the streets, crusts of it."

"Indeed!" said Nancy politely.

"Yes. And I had hoped this war . . . brought on us by the sins of a reckless generation . . . would have taught the community a much needed lesson of thrift. Oh, dear me, now my wool's dropped down. Has it gone into the flower bed, Nancy? Never mind dear, I'll just snip it off. A few inches of wool doesn't matter. By the way, I'm rather surprised that your father planted flowers this year. I should have thought, with his far-sightedness that he would have filled up the borders with radishes."

"We have put potatoes in all the back beds but Mamma said a cheerful exterior was often more valuable than a stuffed interior. Though I, myself, did suggest we could have got a few turnips in between the verbenas."

"A friend of mine, rather I should say the aunt of a friend of mine, has filled the window boxes of her London flat with cabbages."

"Oh, but it's awfully expensive to do that. Eleanor told me, and she was on the Conservation of London Food Supply that they worked out it cost three times as much to raise a potato in a town as to bring it from Australia. There's something wrong with the soil."

"That has always been our ruin, taking from other countries. This generation has never had to depend on itself and you see the result—war."

"We have never been allowed to depend on ourselves," protested Nancy.

Mrs. Hearth smiled cynically and knitted on.

The red and white verbenas glittered in the sunlight. Here and there was a single plant of lavender purple. Red with a white centre, lavender blue, and red, they lined the path as rhythmically as the stitches growing under Mrs. Hearth's fingers.

TWO SELVES

"Shocking. Shocking our negligence. Have you heard, Nancy, about the statue of Achilles, the one near Hyde Park Corner?"

"No. Was it struck in an air raid?"

"You don't mean to say you haven't heard." Mrs. Hearth looked round cautiously, leaned over toward her and whispered: "they say there's a secret passage inside that statue and at night the Germans signal there. Out of the eyes. Red lights, green lights, and sometimes a yellow one. If you pass at dusk you can see it. A yellow light means 'no raid.' A green one means 'aim to the left for Buckingham Palace.' And the red one," she stopped speaking, all terrified excitement.

"What is the red one for?"

"Well, they are experimenting with a new gas. At Essen. The day the red light shines London will be annihilated. We shall be petrified as we are . . . knitting, making a bed up, reading the news. I do hope I shall be doing something useful . . . It would be awkward to be changing one's linen, for instance or taking a bath."

"But why don't they stop them signalling?"

"Why, why indeed! Our high places . . . not always as high as they might be. Though I will not have a word said against the dear Queen. A virtuous woman is a treasure from the Lord."

A slight wind stirred the flowers and the apple tree over the hedge; between the lattice Nancy could see the bulbs drying in the spare patch of ground behind the kitchen garden. "I really came to see your mother," Mrs. Hearth laid her scarf down in her lap, "about a vacancy in the local Food Control. They need an extra girl in the office."

"Oh!"

"I thought it would be a lovely chance for you, dear. It's quite *unskilled* labour. Just sorting cards. The hours are from nine to four."

"That's very kind of you but . . . "

"You are very young, Nancy, but it would be a privilege for me to feel that I had persuaded you to realize your duties toward the community. Think how happy you would be with our ration cards in your hands. How glad, when the Peace day flags are flown, that in the small way we civilians are privileged to share, you also had helped to annihilate the Huns."

"I wonder if I should like to feel that," Nancy questioned. It was wrong, terribly wrong of her but Mrs. Hearth always freed her usually dormant sense of mischief. "And you see, I have work to do now, important work." She tried to look mysterious.

"Oh, my dear, what is it?" Mrs. Hearth, her face an interrogation, leaned forward. She must know . . . she must know . . .

"Oh, here are the others back again," Nancy turned, evading the question.

"I don't ask you, Nancy, in any spirit of vulgar curiosity, but I've known you all my life. Whisper to me what you have taken up. I will respect your confidence . . . " Mrs. Hearth's eyes almost projected the vision of the bandage making room where she would say next Monday, "that girl, you know, has come to her senses at last. Not spoilt as you might think. She has taken up (was it a crêche, motor driving, painting aeroplanes wings) she has taken up . . . " Mrs. Hearth hurried behind Nancy down the lawn. "You will tell me, won't you dear?"

"What it is I am doing? Oh, I must be getting off to my lesson. Thank you so much for being interested."

"But *what* is it?" begged Mrs. Hearth piteously. Nancy turned with a smile.

"I'm learning Greek."

CHAPTER XI

MEETING

"IF YOU'RE cold there's a spare blanket at the bottom of the bed."

"Thanks but I'll be all right. I've got on woolly pyjamas."

Nancy lay watching the stars set overhead like a thousand stamens in some purple daisy. The tall silver leaves of a eucalyptus tree fell over the parapet about the flat roof. She had always wanted to sleep out of doors. And this was like being on the deck of a ship with the Newlyn lights, tiny flashes of gold, cutting between the branches. If one raised one's self, one saw the black masts of boats.

"What fun," said Doreen.

"I should have thought it would be colder."

"The roof is dry. That helps."

Over the trees behind them day fell, a wild rose dropping on dark brambles. There was the hoot of an owl. The bark of a dog. Footsteps. Sounds were silver in this night that had hardly faded from twilight. Strange how right poets were; if only one had a chance

281

to test them. Nice word of Middleton's, "twitterlight." It suggested the movement of shadows. America lay over the water, China. The black convoy. The same convoy as two years ago, sailing past. Beautiful light of boats, beautiful stars. "Can't help seeing the stars as beauty, to-night. If the way I say it is a cliché." Stars, stamens of wild rose, sky. One thought of the night as that, automatically. Hoot of another owl. Dark grey against the silver.

Owls are soft and warm, like baby gulls. Like Greek words.

"Strange she should be so near," said Nancy, thinking of the letter she had just posted.

"Oh, Cornwall's a great place for poets," Doreen said, too calmly.

"If she doesn't answer, I'm going to fall into the cove and she can hardly refuse to let me sit by her fire and dry my clothes."

"You could say you had seen a spy signalling from the cliffs and would she mind if you watched from her garden."

"I might offer to sell her a pot of jam."

"If she eats it."

"True. She may not worry about such matters. I should think she would though. Most poets are interested in food. There's hardly an Elizabethan play without a banquet in it and the Greeks must have been frightfully particular about their meals to judge from the times fat roast kid is mentioned. Anyhow I'll get there some way. The cove sounds the best idea. I could hide some dry clothes in a furze bush and dip the others in the sea. She may have a cook though. That would be awkward."

"She may answer your letter."

"From a stranger? I doubt it. I could always say a bull was chasing me. Funny she should be so near."

"There's another owl. Hear it?"

"Yes. I'm worried about those stars. They're really yellow, you know, or primrose. But that's been said too often. Must say things a new way or cut them out. Do you think anyone's had 'moon-green?' No, that's too clumsy even if they haven't. They're not yellow enough for honey. Too cold for honeysuckle. Tell you what they're a little like . . . the phosphorescence in the Naples bay."

"Let the stars alone. What happened to your novel?"

"Oh, that. I dropped it on some publisher's."

"Did they take it?"

"No. Wrote me after they'd had the thing two months to go and see them. They were more interested than I was. Asked me to give it a romantic ending and take it back to them."

"Are you going to?"

"No. I don't feel romantic. And I have to feel things before I can write them. It would be much more fun to write a book on modern American poetry."

"Those eucalyptus leaves keep away the flies."

TWO SELVES

"What nights we've wasted. If only we had slept out other summers."

Scent of lavender and beans blew up . . . cool . . . cool . . . under the wide blue-purple sky. Knife of salt the air. Bees in the garden. The gold hive. World was poetry if one were let alone. Free. A poet near. Would she answer? It was too late anyhow. Too late to have a friend. To see, speak once or twice. Why live if one could not be free? Speak one's own thoughts. Be answered. Too late. Hylas, "a shooting star headlong in the sea." Why the salt wind stealing through the pansies? Calling. Silly to feel the sea call still. Not to go back to London . . . to the same thoughts . . . eating one's own mind in a narrow room. Oh, the wild rose of the sky. Darkness, darkness, not to sleep, to be . . . adventure.

"Doreen, the stars . . . "

"What?" grunted a voice sleepily.

"I've got it. Cowslip buds . . . they're cowslip yellow."

The tide surged between the moving leaves, out to the far ships, called, crept in again. Night was anchored to the branches. Birds were still.

"What do you want, Nancy?" Doreen grumbled. They were lying out on the sand opposite a large white gull. There was a tiny crust of foam beyond them where the tide crept gradually out. "How would it be

MEETING

different if you went away? You don't seem to want . . . what most girls want."

"I don't know what most girls want. They bewilder me. If I went away it would be different. It would be action. I would stop in England but I'd clash with people I had known. I could be myself better in another country."

"But how aren't you, yourself, now?" Doreen was a little peevish.

"I am, lying here by this sea." Nancy assured her.

But she wasn't herself really. Only she could not explain this to Doreen. She could not tell her bluntly . . . if I did what I felt and shouted poems to the waves, to the gulls, you'd think I'd gone mad and you'd say, "stop being soft." Eleanor would understand my shouting stuff but she would not get why I would rather lie here thinking about a word than climb that cliff with her. You can't explain yourself to people when they don't know what you feel.

The gull flecked some sand specks from its wings. Spread the tips of them, met a wave. And then flew out of the water across the silver crests running to the shore, straight toward the open sky.

Schools ought not to do things suddenly to children. It was all that day at Downwood. Something had cleft her from herself. She was two personalities now, sitting on the sand. Something, like an axe, had hit her and taught her to keep hidden in herself. Because

285

people found out what you cared about and hurt you through it, when you would not agree with them.

Keep the mind straight. Nothing else mattered. It was very funny. Only they had shut the girl round the corner up. Easy enough to call anyone queer. Good thing perhaps—this disassociation trick. If you spoke straight out your thought they called you queer and shut you up. That was if you were rich. If you were poor and spoke your mind you lost your job. Then you starved. So it came to the same thing in the end.

Civilization . . . fighting for civilization! Had anyone stopped to think what a rotten substance it was?

With Carthage a flame and with Troy broken there was one way out.

Ah, not to live a slave, not that.

Shrug one's shoulders and watch the sea. If there were no other way, walk forward. Into the waves. Life was straight and death was straight but between them was a lie. Life one loved. The gulls, the wind. But if it were impossible to have truth otherwise, go forward. Till the water clashed into the ears. Arms at the sides, the Viking way.

All the wisdom that one had not learned. Curious insistent memory. The sea below Corinth.

It would have to be decided soon. It was a pity to throw life away, yes. But if one didn't have life?

"Perhaps you'll be able to make this writer you've written to, understand what you mean," Doreen suggested grimly.

MEETING

"Oh, it will be amusing to see her. But I don't expect much from the meeting. Writers are disappointing after their books."

She could not wish even, any more. "Come along, we'd better start up the hill. It's getting late."

She must not be eager. She must not expect. Could she stay longer than an hour? To meet poets, people said, was always disappointing. Especially if one liked their work. But a writer would know about books. One could forgive much to a mind that felt as one's own mind. That could write in words the beauty that left one dumb. Only she, Nancy, had nothing to offer to a poet in exchange for life or words.

She had never heard words spoken. Real words. Only the headlines of the papers repeated over and over again. Or the phrases of an older generation that had no link with her thought. Never words leaping, shining with meaning, saying a fact.

A brown calf trotted toward the sea. Foxgloves, wet with rain, spiked the bracken with their Tyrian bells. It was an old Phœnician path that curved, black earth between grey stones, along the line of the hill.

Beauty was escape; beauty was another world. Greek chariots, the rainbow of the ships. That childhood in Sicily long ago. (Almond blossoms, you are soft, you are the dove white rain.) The mad rough world of Middleton. Knossos of the scarlet poppies. I understand her mind. Thoughts, thoughts.

"What have you read?" That would be sure to be the first question. She knew the Elizabethans backward. "No, I never got through the Arcadia but I like Euphues." She ought to be all right on the French stuff. Twenty four. And she had read everything she could in preparation for this day since she was ten.

There was a noise of bird songs. The brown butterfly speckled wings of a hawk fluttered from the cliff. Was something going to happen to her at last? It was too late to care.

If she found a friend they might shut her up. Everyone, Eleanor, Doreen, Downwood. Because if she had a friend something would burst and she would shoot ahead, be the thing she wanted and disgrace them by her knowledge. Because she would care for no laws, only for happiness.

If she found a friend, an answer, the past years would vanish utterly from her mind.

At all costs they would fight to break this; everyone she had known. They tried already when she had no friend.

"Why do you want to go to America, Nancy?"
"Why can't you settle down?"
"Why can't you behave like other girls?"
"The trouble is, you've had your own way too much."

MEETING

An eye for an eye. A school for a school. Something deep and slow and vengeful had grown in her. She wanted her experience to triumph, her sense of truth. To sow beauty, to sow happiness, where Miss Sampson sowed acquiescence and a nation sowed brutality.

Better not try to find a friend. Better drown under the cliffs. One stab of water and no fear more. "Dying is ceasing to be afraid . . . dying . . . is ceasing to be afraid." Wycherley was a moralist and they put him in prison. Wycherley laughed at the horde; they broke him. "Ceasing to be afraid," he said. Better be done with it, under the cliff, forget the anemones, the sea call, the adventures. One choke of water and no fight more. Better not try to find . . .

But the Phœnician path stopped at a grey cottage that faced the south-blue sea. Familiar yellow covers, French books, were piled at an open window. Better not try to find . . . oh, take a chance on adventure.

This was the place. She knocked.

She was too old to be disappointed if an elderly woman in glasses bustled out. Poets, of course, were not what they wrote about. It was the mind that mattered.

A tall figure opened the door. Young. A spear flower if a spear could bloom. She looked up into eyes that had the sea in them, the fire and colour and the splendour of it. A voice all wind and gull notes said:

"I was waiting for you to come."